I0524357

Brass Ring Sorority

CHASING LACEY

JANUARY BAIN

Chasing Lacey
ISBN # 978-1-78686-363-8
©Copyright January Bain 2018
Cover Art by Melody Pond ©Copyright June 2018
Interior text design by Claire Siemaszkiewicz
Totally Bound Publishing

CHASING
LACEY

Dedication

I cannot say enough good things about the process of creating Lacey and Will's story with the people I have been blessed with in my life, and I would like to take a moment to say a proper thank you.

To Rebecca Fairfax, you are my rock when it comes to all things Story. Your vision and brilliance have helped this author to become so much more than she could ever have hoped for. For that, and your continued friendship, I thank you.

To my fellow authors at Totally Bound and the incredible, helpful staff and administration, thanks for making this journey so enjoyable. You guys are the best.

Thank you to my mother, who taught me how to be a strong woman, and who made the heroic effort to read to her family when we were but children. You planted the seed.

And, as always, thanks to my beloved husband for sharing his life with me, and for creating Buttonland. I am one truly lucky woman.

Chapter One

"It's a front row seat to the Greatest Show on Earth."
— Robert Scott, private investigator

"Happy ever after. Ha. It's a myth, Lily. A legend. A shell game meant to sell more expensive wedding packages." Lacey Cameron gave a snort, glancing away from the awesome view of crystal-blue water, fluffy white clouds and careening shore birds to stare her monozygotic twin right in the eye. Her carbon copy made that face—the one that suggested Lacey was being a pain in the butt. *Again.*

"Just because our parents couldn't make a go of it—"

"*Make a go of it!*" Lacey could hear the shrillness in her voice and took a deep breath to quiet the tinnitus that immediately pounced, dulling and annoying at the same time. The day loomed too beautiful and too shiny, a virtual Christmas package floating in cyberspace, to have this conversation. Besides, they were just about to the correct location to weigh anchor—the coordinates she was certain would bear fruit. Of the golden variety, of course. This was her number one bucket list item—diving for sunken treasure off the Florida Keys—and nothing was going to spoil it, especially memories best left in the past.

"It was far worse than just not making a go of it, as you darn well know," she growled, refusing to go there, to relive the pain of her childhood. How Lily could was beyond Lacey's comprehension. Best to outrun it and keep running. That had worked for her until now, so why change what worked?

She swung the thirty-six-foot Nautitech catamaran around. She stood in the cockpit, feet planted, savoring the most amazing panoramic view provided by any of the boats offered for charter. She preferred the stability of the twin-hulled dive boat and was pleased with herself for coming down a day early to get her safety competency card and boating license. A rarity for her, that much planning. But the freedom of being her own captain far outweighed any inconvenience.

"Well, I think Casey and Truman *will* make a go of it," Lily huffed. "They're good friends, like to do the same things, both love adventure and they have a ton of other stuff in common. Frankly, I think they're a good bet."

"Yada, yada, yada. Careful. You'll jinx them." Lacey smirked. No way was she ever going to latch on to one man, no matter how good a friend he was. No, not a chance that was ever going to be part of her life plan. She had decided on a different approach, brought on by her recent karate training at the dojo. It was based on the warrior mindset and had brought her some clarity, some purpose. Learning all the five hundred-plus techniques was going to take far longer than embracing the philosophy, but it was a beginning.

All she got for her trouble was the expected disgusted glare when she glanced Lily's way for a split second. But it was the twinge of deep hurt that also crossed her twin's face that flung the worst arrow. She'd just been reminded of her warrior creed, her sworn duty to protect the innocent, and if anyone was innocent it was Lily, incapable of seeing the world through anything but rose-colored glasses. How that had happened was beyond Lacey's understanding. They had both been raised in the same dismal household.

"Hey, maybe it will work out for them," Lacey reasoned in a more level tone of voice, swallowing hard. "Lord knows, it has to for some, right? Otherwise, why have the institution?" She pushed back a strand of bright red hair broken loose in the wind created by the boat flying across the water at an exhilarating speed. She tucked the hair under her ballcap and breathed in the fresh fragrance of the salty foam churned up from the propellers. *Ah, the smell of adventure. Bring it on, world.*

"We don't have to let the past destroy our chance at a good future, do we, Lacey?"

Damn it. This wasn't on the agenda for this gorgeous summer morning. Why was the past visiting now, when it was her turn? The much discussed, much anticipated week of treasure hunting?

"Honestly, I don't know. But I find it best to just forget about it and keep moving forward." She shrugged, not trusting herself to look at her sister. "What else can you do?"

She powered down the twin engines of the catamaran. They had arrived. The perfect time to end this verbal wrestling match that could never resolve things, anyway.

"Come on, let's do this thing. Leave the past where it belongs." She pushed the button that would drop anchor and stabilize the boat. This was the moment she loved best. The anticipation of things to come. The only thing that would beat it was holding some amazing treasure in her hot little hands.

Lacey grabbed her dive suit and hurried to step into it, tugging it up her body and zipping it in place under her chin. Hefting her air tank, she took a moment to check the equipment was working properly before setting it in place on her back. She watched Lily finish suiting up, then gave her twin two thumbs-up.

Seconds later, they were in the water.

She vanquished all thoughts of the upcoming nuptials of fellow Brass Ringer Casey and her fiancé Truman, because nothing was going to be allowed to interfere with the clear level-mindedness that diving in the waters off Little Conch Reef promised. The blue jewel of Plantation Key, especially when surrounded by a mosaic of rainbow-colored fish that immediately began to dance with her, made everything seem possible. It was the sea version of that Hollywood blockbuster, like her sister was blabbing on about with all the false promises to love and to cherish until death do us part. What was it called again? Oh yeah, living in *La La Land*. She was too smart and too burned for that trap.

The exhaled bubbles rose steam-engine-style around her while she used her flippers to propel herself through the clear water. *Absolute pure magic.* A poet with a great deal more talent than her would have some struggle capturing this moment of sublime freedom. The tinny sounds vanished from her mind, leaving only anticipation for the immediate future in their wake. She thrust her body back and forth on a downward trajectory, moving away from her twin like a mermaid-in-training, her long hair streaming behind her.

Finally. It was really true. She wanted to pinch herself just to make sure, but it was past time to get to searching and find what the depths would reveal to her that day. What King Midas had in store for one Lacey Anne Cameron. Excitement glowed from an ember to a raging wildfire within her body in a split-second.

She swam parallel to the ocean floor, checking every nook and cranny of the Spanish galleon *El Infante* for a glimpse of something, anything, manmade. That brigantine lay battered and almost unrecognizable on the white sand ocean floor, a victim of the 1733 hurricane. She really didn't expect to find anything at the actual wreck site — its bones had been picked over years ago — but farther out... Now, that held distinct possibilities.

The morning passed in the sweet sense of being on point, of something just over the horizon waiting for her to discover. Yes, the best of times for her was just before something occurred, the quiet of the hush. But still, this was taking longer than she'd imagined. She'd been certain that she'd bag important treasure before her sister. It had always been a contest to see who could beat the other to the prize. The only other person whose competition gene rivaled her own was Will, her best male friend and hang-out buddy. And today, this was going to be her day. She felt it deep in her bones.

She checked the tank monitoring system occasionally, making sure she had sufficient air to continue. She swam in and out of an underground cave, caught up in the mystical flow. Then a glint under the shifting sands at the cave mouth drew her eye and she was on it in an instant. Fanning the sand away, she worked to uncover the find.

It was deeply planted, the ocean reluctantly giving over its hoarded treasure only after a major tug-of-war. A large golden cross nearly eighteen inches across with a number of encrusted gems. A find worthy of King Midas himself. *Ahhhh.*

Then everything changed in a split second.

The reef hushed, gone silent.

The brilliantly hued school of fish abandoned her, skipping town like an old western's inhabitants during a showdown at high noon, racing for the security of the reef and the bleached bones of *El Infante*. Even the sea anemones shut their flower-like structures, closed to business, paled to gray to match the death-like scene.

Why?

Lacey's heart nearly stopped, skipping a full beat and making her chest bone shudder.

A lidless black eye. Unblinking and cold as sin. And with the audacity to materialize right smack dab in front of her face.

Sneaky freakin' bull shark.

He'd blindsided her, swimming up silently in the warm waters off the Florida coastline while her attention was diverted elsewhere, digging for treasure. She sucked in a lungful of air, almost biting her mouthpiece in two.

Breathe. In and out. Slowly. She didn't want to die on a beautiful summer day by increasing the air bubbles in her bloodstream. That would be a stupid rookie mistake and she was no rookie.

The opportunist slid past her shoulder, casually wheeling around to look her over. He was playing with her, his head the massive size of the front end of a fifty-five-gallon oil drum. Nine feet long, if he was an inch. The shadow cast leached all the warmth and light from the day.

She looked around frantically for Lily and spotted her twin fanning the bottom of the white sandy beach, searching for her own treasure. *Damn it. Too far away.*

She peered at the Spanish galleon. Out of striking range.

She glanced back at the advancing shark now giving an impressive demonstration of his awesome ivories. Each was shaped like an arrowhead, a perfect isosceles triangle, razor-sharp, capable of tearing through flesh and bone like a hot knife through butter. *Breathe.*

He made a second pass. Fast. Too darn fast. A marvel of evolution. Huge yet agile with lightning-quick reflexes. She looked longingly at the surface where the boat bobbed enticingly in the soft blue haze, its white anchor line curving upwards. She'd been caught out in the open. Oh, he was sneaky and smart. Or maybe just another opportunist hungry for its next meal. *Not going to happen, buster.*

Okay. Move slowly. Face him. Prepare.

She reached for her spear gun. Where the heck was it? Not that the gun would stop a monster of this size, but it might possibly buy her time to escape. Of course, she'd nixed the communication devices this morning. With the wreck sunk in shallow waters, they'd seemed pointless. *Good call, Lacey.*

Another pass. He was enjoying playing with her. *Breathe, just breathe.* The diver's mantra kept repeating in her head over and over. Bubbles from her air hose swirled around her. *Good, proof I'm still breathing properly.* Her fingers fumbled at her belt again. Came up empty. The missing gun—oh right—in the hands of a fellow diver, lent just that morning after a sob story. She cursed her generous Irish heart and yanked out from the bag tied at her waist the jeweled cross studded with gemstones. It would have to do. And he'd better not damage it, the bastard.

Okay, no other choice. Stand my ground. Aim for the eyes or gills. Sharks are no fonder of pain than us humans.

Grasping the cross like a vampire hunter and mentally crossing herself with a prayer, she kept the leviathan in her sights. A macabre dance with death began. One she was determined to win — had to win. It would have been made a whole lot easier with an outcropping at her back, but she was in shallow waters, close to shore with no hope of that. He lunged without warning, opening his mouth and re-exposing ivories gleaming evilly in case she'd missed them the first time around. *Don't worry, I get the picture.* His humongous body moved fast as sheet lightning, preparing to strike.

Steady. Steady.

But instead of grasping the expected flesh and bone of a leg, he got a sharp jab in the eye for his trouble. Her father's angry face flashed in her mind. She struck out. Harder.

Take that! If only her mother had flattened him just once, had fought back, like she herself did when practicing her karate moves. No man was ever going to get the drop on her. She'd fight tooth and nail, take them down with her, if necessary.

But the big fish didn't learn his lesson either. Kept coming. *Need conformation, eh, that I'm a force to be reckoned with?* She struck again, punching him right in the snout, the cross a decent substitute for the spear, if she didn't mind the close, disgusting quarters of a shark with food stuck in his teeth. The guy needed a good dentist. Pronto.

Breathe.

He backed off. She threatened with a gesture.

He parried again. A shark who obviously practiced evasive sword-fencing techniques. What was his problem? If it was hunger, she was less than sympathetic. Besides, to this gigantic beast, she was just a morsel. *Go after something your own size.*

A movement in the water to her left drew her attention for a micro-second, but she could ill afford to check out what her peripheral vision hinted at. *Keep your eyes on him. Turn from a shark, especially run from a shark, and he thinks he's found his din-din.*

A spear whizzed by her shoulder, but instead of sinking into the sand-paper-like thick hide, it flew on by, entirely missing its target. She groaned and quickly moved her physical body between her sister and the shark, her heart in her throat. Had Lily missed because she couldn't bear to hurt another living being, or because she was a terrible shot? Because now he was a whole lot more confident, looming larger than life and almost grinning at his prey. Them.

Without taking her eyes off the shark, she thrust the cross into her belt and gestured for the power-spear, praying Lily would have the good sense to give it to her. For a moment her hand remained empty, then the tool was handed over. *Thank God.* The shark was ready. He lunged at her, giving her no time to think, to prepare.

She slipped sideways, bringing the spear up and firing instinctively, his mouth gracing her thigh on the pass by. *Please, please don't let me bleed out.* Blood spelled *doom.* The bloodlust of the bull shark was legendary. A frenzy that would guarantee the Camerons' Armageddon.

When he turned and swarm back toward her, she saw that she had indeed hit her target. Hope exploded in her chest. She had weakened the enemy. But was it a mortal blow? Or would he now become even more desperate?

The shark hung in the water, considering them. She kept the spear pointed right at him, ready to use it as a bayonet if necessary. Two fighters for the price of one must have finally gotten through to his feeble brain. Twice the trouble. How much more could he possibly have to think about? *Just remember who you're dealing with here, asshole. Go. Away.*

An eternity passed, though not enough time to observe all the follies of her life. *Nah, I wouldn't change much, well, except for maybe holding on to my own power-spear.* Having to use her sister's sucked.

He pretended nonchalance, the equivalent of a human saving face before turning and swimming lazily away, giving a defiant flip of his tail. A final human-like gesture that earned him no respect.

Lacey would have loved to embrace her twin to reassure her but getting to the surface was a tad more important. Though she did take the time to tuck the cross safely back into the bag tied to her waist. No point in coming back later for it. Someone else might have nabbed it by then. And she was determined to have something to show for the day's efforts. No shithead shark was going to win.

They swam side-by-side, grasping the vertically hanging anchor line to pull themselves up hand-over-hand, bobbing to the surface a few precious seconds later beside the catamaran. Diving in shallow water of less than the thirty-three feet deep meant a painful case of the bends was not remotely possible, thank goodness. And she couldn't have even been hurt enough to draw blood when the shark had come too close, otherwise she'd not be here to even think about it. Her heart lurched at the thought and she forced the visual away. Not the moment to relive that experience. *Just keep moving, Lacey.*

She pulled herself over the side of the boat, hauling her butt over the rail. Lacey disengaged her equipment and unzipped her wetsuit. Lily came up right behind her, yanking off her own tank and air hose like all the hounds of Hades were fighting for her mortal soul. *Oh, boy.*

"Wow, that was something, eh?" Lacey said as neutrally as possible while taking her first sweet I'm-out-of-immediate-danger breath, thrills still coursing through her bloodstream like a tilt-a-wheel at the county fair. The cost of a shark attack. *Endorphins. Should last till Christmas. Or tomorrow.* Adrenaline — her opiate of choice.

"Why the heck didn't you have a power-spear?" Lily accused, her voice unusually squeaky and her face one big red blotch of righteous anger. Not an attractive look for either of them, being fair-skinned redheads.

"I lent it out and I was doing just fine. The cross saved me. Not that I'm all that religious, but it does make a girl wonder." Lacey pretended nonchalance at the near miss, earning a look of disgust from her twin. After all, she had a reputation to uphold as being the most badass of the two. She took the moniker seriously. And being the oldest by three minutes, twenty seconds gave her awesome power.

"You could have been killed! We could both have been killed!"

"A bit of hyperbole, Lily Cameron," Lacey deadpanned. She loved using fancy words to annoy others. *Blame it on my inherited Irish badass-ness.* Or the short time spent in a high school teaching her love of the English language to students. Well, of course, that had only been a few hours in total. *Turns out, students can be darn annoying. Maybe I should have chosen to teach physical education? Made them run around the gym, burn off some of that annoyance factor...*

"Hyperbole, is it! Did I not just rescue you from a bull shark the size of a freakin' tank?"

"You should have stayed away. I had him cornered, hitting him with the cross. That reminds me..." She stopped to check on its condition, dragging it from her goody bag. "Whew, still fine."

She held it up for her twin to admire. The encrusted jewels gleamed brightly in the late afternoon sunshine.

"What do you think? Is this sweet or what!"

Lily remained silent, working on getting out of her scuba suit, giving her the cold shoulder.

She rinsed the treasure with fresh water and dried it with a soft cloth, laying it reverently on the deck near a few coins—the tally of a day's efforts. Lacey glanced at her sister again. Lily's lips were pressed together so tightly they were in danger of disappearing from view. Lacey might have gone a tad too far this time.

"Robert Pattinson or Liam Neeson?" Lacey asked, exaggerating the actions necessary to wiggle out of her diving suit while she pretended to consider her choice. She pulled on shorts and a halter top over her skimpy red underwear that nicely matched her waist-length curls to a T—the effect desired in certain situations, though perhaps not this one. She answered her own question. "Difficult choice, eh? They're both hot. Hmm, so, sweet sensitive guy versus action hero? Liam, I think. He's strong, but he can be sensitive as well. I like a multidimensional man."

She glanced at Lily. Still nothing. Just busy stowing her wetsuit.

Finally, Lily spoke. "I'm not going to let you brush this off so easily, Lacey Anne Cameron." Probably not if she was using her full name.

"Want to head into town? Celebrate our find?" *Get Lily's mind off the attack.*

Lily shrugged. "Whatever."

"Great." Lacey pretended the indifference didn't bug her. Much as she hated to admit it, she liked being best buds with her twin. Perhaps she had overstepped the mark this time — set herself up for the problem. Nothing she couldn't handle, of course — part and parcel of being out on an adventure. Still, she didn't want to worry Lily. Thank goodness, her twin never held a grudge. Of course, Lacey had never put them in peril quite like that before. *Take responsibility. Warrior up.*

"I'll buy a new spear. ASAP," Lacey promised.

Lily just shook her head. *Not going to be an easy nut to crack.*

Lacey picked up her phone to check for messages, pushing her damp hair from her face while she read the most recent one. "Do you remember Megan Wright?"

"Sure, she graduated with us. She has a brother — Danny — a year ahead of us. Why, is something wrong?"

"I don't know. She just says she needs to see me."

"Is she here in the Keys, then?"

"Yeah. She's waiting for me up at the marina. Our celebratory drink will have to wait." *Why has Megan tracked me down? Does she live in Florida now?* But something stirred in Lacey's gut, a sixth sense that this was not a social call.

"Okay, you bring up the anchor while I stow our stuff," Lily directed, ever the practical one.

"Already on it," Lacey countered, before getting down to the business of maneuvering the catamaran safely back to the dock, definitely her new favorite toy.

Twenty minutes later, Lacey pushed open the door of the Four Seasons marina, glancing around for Megan. The place was nearly deserted and she spotted her at the bar, looking out across the emerald waters of the Gulf of Mexico. A few miles to the east and she'd be looking at the Atlantic Ocean, Plantation Key being one of a group of islands dividing the two bodies of water.

Megan caught sight of her. She immediately stood up, embracing her.

"Nice to see you."

"Thanks. You too."

They pulled apart, both sliding onto bar stools. It had been only a few short years since graduation from the University of Manitoba back in Winnipeg, Canada, but her fellow collegian had changed. A lot. Megan's shoulder-length dark hair had lost its luster, pushed haphazardly behind her ears, and her brown eyes were obscured by dark-framed glasses instead of shining from behind her unusual contacts. A few tight lines were even developing around her mouth and there were creases in her forehead. Lacey's gut tightened further. Now she was worried. *Is Megan ill?*

The bartender nodded and gave her an approving look. "What will you have, beautiful? First drinks on the house, rest are on me," he said with a smile meant to be charming, his approval of her appearance obvious.

"Why, thank you." She was about to automatically launch into her usual banter when she stopped herself. *No. Shut it.* Megan needed her attention more than Lacey needed free drinks.

"Okay, so tell me, what's the deal?" she asked, nodding her thanks to the waiter, who dropped off a pitcher of free margaritas before leaving. "You living in Florida now?"

"No, living in Toronto, and I see nothing's changed. Still attracting the men in droves, eh?" Megan's tone had a distinct edge. She'd dodged Lacey's questions, taking a big swallow of her drink instead. She'd had a few too, judging by the slight slur to her words.

"And you're here in Florida to check up on my love life? It's been years since I dated Danny. That was a high school romance that wasn't made for the real world."

"No, of course not." Megan shook her head. "Yeah, I know. But you guys were good together. You kept Danny on the straight and narrow. After you broke up, he was kind of lost, fell in with the wrong crowd."

"I'm sorry about that, but we weren't meant to be together forever. Now, seriously, tell me what's wrong." Images of high school flooded her brain. When she'd met Danny Wright, she'd thought he was the one. The one who was going to rescue her. He'd been so sympathetic about her home life, listening for hours while she ranted on and on about how her mom put up with her dad. How she'd never allow that. Back when she still believed in chivalry and true love. They'd leave Winnipeg in the dust and head for greener pastures. Danny would be a big-time promoter with his buckets of charm and she'd help out in any capacity possible. Be such a perfect person that their lives would unfold without a wrinkle. Now, looking back, she could see what a cotton-headed, starry-eyed fool she'd been. *The warrior learns from his mistakes and grows stronger, more powerful.*

"It's Danny. He's—he's dead." Megan's eyes filled with tears. She wiped them away angrily. "Lord knows he's not been a saint in recent years, but he didn't deserve this."

Lacey sat in complete shock. *Danny. Dead.* That handsome charmer filled with so much life? It didn't seem possible—she expected even now to see him show up in the bar, to fill the place with jokes and laughter.

"I'm so sorry, Megan," she managed to say, trying to gather her thoughts.

"I'm still finding it so hard to believe." She swiped at the tears that flowed from her eyes. "But I need your help, Lacey. That's why I'm here." Megan sat up straighter on her stool.

"Danny was murdered, a victim of a mugging. I want you to find out the truth. I think things are being covered up."

This made no sense at all. *Who is covering up what? Time to grab control of the conversation.*

"How about you start at the beginning? Fill me in on what he's been doing. He married an American woman and moved to Vegas—right?"

Megan nodded, her eyes glinting. "Yeah, right after graduation. Angel Marcos, a casino worker. They met on spring break a couple of months before he graduated. Married far too quickly, in the whole family's opinion." She shook her head, biting her lower lip before finishing the rest of her drink. She poured another and continued speaking, in a darker tone.

"A quickie marriage they didn't invite the family to. She had a child from another man before they got married, a boy named Mathew. I've only seen photos. Angel is more about her own family, not ours." The bitterness spilled over. "I hate to say this, but I think she had something to do with Danny's mugging."

"Why?"

"In the past year, he applied for three insurance policies that paid a high premium on accidental death — all going to the widow. That's why I'm here. I know you're damn good at investigating fraud. I need you to find out what happened. Was he hurt because someone wanted the insurance payout? My money's on Angel being involved somehow."

"Tell me all you know about Danny's attack."

"I've got the police report right here." Megan leaned down to reach under her stool and pulled a folder out of her tote bag.

Lacey opened the cover, glancing over the first sheet of information to get a grasp of the situation. She'd study it later. "It happened in the Philippines?" She looked up at her friend, surprised.

"Yeah. Mugged near the hotel he was staying at, behind a place called the Dollhouse. Don't know what it is, but I can guess. Like I said, my brother's not been living the life of a saint."

"Was he there by himself?" *Dollhouse. Most likely a house of prostitution.*

"I don't quite get why he went there alone." Megan pursed her lips. "Angel has family in Manila, so maybe it was to give her an alibi?"

"Maybe." Lacey shook her head. "Looks odd on the surface, all right, since her family lives there. Anyway, the polices will have red-flagged this, with the death occurring overseas in the Philippines." Insurance companies usually paid investigators well for uncovering fraud. This wouldn't cost her friend a dime.

"I need you to look into it for me. Please, Lacey, find out what really happened. The insurance investigators don't care like you would — you were like family to us, always at our place instead of yours. Besides, you're the best at what you do. I don't think I could live with myself if justice isn't done for Danny," she said, choking up, tears spilling over. "And you really liked Danny, right? Otherwise, you wouldn't have dated him all through high school. And I know you don't want to hear this after what happened, but he always loved you. He just got drunk that one night and made a mistake with that skank. He was so young at the time — easily influenced by peer pressure. If you hadn't had that fight, none of this would have happened and Danny would be with us today. He married on the rebound. I know that in my heart."

Lacey cleared her throat. The accusation hung between them. Yes, she did feel some responsibility to help her friend, but reliving the painful past, that would take strength. Maybe more than she possessed. *The warrior must stay true to his course.* Was this it? She'd always believed in fate and could never ignore a cry from a friend. Which was why she now practiced karate, to keep her body and mind sound, knowing her weakness was to run into the fire, not away, like any sensible person would. But how often had she thought, if only someone had rescued her mother?

She straightened her spine. Now. This moment — this was what mattered. This was the true course. "Yes, I did care for Danny. I'll see what I can find out."

"Oh, thank God!" Megan swiped her tears away with her fingertips. "I can pay for your time. I have a good job now, working for a book marketing company in Toronto."

"No worries. One of the insurance companies will pay to save doling out that kind of cash. And if not, this one's on me. I want to see Danny's killers brought to justice almost as much as you do."

* * * *

"No way! After what happened today, you're not going to Manila by yourself!" Lily squawked, sitting on the bed beside her with her arms crossed over her chest.

Now Lily gets stubborn? Just as the video conference with their Ringer pals was beginning. And on the first day of hunting treasure when she'd found a big prize. One with a new line of provenance sure to add value — verifiably used by new owner to fight off a shark attack and the human won the day. She had it safely tucked by her side, ready at a moment's notice to show off to her beloved Ringers.

"Megan needs my help. I have to go." Lacey was equal parts exasperated and sympathetic, busy working the keyboard on her laptop. "Besides, Manila is safer than a shark." Lily scooted in closer on the hotel room bed to make sure her fellow Ringers could see them both on camera.

Then a montage of happy female faces filled the screen of her laptop as the video conference pinged like circling sonar into reality. Lacey couldn't hold back a warm smile at the big reveal. There sat Rebecca, her writer friend who looked exactly like a young Kathleen Turner with the sexy voice to match. Miranda, the sweetest pixie in the world, even if she liked to hunt UFOs and paranormal activity, and debunk them, of course. Ava, their lawyer, was right there beside Elin, the awesome Swedish goddess, and Tessa with the gorgeous curls and unmatchable musical talent. And, of course, Casey, bride-to-be, full-time professor of archeology, looking nervous as heck perched smack-dab in the middle of the crew. *Hmm.* At least that made sense, her looking shell-shocked with nerves. She was about to get married, tie herself to one man.

Lily was still ranting away at her side, drawing the attention of the Brass Ringers before Lacey could get a word in edgewise. "Yeah, right, lots of human sharks in Manila. You always do this! You run off like you're the only one that can fix things. And how about your treasure hunting? You planned for years to do this. Are you just going to say that's it—take off like a crazy woman on steroids? Surely Danny's case is being investigated by his insurance companies? They'll be able to take care of it just fine. You're not the only investigator on the planet, you know."

"What's this about you going to Manila?" Ava asked, pushing in closer to the screen. *What the heck, Lily, are you setting me up?* The last thing Lacey needed was all the Ringers on her back.

"You guys talk some sense into her," Lily huffed with obvious exasperation. "She thinks running right into the thick of a problem is the answer—yet again. It's Danny Wright. He was mugged in Manila. I'm sorry to say it, but he's dead. And his sister Megan wants Lacey to go there and investigate."

Murmurs of *I'm sorry to hear that* filled the airwaves.

Lacey saw her chance and weighed in. "And Megan's counting on me. She's asked me as an almost-sister to help her." She hated to use that, but pressed on anyway, not happy that all their friends had to be in on the family squabble. "If anything happened to you, I would go to the ends of the earth to get to the truth, to nab the perpetrators. Megan's family—I have to do the same for her. She's so broken up over what happened to Danny. I need to do this, Lily. Surely you can see that. Yeah, *I know, I know,* I've made mistakes in the past, run into situations too quickly without thinking it through, but this, this is important. I have to do this." She stopped, waited, reading the indecision on her twin's face. She also saw the exact second a new idea was sparked.

"I'll make peace with this if Will can go with you."

William James Thornton III. Her best friend in the whole world. Even if he usually owed her one due to a lost bet, it didn't set right with her to call on him too often. *Save the get-out-of-jail card for a dire time.* And she already had some secret plans she wasn't sharing with anyone, which reminded her—call The Doctor tonight and set things up for the forgery work she required. No, best to be footloose and fancy free in Manila.

"No, I don't think that's a good idea. Will's been so busy. I wouldn't feel right bothering him." And lately, if she was being honest, it had been getting somewhat awkward between them. She wasn't sure why, but she had no time to find out, and especially not right now.

"It's Will or you're not going! I will absolutely disown you, Lacey Anne Cameron! You can do all the business from here on yourself. I will dissolve this partnership and disappear for parts unknown. See how you like it, doing it all on your lonesome."

A full-name warning. *Again. Not a good sign.* Lacey chewed on her bottom lip, looked away from the laptop and stared out at the brilliant water lapping at the shore not ten feet from their balcony. And she could not even consider running their business without her sister's goodwill. She counted on Lily more than she cared to admit.

"I'll think about it. Okay?" *There. Buy time as this is really not the proper moment to be discussing family business.*

"Not good enough. You call Will or I will."

Just when did Lily get so damn stubborn?

"Okay, okay. I'll call him later," she said in exasperation. "No guarantee he'll want to go anyway. What then?"

"Oh, he'll go all right. I'd bet the farm on it." Lily gave her a mystifying look, lips quirked in a weird grin. Lacey didn't get it. *What's the big deal? Really? One little shark does not an unsafe world make.* Okay, he'd been as big as a whale, but she'd had him cornered. Anyone could have seen that.

"But first I've got something to share with the Ringers." She tugged the cross into plain view.

A chorus of ohhs and ahhs quickly followed as the gleaming object caught the light, sparks glowing off the encrusted jewels embedded in the gold.

"And this time I win the bet — getting the treasure on day one, in the a.m., thanks, Lacey," Miranda said with a smirk. "And guess what I've got planned?"

The mention of the Ringers' bets reminded Lacey of the last treasure Casey had found, that one in Dawson City in Canada's Yukon. Soapy's Gold. And that find had helped to finance this trip. It was what the Ringers did — finance one Brass Ringer's wish at a time. It was how they'd gotten their sorority name. And what the chosen Ringer had to do for the winner who guessed the hour of the find was always too delicious. She squirmed on the bed, remembering the pole dance she'd done for Will. It had been entirely too much fun enticing him. She'd never gotten to know what he really thought of it — her spectacular display had rendered him speechless. She'd practiced for weeks to get the moves right.

"And guess whose turn it is to step out of their comfort zone?" Miranda wiggled her eyebrows, her tone smug. "Drum roll, please."

A chorus followed.

"Rebecca!"

Rebecca gave a huge groan upon hearing her name. "Okay, okay, tell me and put me out of my bloody misery."

"Ha, this is going to be such a fun one. I had all winter to come up with it. You have to go to England and kiss a duke. A real kiss. And not a fake duke, but a real one who still lives in a castle or a fancy manor house with all the ancestral lineage to boot. Is that perfect or what?"

"What, only a kiss! I had to do so much more when I did that pole dance for Will. Not fair!" Lacey objected.

General mayhem broke out as the Ringers hooted and hollered, overruling her objection. Well, Rebecca was notoriously shy around the opposite sex, so maybe it was enough.

Ten minutes later and the conference ended. Lacey set her laptop and the new treasure aside, ready to do battle with her twin, knowing Lily would be jumping right back into the argument.

"Okay, the phone's ringing for Will," Lily said with no warning, thrusting the bright pink cell phone at Lacey's chest. She'd missed seeing her take it up and punch in a number.

Lacey took it, rolling her eyes. "Just this once, you get to call the shots, little sis. And it's only 'cause I want to get on with helping Megan ASAP. Otherwise— Hey, you," she spoke into the phone as Will picked it up.

If she were being honest, maybe the excuse to call Will wasn't the worst thing to happen that day. After all, he had lost the last bet. She often teased him about not going to Vegas as he so often lost bets to her. And he always manned up and paid whatever price was requested—after much grumbling, of course.

"Lily?" His tone was cooler than she'd expected.

"No, it's Lacey. Lily made me call on her phone. You okay? You sound off." She gave her twin a well-practiced pout.

"No, I'm fine, just woke up." He cleared his throat. "How's the treasure hunting going?"

"Good. Found an awesome jeweled cross today that should bring in a tidy sum. But I'm not making a social call. You remember that bet from last fall in London? When I won that fun game of pool? Well, I need to collect. ASAP."

The scene was still fresh in her mind, her watching Will's amazed expression when she'd cleared the table of all the balls. *The warrior is always one step ahead of his enemies.* Not that Will could ever be that, but being able to surprise him like that? Priceless.

"You cheated, not telling me you had spent your university years practicing. Oh, and you wore tight jeans and a low slinky top, just to distract me. Why should I pay up?"

"Ha! Saying you can't handle a little distraction like cleavage? A man of the world like yourself?"

"Little distraction is a vast understatement. You, my friend, are a major distraction." He sighed. "Okay, I'll pay up even if you cheated. So, what's the deal? What's going on?"

She explained the situation while Lily kept close watch, even having the audacity to make the ubiquitous sign of eyes glued to her with an effectively mimed gesture. She almost laughed aloud, forgetting her anger at being cornered. Pure Robert De Niro in *Meet the Parents*. Besides, Will could use his Learjet to fly them first-class. Not exactly the hardest concession to make. But she'd never share that.

"Okay, I got something I have to do first—that charity thing my father has arranged to raise funds for the Human Rights Museum—but I can be there by daybreak. We can leave directly after for Manila," Will said, sounding exactly like he was—a good friend who was always there for her and Lily. Even if lately he'd been so preoccupied. She was a little disappointed he had something to take care of, but she could hardly complain about a charity event. She had to admit, she felt a special thrill knowing he'd be there come morning. Will was Will—no other man could hold a candle to him. Too bad they could never be anything more than just friends, but her life's plan did not include male complications. She knew all too well what that could lead to.

"Thanks, I owe you one," she promised.

"One," he grunted in that great radio voice of his, all deep-toned and reassuring, that always resonated all the way down to her toes. "Beautiful, you must owe me a trip to the moon by now. I'm always the one sorting out your messes."

"Then you'd better start making smarter bets and stop losing so many to me. Besides, Lily said she's paying personally for this one, since she's the one insisting on it," she teased, pleased at the astonished look her words brought to her twin's face. *Good.* Lily needed to be put in her place. And besides, Will preferred Lily, would do anything for her. And who could blame him? Lily was far more stable and level-headed.

"Not fair!" Lily screeched. "You're the one getting to go to Manila while I get to take care of the bail-jumpers and the bad-husband cases and all the paperwork you always leave for me—"

"Yeah, yeah. Suck it up, buttercup." Lacey broke off the call and tossed the phone back to her sister. "I gotta pack and do some research on the case before we leave in the morning. I have so many unanswered questions about Danny Wright and what he's been up to since high school. And what he was doing in the Philippines in the first place without his wife?" She swallowed hard, still reeling from the knowledge of his death. He'd been so young. *How can this have happened?*

"You'll be back in time for the wedding, right?"

"You bet. I wouldn't miss Casey and Truman's wedding for anything in the world."

Even if I don't believe in fairy tales. The days ahead would be challenging, having Will along while she worked the case. And Will was enticing, no doubt about it. Good thing she was prepared, Teflon-coated against such an attraction by a whole lot of life baggage and experience. *Yeah, damn good thing.*

Chapter Two

"Conquer the self and you will conquer the opponent."
— Takuan Soho

Will sat on the edge of the king-sized bed, naked, and ran his hand over his thick beard. *Lacey. God, woman, what am I going to do about you?* He shook his head and stood up, ignoring the erection that talking with Lacey over the phone had produced. He pulled on underwear and stared down at his right leg. His limb was sound. An image of his best friend, Charlie, attaching his myoelectric below-knee prosthesis every morning for the rest of his life crept into his brain.

I need a shower. He required a clear mind and firm resolve to tackle his father. He took a deep breath. *What a fucking hypocrite. Human Rights Museum, my ass.* His dad wouldn't know decent behavior if it bit him on his stubborn, workaholic ass. It was always about the money.

Thirty minutes later, Will exited his penthouse condo dressed in a black tux, the expected attire for the gala event. Though he'd have been much more comfortable in jeans and a T-shirt, it wouldn't get patrons to open wallets, according to his father and brother. His mind preoccupied, going over arrangements for the thousand things his life seemed to require now that he was back from service in Iraq and Afghanistan, he missed the woman coming up to him in the car park. *Fuck.* He shook his head. No way to avoid it now.

"Will, wait up. I need to talk with you." A shrill voice echoed around the cement structure.

"Could it wait, Maureen? I'm running late for an event." He didn't turn around but hit the button on his key fob.

The woman hurried the last few steps, her staccato heels a sharp rendition of fake coconuts standing in for a horse clopping in an old western movie. Will bit his lip to hide his mirth. *Not nice.* But the woman just wouldn't take no for an answer when it came to him giving her a good fucking. A man liked to be part of that decision process, not have it taken for granted just because a woman was willing to shell out top dollars to help one of his family's charities. At least he did, since he'd long grown tired of jumping into any old bed, and especially when it was expected.

He turned around to face Maureen, the key fob biting into his hand when he fisted the metal too tightly. Her clothing choice of a long scarlet gown, elaborately curled brunette hair and a waft of heavy perfume surrounding her with the cloying aura of flowers suggested somewhere special. *Please don't let her destination be the Winnipeg Convention Center.*

"That's what I want to talk to you about." She sounded out of breath, her tone exaggerated by self-importance.

"Hmm. What is it?" Will held onto a thin thread of patience by counting to ten. These damn charity gigs set up by his father's trust were not cutting it anymore. Not how he wanted to spend his time at all, not when it could be better passed with those really in need. Like yesterday's work with Charlie Goodman, working tirelessly on a new prototype lightweight titanium 3D printer to cheaply and quickly replace limbs lost to landmines and injuries caused by war atrocities. Now, that man was really on to something. How to truly help. Not just throw money at a problem, but figure out how to benefit in some definite way.

"I thought we might—you know—discuss this over drinks?" She gave him a coy smile, her red lips, most likely enhanced by fillers, far too pouty for his liking. Why were women not aware that what nature intended was just fine? Fresh-faced from the shower did it for him every time.

"I don't have much time tonight, Maureen, sorry. But my brother or my father could help you. I'm sure of it." *Perfect. Sic my problem on the right party.*

"Not who I want to talk to. Not at all." She shook her curls and leaned in closer, pushing her perfume bubble right into his personal space. He held back a sneeze, frowning.

She reached up, straightening his black tie. "I got a check with your name on it already prepped." She patted his chest, then slowly let her hand drift downward to his belt. "My, you must work out a lot. Abs like steel. You'd make a great Viking, darling."

"I do my best." He carefully directed her hand off his body, earning another pout.

"I had hoped..." She shrugged, pretending indifference. He caught the look of instant fury before she shut it down. *A woman scorned. Just fuckin' great.*

"I have to go." Then his conscience squawked. The woman would assist the family foundation with her deep pockets, and the charity did do some good, even if its recipients were not the choices he would make. Those he intended to pay for on his own. And he couldn't totally blame her. It wasn't as though she hadn't heard of his reputation of being the bad boy of the charity circuit. *Reforming. Not easy.* "Okay, one drink."

"You're not saying that like you mean it," she pouted, her lips down-turning even further.

One. Two. Three. "Please, Maureen, would you care to join me for a drink later? I'm buying." He invited her with sincerity, replacing her image with Lacey's.

"Okay, when you put it that nicely." She punctuated her remarks with a conspiratorial wink. Visualizing Lacey in her place had worked a tad too well—his blood flowed freely again to body parts below the waist. *Damn it. I should have taken care of it earlier.*

Ten minutes later and the valet slid in behind the wheel of Will's Mercedes-Benz SLS supercar, the wide grin on the boy's face expressing his delight at getting to drive it. *Have at it.* Not like he'd buy it for himself anyway. Dear old Dad had presented it at Will's homecoming, though it was more likely to impress his cronies than anyone else.

Will swept through the front door and took the escalator to the concourse, alert, scanning the crowd.

"Hey, Will." Charlie came forward, dressed in a tux, his limp barely detectable. He was carrying two glasses of champagne in his hands and held one out to Will, his boyish freckled face widened by a grin, his ginger hair flattened into submission.

"Here. This will help."

"Not as much as a good bottle of Scotch," Will said, catching sight of his father in deep conversation with a young woman near the ballroom's entrance.

Charlie nodded at the pair. "You know who that is?" he asked.

"No, but she does look familiar." Where had he seen her? The young woman had a sharp, intelligent aura to her with her brunette hair fashioned into a sleek bob, bright red lips and dark-framed glasses perched on her pretty face. *Hmm, going for the sexy librarian look.*

"Porsha Evans, a feature writer at *Maclean's* magazine. I wonder if she's on a story."

Right, the small photo on her by-line. A frisson of dread flicked over Will when his father looked over and gave a commanding nod of his silver head. Women considered his father a handsome man. And he did enjoy women, having stepped out on his marriage contract twice that Will was aware of. Will gave him a perfunctory smile in return but didn't move toward him. Soon enough he'd be trapped with him at the same dinner table.

"Let's head in." Will nodded at the wide entrance when a small group of people obscured the view between him and the family patriarch.

Charlie had the good sense not to question, but continued the talk while they strode inside, filling him in on more details of the work they were both most interested in, the prototype prosthesis for children suffering from war injuries, requiring a missing limb to be replaced. Will steered him to the bar and was about to order a double Scotch on the rocks when he remembered where he had to be in a few hours.

"Bottle of water." He gave his order to the bartender.

"And I'll have one as well." A woman came up beside him, drawing his attention. Porsha Evans. Her voice came across as crisp and precise as her feature articles.

"You're a hard man to track down." She gave him a level look.

Will shrugged. "No harder than anyone else. Did you call my office for an interview?"

"Going to play it that way, are we? I thought it would be better to get to see you in your own element. Home-town-hero stuff."

"My element?" Will scoffed as Charlie deserted him, taking his double Scotch and hightailing it away. "I'm hardly a hero. I would recommend you find someone else for that angle. It is a story you're after, Miss Evans?"

"Porsha, please. To answer your question, yes, I am on a story. *Maclean's* wants me to do a feature on you." She took a deep breath, slanting her eyes at him. "Don't you think it's a bit unusual when a rich man's son—especially one reputed to be able to spin straw into gold—volunteers and goes off to war and comes home a decorated war hero? It's not like that happens every day."

Spinning straw into gold. Pffth, more like filling barrows of cash off the backs of other men's labors. Though the worst part wasn't the company doing business. It was one specific business, the one that had begun the family wealth, he objected to. The kind that blew off limbs and left good men and women dead on the ground. *The armament business.*

"I did nothing more than any other soldier does every day fighting for his or her country. Now, if you'll excuse me…"

"Ah, you've met." His father snuck up from behind and threw his arm around him, not in support, but to keep him in place. "I promised this young lady full access to your story, Will."

"Sorry, but I'm going to have to let you both down. I'm off to Manila in a few hours to help a friend." He pulled out of his father's iron grip, hot anger flaring. There was nothing he disliked more than being set up.

"No problem. I can easily arrange to go with you," Porsha responded too smoothly, the consummate professionalism obvious even through her charming smile that was meant to disarm. A barracuda no doubt lurked. Or maybe he was being too rough on her — maybe she was just trying to do her job, after all.

"Sorry, that won't work for me." He pressed his hand to his chest, touching the dog tags, his talisman, through his shirt. He had to give her something or she'd become a bigger pain in his ass. "Okay, when I get back, I'll make some time."

"When do you expect that to be?"

"I'll call you. I'm rather at the mercy of my friend on this one."

"Who are you going with, son?"

"Lacey Cameron." No point in hiding it.

His father's lips thinned, but he didn't take the bait.

"We need to talk. About business," Will pressed.

"You do have a poor sense of timing." He gave Will a look designed to cow business rivals. It usually worked, but not with Will. Will had seen every play in the book and waited him out.

"Fine, walk with me."

They headed out to the mezzanine. "Okay, say what it is you feel so compelled to share."

Will cleared his throat. He needed to get this right. "I want us to consider moving on from the armament business and into—"

"What? The very business our wealth is based on! The one that brought bread and butter to our table? That provided all the luxuries you now enjoy."

"And the one that kills and maims human beings. Is it so easy to forget about that? The price of war and profit is human lives. I want to see a new vision for us. I've just started a new venture with Charlie. He's developed a prototype for creating artificial limbs on 3D printers that cost a fraction—"

"And you think that can replace the lucrative armament business?" his father interrupted, the derision obvious in his scoffing tone.

"Not replace it right away, no, but surely we can transition to other companies that are just as profitable but that don't result in damaged lives. Besides, you're as rich as King Midas. Why are you stockpiling so much gold? We could manage to slow down profit and give back to the community and you'd never notice the difference."

"I earned my money the hard way. I do not apologize for the how to you or anyone."

"I didn't ask you to apologize—"

"Ladies and gentlemen, if you would take your seats, we're about to begin serving dinner," a loud voice came over the speaker above their heads.

"Time's up," his father chirped, a gleam of satisfaction in his eyes.

"This is not over," Will warned. But they headed back into the venue, conversation halted for the moment. Duty called.

Two grueling hours later, a few extra minutes spent buying Maureen the promised drink, and Will slid in behind the wheel of his car, relieved the evening was over. Then someone opened the passenger door and jumped in the other side. The exotic jasmine fragrance wafted his way. *Porsha Evans.*

"What do you think you're doing?" he asked, outraged.

"I wanted a few minutes alone with you. Seemed the best way," she said with a small shrug. She had the audacity of a good-looking woman, knowing she could get away with more than her less-endowed counterparts.

"Best you get out right here. I don't have time for —"

"Just a few minutes is all I ask. Drive me to your place and I'll take a cab back. I don't like that we got off on the wrong foot." She bit her lip, the first honest expression of the evening. "Please, I have a job to do." She laid her hand on his arm and he relented.

"Okay, just back to my place. I have to pack." He started the car.

"Fine. Do you mind if I tape the conversation?"

"Is that strictly necessary?"

"Not if it makes you uncomfortable."

"It does."

"Tell me about your life growing up? You come from a very rich family — that must have had some influence on you?"

"Well, no one has a choice of who their parents are or what socio-economic group they're born into. I admit, I was lucky in some ways. Went to some nice schools, had the best money can buy."

"And not in other ways? You obviously have some ideal you want to live up to. Does it have something to do with why—" She froze in mid-sentence, the loud police sirens drawing her attention. Will yanked the wheel hard, directed the coupé to the curb and took his foot off the gas. He slammed on the brakes, stopping on a dime. Another driver who wasn't so quick rolled right into the intersection.

A terrible pantomime unfolded in real time. Screeching tires. Crunching metal. The car ahead of them, unable to stop, torn nearly in half by another speeding vehicle T-boning the passenger door. A police cruiser entered the scene, chasing the first.

Will checked his rearview mirror. Others had pulled up behind them. He shut off the motor and turned to his uninvited guest.

"Wait here," he ordered. He opened his door and climbed out into the unknown, questions flooding his brain. *How badly are the people hurt? Is there anything I can do?*

The moisture-laden night air stank with the sharp odor of gasoline and smoke, rising in a soft billow from both the crushed car and the instigator vehicle. His clinical mind and military training took over. He raced to the small sedan that had been T-boned. It could have been him and Porsha, next in line to drive past Winnipeg's Confusion Corner, the notorious section of the city where the three roadways of Osborne, Corydon and Pembina Highway met.

He yanked on the passenger door. Though he pulled on it with all his might, the door was stuck fast, crushed in tight against the body of the car. Inside he could see the airbags had exploded and an elderly man had been flung back against the bench seat, blood streaming from facial lacerations.

He ran around to the driver's door. Thank God it opened. He checked the older man's pulse, laying two fingers gently against the carotid artery in his neck. The man had to be in his eighties and too much pressure on the artery could cause a heart attack all on its own. No pulse. He looked around frantically, but the lone cop was busy with the culprit, getting the young asshole into handcuffs. It was up to Will to keep the man alive until paramedics arrived.

He tore the airbag out of the way, exposing the man's chest. Was he having a heart attack? After unbuckling his seatbelt, he picked him up, laid him on the ground and began rapid-fire chest compressions, alternating with bursts of air into the man's frozen lungs. CPR training was something one never forgot after war. *Ever.*

The machine-like rhythm occupied all of him, sweat dripping into his eyes, his own heart rate thundering in his ears. An unknown amount of time passed. Still he kept up the repetitions, only stopping to check they were still necessary every few minutes, making him nearly jump out of his skin when the reporter asked loudly near his ear, "Is he breathing?"

A quick glance confirmed his suspicions. She was recording the entire episode on her iPhone.

"Don't you have anything better to do?" he snapped, adrenaline and hundreds of hours in his home gym giving him the stamina to continue indefinitely. It was always the same in the modern world. Style over substance. Video over action. Easier to observe than to do the right thing.

"Will, people need to see how it's done," Porsha said, her voice filled with a chiding admiration. Guilt struck. He should have thought of that.

"They should take a course." Sirens flared then ground to a halt close by. Help was here. Seconds later, paramedics equipped with a gurney and portable equipment rushed up. The pair of professionals assessed the situation, laying out their equipment, preparing the defibrillator.

"Thanks, we'll take over from here."

Will removed his hands, got out of the way quickly, and let the trained men continue his work on their patient. He pressed his lips together and offered up a small prayer for the man and his family. Even throughout the war, Will had not lost his belief in a higher power, though he'd lost some of his enthusiasm for his fellow man after observing first-hand what mankind was capable of. *War can do that to a soldier. Make them question.* Something his father was none too pleased about. Or his brother.

Adrenaline fled his system with the crisis over, his body no longer requiring the extra fuel. Exhaustion set in almost immediately, his arms tingly from the extreme muscle actions, his mind clouding over. He sighed. He still needed to pack and head to Florida ASAP. But first he'd have to give a statement to the police then deal with the reporter. And the hardest thing of all, what to do about his growing feelings for Lacey that had gone well beyond seeing her as a friend? His mind segued to imagining getting the better of the woman who so loved to play practical jokes on him.

Hmm. A diabolical scheme shot into his mind in an instant, throwing off the tiredness playing havoc with his system. *Yes.* He'd get her to stand up and take notice.

Chapter Three

"Argue for your limitations, and sure enough, they are yours." — *Richard Bach*

Ah, the Florida Keys. The heartwarming view from the boardwalk of sailboats and families carousing in the water added a spring to Will's step as he strode along. The passing sounds of a tug boat warning of its approach assailed his senses, along with the sharp odor of brine and fish. The sun was already tracking its fiery course across the summer sky when he stopped to pull open the wooden door of the Sugar Shack. He'd gotten the message at the hotel that Lacey was having brunch at the local eatery. He was a bit behind. It seemed like anything that could go wrong this morning had, from finishing up business details to running the gamut of that nosy reporter. But one thing had gone very right. The Ringers had asked for his help in protecting and keeping Lacey safe in Manila and he'd given his solemn word she'd come to no harm on his watch.

He gave a quick perusal of the joint, letting his eyes have a second to adjust to the lower light level. His breathing dramatically increased as he took in the image of Lacey, frowning and busy with her stuff all spread out around her, sitting at a bar table.

"Meow." A tiny kitten, bedraggled and sitting in the middle of the chaos, made the first move.

"Will," Lacey said, giving him a grin. One hand clutched a file and the other a coffee cup, her laptop open. Bending down to kiss her check, he caught a whiff of the Irish coffee fragrance that lingered on her breath. She was dressed casually in white shorts and a flowing sky-blue tank top, managing to make the outfit look fancier than some women did full evening dress.

The black kitten with one white patch of fur surrounding a golden eye took his measure at that moment. It stood up in the center of the table, arching its approximately six-ounce body in a feeble effort to look larger, and made the most insistent hissing sound imaginable at him.

"Will, meet Jolly Roger. Doesn't he look just like a pirate with the patch on his eye? I found him abandoned on the beach this morning." Lacey looked so pleased with herself, but he just shook his head. *So Lacey. What's she thinking?* Now they'd be delayed finding a shelter that would take the scrap.

He reached out to pet the sad excuse for a feline – it had to have been the runt of the litter – getting a bat of its paw for his efforts. A dew claw dragged along the back of his hand for extra emphasis on exactly how the kitten felt about his presence.

"I don't think he's very jolly," he said, arching an eyebrow and nodding at the waitress picking up a carafe at the bar to bring him some coffee. He waited while she poured him a mug and offered a menu he refused, before walking away. "Do you really think you should name an animal you'll just have to abandon here anyway?"

"Maybe he's concerned you're so late this morning because you were busy rogering someone last night." He noted the edgy tone.

"Then I'm the one who should be jolly. But for your information, I was too busy getting ready to escort you to Manila for any rogering last night. Not that it wasn't offered."

"I'll just bet," she said, thinning her plush lips into a firm line.

"People change, you know. Grow up. Decide to set a new course."

"Your course has always included being the epitome of a playboy. Why change it now? Works for business and gets you what you want — an endless string of women to warm your bed — and other things."

The accusations hurt, mostly because it had been all too true. Since he'd come home from this last tour of duty, he'd lost control of his destiny. But all that was going to change. In fact, big changes were underway already, giving his life more meaning. Giving him a reason to get out of bed in the morning and keep it empty of the wrong company. But now was not the time to get into it with Lacey. The current mission was to safely escort her to Manila and see it through, under the guise of a lost bet.

"Where's Lily? I thought she was with you." Maybe Lily could deal with the kitten, maybe even take him home for her sister. No, that wouldn't work. Border agents would put the kibosh on that idea in about three seconds flat. And that would upset her too much.

"Went home this morning."

He took a large gulp of coffee. Though distracted by the new case, Lacey looked good, really good. And smelled even better. Vanilla always wafted off her in waves, reminding him of sugar cookies, his favorite cookies to nibble on. Being around her made him horny and hungry.

"I'm sorry to hear about your friend Daniel Wright." *Who exactly was he to Lacey?* The Ringers had filled him in some, mentioning Lacey had dated the guy in high school. How serious had the relationship been? His stomach tightened just thinking about it. He'd always been under the impression she was as footloose as him, but with more restraint. He hadn't seen her date anyone more than a couple of times.

"Thanks. I feel so bad about Megan, his sister. She's all torn up about it."

He cleared his throat. "So, you'd better pack up. I got a jet with your name on it waiting, beautiful."

"If it has my name on it, it can wait," she said, pursing her lips but also powering down her laptop. *So like Lacey, always needing to be the one in control.*

The kitten jumped onto her lap and she stroked its fur, the sounds it emitted surprisingly loud, like the little steam engine that could. The stroking was bad enough, but then she picked him up and tucked him — if it was a him — into her tank top, tying the ends over her trim belly to keep the animal cocooned inside. *Lucky fucking tyke.*

"Pick up your stuff. We'll need to find a shelter for Jolly Roger." He softened his directive by helping her gather her things. But one horrified glance told him he'd gotten something wrong.

"What?"

"JR goes with me." Ah, there was that no-nonsense tone she was famous for.

"Lacey—"

"A warrior stands up for those who are weak, for the innocent, for the vulnerable," she quoted.

"Not sure the samurai meant strays. But fine, he's your problem." Though he was secretly pleased he could offer private travel to prevent anyone taking the little guy away from her.

"Not up to helping with one tiny little itsy-bitsy kitten? My big strong warrior's been felled by six ounces of spit and vinegar," she teased, tucking her papers and laptop into a large bag hanging off the back of her chair. Her luggage stood to the side of the table, a carryall on wheels stuffed to breaking point, its sides bulging alarmingly. They were the only two customers in the restaurant.

"Hardly," he scoffed, grabbing her suitcase in preparation for leading the way. He had been given carte blanche to deal with her and he intended to honor it. And he had a surprise up his sleeve that would have him finally winning a bet. Even though winning with Lacey was usually best done by losing, this time he intended to win. Big.

* * * *

"Okay. Ground rules first. You are not to run off half-cocked any old time you feel like it. And you're going to stay by my side for this entire trip. It's my job to see you home safely. I've made promises to certain parties and you know I never go back on my word, unlike some I won't mention," Will said after she'd gone to all the trouble of filling in him about Danny's tragic case and the need for prompt action. What part did he not get about how vital it was that they use every moment to get to the bottom of things? He was smoothly working the controls of the Learjet as they flew through clear skies toward the Philippines, obviously not as invested in the case as she was.

"What! I can't promise that. What's got into you? You've never made me promise stuff like this before," she complained, taken aback. Will was her golden ticket, usually amenable to her wishes, well, honestly only after she'd explained the urgency of things. But still. She grabbed the half-empty mickey of McGuinness whiskey from her bag and took a swig. JR was sound asleep on her lap, occasionally trilling as if he had a hyperactive purr mechanism, succeeding in endearing himself all the more. He'd given up playing with his favorite toy, a shark tooth on a string, bought at the gift shop. No way would she ever tell Will about that encounter, not if she wanted to avoid another long, freakin' boring lecture.

"Yeah, and you've gone to the Philippines looking into a murder case before, right? You are aware of its well-deserved reputation for making tourists vanish? Permanently? No. We do this my way or I'm not landing. I know you all too well, Miss Cameron. Your track record stinks. You don't know when enough is enough."

"Now you tell me," she grumbled. "What Lily doesn't know won't hurt her." She had to be the culprit behind this assault, even if he wasn't fessing up.

"Yeah, well, when I promise someone something, I keep my word." Will's lips thinned as his jaw hardened.

First Lily, now Will. What was the world coming to? Maybe she could be impulsive, but she had the proverbial luck of a cat. She'd proved that many times. Life. Meant to be lived. Be like water. Water is very difficult to stop. It finds the smallest crack in an object, invades and fills any gap, wears away defenses, goes into places unseen and overcomes the strongest obstacle. Water supports the largest ship. She decided to ignore the last part of the refrain about water also being capable of overturning a ship. She knew how to swim — even with sharks.

"You need to loosen up, William James Thornton III. And I'm just the woman to teach you."

He snorted. "Your feminine wiles have no power over me, beautiful. Save that for a weaker man. When I want a woman, I let them know. Make myself indispensable, for one."

Wasn't that exactly what he was doing right now? Was he suggesting he wanted more? Her heart rate quickened. "Okay." She made the sign of the cross. "I promise not to go out of my way to ditch you." *Could happen by accident, right? Not going to be hamstrung in Manila. And plans made beforehand don't count at all.* What Will didn't know about the Tiger's Sword couldn't hurt him. It had been years since she'd mentioned it, anyway.

"Your word's gold. Remember that."

She squirmed uncomfortably. Will had changed since he came back from his last tour of duty. Darker. Edgier. Coming and going without explanation. Maybe having his friend Charlie lose his lower leg to war had affected him more than he let on? But, no, he'd taken it fine, exhibiting his warrior ethos and helping Charlie through it. Everyone's rock.

"You look like you've lost weight," she said, sizing him up from under half-closed eyelids as she leaned back in her seat, admiring the dark tribal tattoos that snaked their way down both biceps. The artist had done a good job of making them appear 3D.

He shrugged. "Maybe," he said noncommittally while checking the instrument panel.

"You still seeing that army shrink?"

"Sometimes," he admitted. "Not sure it helps much."

"Yeah, I know what you mean. Most shrinks are more like rubbernecks at an accident or too busy trying to figure out their own shite," Lacey grumbled. Besides, dragging some stuff into the light of day was far too painful. But she had the cure. Just keep movin' and the shit don't stick. Of course, that personal philosophy predated her warrior creed, which had a nicer ring to it, but it still got the job done.

"I got us an invite for tonight at the governor's mansion." Lacey savored the moment. As expected, Will's dark eyebrows rose over his eyes, eyes that never seemed to miss a thing. A definite Zac Efron type, though a whole lot bigger, hence his nickname, the Wall. "You should shave that thing off, you know. You're far too handsome to be covering up that mug, even if it's in fashion." To underscore the point, she reached over and tugged on the full beard. *Hmm, plusher than expected – not so rough.*

"That was quick. I do admire your style, Miss Cameron. And I've had a beard before it was in fashion—so lay off," he warned, sharing a smile to lessen the sting. "Not that I look forward to dressing up in a monkey suit. But how exactly did you manage that? Or aren't you free to share Cameron state secrets?"

"Scoped out the guest list, of course. Easy to add our names."

"You mean you hacked into it." Will snorted. "What about the formal invite—the one you normally show at the door? It's a museum fundraiser with priceless artifacts. There'll be security checks. You can count on it."

"Don't worry about it. I got that covered too."

"That's exactly what I do worry about, beautiful." He shook his head, his lips tightening.

"And I thought maybe, with your special connections, we might gain access to—"

He interrupted her. "I've been doing some serious thinking about that since I got back, about leaving the family business in my brother's more than capable hands. Strike out on my own, get away from all things to do with the war."

"Hey, don't cop out on me now. I may need your special connections and talents in Manila." She'd heard this song-and-dance routine last time he got back from his tour of duty, when he and Alexander had gotten into it about a part of their business that supplied contracts of armaments for the war. It had involved ethics or something like that. He just needed her to shake him out of it. Again. "And, you know, Alexander and your dad are not going to make it easy for you to leave, right? Aren't your charity fundraising events enough for you? It's more than most rich playboys manage. Why spoil a perfect gig?"

"Do you want kids one day?"

"What? Where are you coming from with this?" The complete change of subject threw her into confusion.

"Just indulge me. I'm escorting you all the way to Manila, so the least you can do is answer a simple question. Do you intend to have children one day?"

"I don't know—I guess. Haven't given it much thought. But since I'm never, ever getting married"—she shrugged—"I'd need to plan carefully. You know—put money aside. Find a sperm donor." She snorted at the crazy image of being artificially inseminated, remembering a movie that had used a baster for the procedure. Not exactly her style.

"A sperm donor, eh?" He smoothed down his beard, obviously thinking. "Okay. I volunteer when you're ready. I think our genes would click perfectly and create a super kid."

"More like one that runs off and joins the circus or gets themselves into all kinds of hot water if it gets endowed with my temperament."

"Your temperament's not your problem. You're a lot of fun to be with."

"Oh, so I do have a problem?" She pretended the words didn't sting.

"No, it's your headstrong need to rush in where fools fear to tread. I don't see all this warrior doctrine you've been spouting really helping you that much. You appear to be the same Lacey always getting into trouble and needing someone—namely me—to get you out."

"It helps! I've learned a ton about behavior. I've made much wiser decisions this past year, I'll have you know. When was the last time you got a call from me? And this one doesn't count. I had a gun to my head."

"Okay. I'll give you that. This is the first time this year. But in years past—"

"You're not the only one who can change, Mr. Thornton. I'm quite capable of changing."

"Then prove it. Be careful in Manila."

His words grated. Hadn't they just been over this? "Christ, Will, when did you get so serious? What happened to fun-loving playboy Will? My favorite partner in crime? I want him back. You know — the guy who mooned my entire sorority. I'll bet you're still getting dates over that one."

"Yeah, after you streaked through the cafeteria on a dare. And maybe a guy never kisses and tells." He shook his head, but a twitch at the corner of his mouth gave him away.

"Nice ass, by the way."

"Got your name on it."

"What are you talking about?" She gave him an incredulous look.

"Don't ask. It was another dare. Each guy on my football team had to get a woman's name in ink on some part of their body. You know — sort of like your Ringers tattoo." He meant the one on her shoulder that she treasured as it made her feel she belonged somewhere. *Safe.*

"So you got mine?" She sat frozen, overwhelmed by the implications. Had he really done that and not her sister's?

"Not exactly."

"Then what?"

"I got the words 'your name' tattooed on my butt." He broke out into a belly laugh, a wondrous sound that rumbled through her, making her feel things she preferred not to feel.

She punched him lightly on the biceps.

"Ouch."

"I want to see that tattoo. You must have gotten it after you mooned us."

"So, you did scope out my ass. And yeah, to answer your question, got it about three weeks later."

"Let's not make this trip all about doom and gloom. Promise?"

"Whatever you want, beautiful," he said with a snort.

"Good, glad that's settled. Now, let's get this baby on the ground so we can get to that party. I'm dying to see the collection. Maybe even beat you to finding a small souvenir of our trip. So, what shall we bet this time? The one who finds something special first?" she teased, her drive to outwit Will and find some treasure rearing up as always. They had been trying to outdo the other in acquiring such objects for years. She'd deal with the investigation tomorrow—this was her one chance to nab the sword. General Yamashita's sword. The Tiger of Malaya's samurai sword. The sword she'd always meant to acquire and now had the perfect opportunity.

"So help me God, if you try anything, Lacey Anne Cameron, I will bring my full force to bear down on your head. There's to be no bet this time. Not in Manila."

"Oh yeah! What would you do about it?" Good, her friend was back.

"You don't want to know. But you wouldn't be able to sit down for a week, that I can promise you."

"Hmm, I'd like to see you try! I'd have you on your back in a heartbeat with one of my spectacular karate moves. Don't be provoking me, buster, or it's your ass that will be in a sling."

"I'm bigger than you. I'm stronger than you. Don't give me provocation, beautiful. And I know a few special moves myself." He made the last statement with a smoldering glance that burned right down to her tapping toes.

Her pulse quickened and she licked her lips at the zinger, considering Will's idea of a special move. Exactly what would that entail? Her Will was all alpha male — a prime example of the species if there ever was one. "Yeah, well, I'm quicker than you! Don't forget I ran track at school. Even beat out Casey in the finals."

"Don't push me too far, beautiful, or you'll be the one who loses. I'd do anything to keep you safe — even if it means taking matters into my own hands and giving you that spanking you'll so richly deserve if you put yourself at risk while we're in Manila. It's past time you got a taste of your own medicine." His threat sounded more like fun than real, what with Lacey's mind following the seductive breadcrumb trail to the bedroom. Nah, Will was her friend, not her lover, even if he liked to make seductive suggestions he never followed up on. *Sperm donor, really.* Besides, he was a playboy at heart. A twinge of jealously shot through her.

"I could have gone to Vegas and spoken to the wife first," she said, casually. She might be directing the case, but still, it was helpful to bounce things off him. She glanced out of the side window. Lush green landscape interspaced with Quonset huts followed by the sprawling metropolis of the city came into sharper focus. Will lowered the jet's elevation, the first step in beginning his runway approach.

"No, your first thought was good. Best to get the facts from the source — right where the crime occurred. Then when you interview her, you'll have a better idea if she's involved in anything."

"Okay, I'll stick with my game plan. You're right, I'm usually correct anyway about things," she teased.

"Yeah, most things, beautiful, I'll give you that. But not everything. There's so much hidden that you tend to miss."

"If I miss it, it can't be that important."

"A warrior misses nothing. He understands what is said, and what is unsaid," he quoted. "You've still got some things to learn, Miss Cameron. We all do."

"Ha." She grinned at him, trying to be mysterious. "A warrior also knows to keep his own counsel and his trap shut, even if he knows it all."

"I think you just made that up." He raised a dark eyebrow in her direction. "So, you think you know me?"

"I know you like the back of my hand, handsome. You're an open book—a man without secrets." Even though it wasn't exactly the case anymore, she'd never let on. She needed to feel in charge, that things would stay the same. That she and Will would always have the easy banter and relationship. That nothing would come between them.

"What is your deepest, darkest secret, beautiful?"

"Phhttt." She let out a breath, annoyance twinging at the question. "I don't know. I'm too busy living my life to worry about it. Same as everyone."

"I think it's that you're scared to lose a bet."

"Me scared! I'm the one trying to make one for Manila, and someone's being a party-pooper."

"Okay then, I'll bet you that I can beat you at a game of poker."

"What kind of poker? How about strip-poker, just to up the ante?" She was darned good at poker. This would be a breeze to win. And making Will strip would be too delicious. She'd get to check out that crazy tattoo. "And let's up the payout. I want something special when I win — something entirely different. Say, a fancy new Bose sound system. Then I'll think our national treasure Celine Dion is right in the room with me, singing like a glorious angel."

"And it's not special to have me at your beck and call anymore? How things have changed." He shook his head, but his grin gave him away. "But me, I get a future favor." Now he looked too smug, like he had her.

"On second thought, I think I prefer the future favor too." He was not getting one up on her.

"Too late. You already called it."

"That's cheating. I was still thinking about it."

"Live with it, baby, live with it."

A loud squawk over Will's headset demanded his instant attention. They were landing at Ninoy Aquino International Airport about four miles south of Manila. The thought of a glittering evening's promise lying ahead sent a frisson of excitement racing through Lacey. She grinned at her daring plan. She'd win his silly old game anyway. She had an ace up her sleeve.

* * * *

Lacey made a last perusal in the mirror. Dark wig to hide her own red curls, artfully arranged into a waterfall that defied gravity — check. Makeup enhanced with a modern smoky eye recommended for green eyes and cleverly glossed lips — check. And the coup de grâce, a watered-silk seafoam green dress cut down to her navel front and back in a v shape, requiring two-sided tape that she'd chosen to forgo — check and mate.

"Think I'll catch the big fish tonight, JR?" She twirled around for the kitten's perusal. He ignored her, busily pouncing on his new cat toy lying on the hotel bed, a stuffed gray mouse with a bell for a tail, apparently blithely unconcerned about matters of grooming. He'd left that to her, squawking the entire time she'd bathed him in the flea dip and brushed his coal-black fur to a burnished shine.

"Well, I'd say we both clean up nice."

Her cell phone buzzed with incoming traffic.

Meet you there. Business calls. Car in front for u at 7.

Invite left for u at front desk, she texted right back.

Lacey scooped up her evening purse, tossing in lip gloss and the room key, then added a small canister of pepper spray attached to a penlight. A gal could never be too prepared. Picking up the prerequisite party mask for the masquerade ball, she took a minute to admire its silvery sheen and white feathery fringe before she slipped from the room, tugging the *Do Not Disturb* sign onto the outside door handle to keep JR safe, and sailed forth to the lobby.

The limo pulled into the long lineup in front of Malacañan Palace twenty minutes later. Lacey's fingers absently smoothed and fluttered over the soft feathers of the mask she held in her lap while she waited her turn to disembark the limo crawling carload by carload toward the glittering entrance.

Hmm. Designed by the Spanish with a love of colonial architecture, the neoclassical structure graced the Pasig River. She mentally recited the facts she'd read from the online tourist brochure, admiring the snow-white classical arches and red-velvet rooftop. Now that made her want cake from her favorite Winnipeg bakery,

Jeanne's. Her stomach rumbled. *Okay, think about something else.* Surely there would be canapés at the party. Yes. Some dispute over the origins of the name for the palace. Everything from 'the place of many great ones' to 'place of evil bamboo'. Built in the mid-eighteenth century, the palace was now the official working residence of the current president. *Sweet. Meet the president and son and reconnoiter the sword. Three birds with one stone.*

She held her head high, practicing her model walk from the car through the entrance and into the Rizal Ceremonial Hall, mask in place. Again, a wait. It sucked standing around on four-inch heels. Not her idea of fun. She looked longingly at the benches lined up along the walls, where some people had already claimed a spot.

She presented her ticket to security, heart skipping precisely one beat. Had her guy forged it right? It had been a quick job, then FedExed overnight to the hotel in Florida.

"Enjoy your evening," the man in the black suit said with a bored nod to the group moving through ahead of her. Finally, he turned to her. A headpiece with microphone and a slight bulge in his jacket pocket screamed *security detail* just before his eyes popped from his head, not able to shift his vision farther up her body for a full count of three seconds. *Men. So predictable.*

His eyes met hers, assessing. He'd barely glanced down at her golden ticket, handing it back to her. *Whew.* She tucked it back into her evening bag.

"It'll be our little secret, sweetheart," he said with a small grin as he waved her through. *Fuck.* What miniscule detail had been wrong? She could hardly ask the guy. The Doctor, her usual forger, had had to beg off back in Florida when she'd contacted him, with flu or something, handing the job off to an assistant he swore by. Well, she'd damn well swear at him when she got back home, demand her hard-earned money back.

She took a glass of champagne from one offered on a tray by a black-uniformed waitress and stood off to one side, watching the multitude of guests in their glittering gowns, men in black tie, everyone anonymous in fancy masks. Combined with the impressive enhancement of thousands of pinpoints of light, it gave the occasion a definite fairyland luster. She pulled her phone from her purse and sent Will a quick alert to stand down — the invite didn't pass muster. She gulped the first glass, picked up another from the next tray and took a few more sips, waiting to hear back. She scanned the room, checking the position of the security cameras.

Finishing her second glass, she nabbed a third, with time marching on. *Come on, Will, answer the damn text.* She needed to find some food to absorb the alcohol, but it was hard to relax until she'd heard from him. *What if something has already happened?* She glanced at the receiving line, but nothing looked untoward. The two male security guards working the crowd looked bored as hell. *Good, stay that way.*

"Please don't tell me you bat for the other team." A low male voice interrupted her thoughts. She'd missed him coming up while texting. He towered over her. Not easy to do considering her height of five foot seven and the four-inch heels. Most of the men in the room she could peer down on. What had been devastating in high school was now a cool advantage.

A definite hunk stood confidently before her, his thick hair burnished golden by the overhead chandeliers and his clean-shaven face exposed by the bottom half of his mask, highlighting full lips and a jawline chiseled from pure granite. Just about everyone else in the room being blessed with brunette or black hair and dark eyes made him stand out. She was the tall woman, he the lone male-model type. *Hmm.* She ran the tip of her tongue over her bottom lip.

"Now why would that matter? Maybe my girlfriend is bi," she said, raising her eyebrows at his audacity. She'd heard worse opening lines.

"Not certain a ménage would suit. I'm greedy enough to want you all to myself," he said. A hint of amusement colored his tone, the blue eyes through his black mask alive with devilment, further piquing her interest. He had a great voice, low with a resonance that spoke volumes about his male DNA. She'd be even more interested once she was certain Will had gotten her message. She didn't want him embarrassed by being tossed out of the event, or, worse yet, being detained. The lecture and ensuing guilt she'd get then would rival the time in Maui when she'd nabbed that bicycle from a local eatery, having every intention of returning it as soon as the chase was over. Really.

"Maybe I'm into sharing," she teased back.

"You're Canadian," he observed, accepting a glass of champagne from a waiter.

She nodded. She took a sip of champagne, eyeing him over the glass. "I'm Anne. And you are?"

"Michael—"

She pressed her fingertips over his lips, interrupting him. "Just first names. That's what a masquerade ball is all about. Mystery."

He nibbled playfully at her fingertips, making her eyes open wider when a shiver of pleasure danced across her skin.

"And what do you do, Michael?"

"I'm in town on business. And you?"

"Business as well."

"What kind of business?" he asked.

"Just checking on something for a friend."

"Long way to come to help a friend. You must be very good friends."

"Yes, old friends. So, how long are you in town for?"

"Not sure. Depends on opportunities," he said lightly. His blue eyes quickened with interest when she gave him a quick glance upward from under her thick eyelashes. The mask brought a new edge to the game, condensing it down to what message could be delivered by the eyes alone.

She nodded at the crowd, considering. "Do you know the president?"

"Not personally. But I would hazard a guess that's their party coming in now."

Lacey took a discreet look in the direction Michael saluted with his glass of champagne. Yes, the governor's party had arrived. Her heartbeat increased. She glanced up at her new acquaintance, who was just finishing off his glass of alcohol.

"If you'll excuse me for just a moment? And perhaps you'd like to take a closer look at all the loot displayed for the peons this evening?" he asked.

She snorted. "Sure, that's right up my alley."

He headed in the direction of the bathrooms. The governor's party was working the room. She recognized the older, dignified man while the others orbited around him. *He should be thanking me for what*

I'm about to do — relieving the palace of the sword and perhaps averting a future scandal. It had been stolen in the first place and had a checkered provenance.

"Well, well, who do we have here?" a voice broke into her thoughts. She spun around to find herself peering down at a very slick-looking man — no other way to describe him. Well-oiled hair and a suit that shone like cheap sharkskin. Bad acne must have plagued him as a child, which slightly softened her view. That couldn't have been easy. His photos online must have been retouched to mask the flaws.

"I'm Anne. And you are?"

"Marcus Salang. The governor's son at your service. Any service you need, I'm your man," he said followed by a lecherous grin from under his black wolf mask.

"I'll just bet you are." *Oh God, grant me the patience.* Marcus was obviously used to throwing out who he was to the women present at these official receptions and getting fawned all over. The shaved sides on his scalp, a sort of Viking style haircut, did not flatter. Why were so many males jumping on board with the severe cut? It boggled the mind. Now Will knew how to look good. His haircut flattered, even if it was short.

"You know, for a woman like you, I'd ditch this place in a heartbeat. Got a party with your name written all over it about to start at Club Ten. Ever heard of it?"

"No, can't say I have."

"Only women who are a ten get in," he chortled.

Did you really just say that?

"How about the men? They have to be a ten too?"

Want a man to notice you? Don't play too nice.

He gave his barracuda grin, obviously too confident to be insulted. Exactly what she counted on. He pursed his fleshy lips, giving her a sly glance. "Only a ten in the money department, sugar."

"Salang," she mused, sipping at her champagne, keeping him on the string. "Your family surname means 'in place' and the origin is Tagalog."

"You study our history?" he asked, his eyebrows rising over his dark, beady eyes.

"More like an interest in etymology—the study of where words originate," she said with a small shrug.

"I can forgive that," he said with a smirk. He leaned over and brought his fleshy lips to her ear. "But I have something I think you might have an even bigger interest in."

"And what's that?" she asked, managing not to take a step back from the sharp tang of alcohol on his breath.

"I collect artifacts, many never shown to the public. If you would like a tour, I can easily arrange one. Anytime. Right now, if you like. I have many things I would enjoy sharing with a woman like you. Many, many things."

"Really," she said, her heart rate accelerating. *Perfect.* She could handle this mutt no problem-o. "I have an interest in antiquities."

He ran a finger lightly down her arm. She barely suppressed a shudder of revulsion.

"Would you care to see the public exhibit now, sweetheart?" Michael asked pointedly as he rejoined her.

She'd missed his coming up while listening to the seedy albeit exactly-what-she-was-after offer. She frowned. She'd handled a dozen men like him in the past and easily outwitted them. And this Salang was a big fish, according to her research. And the biggest reason she'd chosen this dress. Checking out his antiquities would be a fabulous opportunity, one she didn't intend to miss out on. Business first.

Marcus frowned at the interruption. "The lady and I were talking. I would appreciate your butting out," he said, his tone growly as a grizzly.

"Sorry, but we already have a date, so I recommend you step back, sir." The 'sir' didn't come out filled with even one small iota of respect.

"Do you not realize who the fuck I am?" Marcus growled louder, his eyes hardening through the mask. His bodyguards looked up from a short distance away, alerted now, their dark stares adding a slice of sinister to the threat.

"No. Should I?" Michael asked, his eyes glinting dangerously.

Just what I need. Two men making a huge scene. With what she had in mind, less attention would be entirely welcome. Talk about bad timing. Michael might intrigue her, but she was not going to alter her plans just to satisfy a temporary itch, no matter how well packaged the gift.

The two men faced off. *Enough of this shite.*

"I'm sorry to break it to you both, but I'm a grown-ass adult and I choose my own direction. I also have a special interest in antiquities —"

"Marcus. Oh, Marcus," a feminine voice interrupted. A petite woman swept up to them, her pink flamingo mask the perfect foil for her dress. Dark glossy curls perked up her appearance. *Damn it.* Lacey might have missed her perfect opportunity.

"You promised to show me Club Ten," the interloper said with a small pout.

Lacey bit down on her bottom lip, stealing a quick glance around for the closest exit. Michael was seething with emotion, his fists clenched at his sides. *This is going so well.*

"Yeah," Marcus said as he appeared to be debating which way to go.

"I saved all this night just for you," the woman purred, sidling closer and placing a proprietary hand on his arm, pressing the side of her breast against it. If she was that desperate, what the hell.

"Another time, Marcus. I'll take a rain check on the tour. It appears your friend is more in need of you right now. But I thank you kindly for the stimulating conversation." *There, tit for tat, Michael. I call my own shots.*

"I will bid you goodnight then, Miss Anne," Marcus said with aplomb, reaching for and raising her hand to his mouth to kiss in one gallant operation. She hid a shiver when he slid his damp mouth over the back of it. He didn't offer his hand to Michael, who didn't appear too upset at the slight.

"Nice to meet you," Lacey murmured, watching the woman's eyes narrow with jealously. *He's all yours, sweetheart. For now.*

She took a drink of the champagne. Damn. She'd lost her big chance to check out future acquisitions tonight.

Michael stood at her side like a grenade about to go off if someone would just pull the pin, but also managing to look smug at having won the first round. Some feat with a mask on.

"That was unnecessary." She released some of her fury at losing out on the tour.

"Do you know who that guy is? A barracuda. A shark in sheep's clothing. An untrustworthy piece of —"

"Don't you mean a wolf in sheep's clothing?" she asked in a chiding tone.

"You know what I mean. You want my advice? Stay away from that guy." His voice held a cold fury. A little overkill.

"As it happens, I do not need your advice." What was it to him who she spent time with? They'd just met, for heaven's sake. Seething, she told herself to calm down, that she needed to direct her energies to the reason she was at the party in the first place.

"Fine. But I'm just suggesting you think very carefully before spending any time alone with him. He's not trustworthy."

"You've voiced your objections. Can we move on?"

"I was thinking we should check out the exhibit."

"Might as well," she grumbled. At least it would get her closer to the part of the palace she wanted to be in.

"Nice tattoo, by the way." He traced the tattoo on her shoulder with a finger before placing a very large, warm hand on her lower back, searing her bare flesh. His citrus aftershave with darker tones of exhilarating male musk tantalized her senses and brought her back into the moment. He directed her steps to the exhibit. She took a deep breath, enjoying the pheromones left in his wake. She'd already lost one big fish tonight — why let her annoyance lose her another one? *The investigation won't consume every hour of the night, right?*

"It represents a group I joined in university. We call ourselves the Brass Ringers. Eight of us, one for each interlocking ring. We all have it inked on our upper shoulders."

"And hence the stylized *R*." He gave a half-smile. "Are they all as ravishing as you?"

"Depends on who you ask. But yeah, pretty awesome crew. Gorgeous, smart and fun."

He leaned down and murmured so close to her ear that his warm fragrant breath grazed the side of her neck, making her shiver. "I'd like to learn more about the 'fun Anne'."

"I'm here on business. Had to leave her at home," she quipped back with a small smirk.

"That's a shame. I'd love to ask her out to play sometime."

She laughed, letting go of the rest of her annoyance. *A warrior knows when to move on — save what they can from any situation.* "I'll just bet you would."

The display cases, guarded by a stony-faced crew, came into view when they turned the corner into the exhibition area. Lacey mentally envisioned the blueprints for the palace while dutifully admiring the treasures housed under the bulletproof glass. None quickened her interest like the sword reported to be housed separately, in a small room off the Hall of Honors. She slanted her gaze to the right, catching the movement of women parading off to the bathroom. A lavish display of foliage discreetly hid the entrance, the security camera not facing that way, but toward the larger room. *Good.*

"If you'll excuse me, I need to powder my nose." She gave the age-old excuse, antsy to get down to the real business of why she was here tonight.

"Sweetheart, if you enhance your ravishing beauty any more, I will not be held accountable for my Neanderthal reactions. A man can only take so much." He leaned forward and lightly tweaked the end of her nose, giving her a wolfish grin and a deliberate wink.

She couldn't keep from smiling. *Audacious as hell.* He wanted in her pants, no doubt, but he had a charming way of putting things. Nothing wrong with instant lust.

Hell, she hadn't been this turned on in ages. Too bad the night's agenda took priority. *Damn.* Too bad all right. But it was her one chance.

"Where are you staying?" she asked, making an instantaneous decision.

"The Mariette."

"Meet you in the downstairs piano bar at midnight if we get separated, sans mask," she said on impulse.

"You can count on it." He took her hand and pressed his firm lips to her palm. She shivered, the feathers of his mask tickling her hand only adding to the sensory overload.

She pulled her arm back and purposely walked away, heading for the ladies' room. *Clear your mind. You've got a prize to collect.*

The line for the bathroom was beyond ridiculous. She waited all of two seconds before giving a disgusted snort, then slipped out behind the covering mass of stylized foliage and down the hallway. Finding it dead quiet at this end of the building, she moved unnoticed through an antechamber, making a sharp right turn at the exit. An image of the Pink Panther came to mind. She held back a nervous giggle.

She was near the back of the palace now, with only one more room before it exited onto the riverbank. She pulled the necessary tool from her purse and unlocked the door. *Now I'm breaking the law.* This was far harder to explain than the cover story of being lost. Her heart rate hammered in sympathy. The door snapped shut behind her. Thunder rumbled ominously in the distance.

Tock-tock-tock. A grandfather clock in an unseen corner of the final room reminded her — no time to lose.

She swallowed hard.

Taking a deep breath, she crossed the final room stealthily, the dark shadows created by the dim lighting rattling her nerves. She didn't want to be surprised by someone looming at her from behind a fixture. *Just a few more steps.* Her ears were acutely tuned to any slight sound or rustle. The cabinet designed to hold the sword upright came into view. Her fingers itched, but her mind focused. All was about to be revealed. Her heartbeat increased further, the sound a thumping echo in her ears.

Was that a noise?

She froze. Sweat trickled down her sides. Fear prickled her scalp. What if she had made a huge miscalculation? No. It was just raindrops hitting the windowpane. She let out an unsteady hiss of breath.

One more step —

Fucking empty? No way.

Her hands balled into fists. All this for shite. The cabinet door left slightly ajar and the sword that had gleamed so brightly in her mind — nowhere to be seen. Someone had beaten her to it. Swallowing the let-down loaded with anger, she crept from the room, retracing her steps back to the women's bathroom where the line was now non-existent.

Disappointed was not a big enough word to encompass what she was feeling. She washed her hands, then blotted her underarms with paper towels. Frowning at her image in the mirror, she wanted to throw something, anything. *God-damn-it-all-to-hell.* Someone had beaten her by only a few precious minutes, judging by the open cabinet. If only she hadn't dawdled. Only herself to blame.

She checked her phone on the way to the exit, signaling for her car. Just enough time to get back to the hotel and meet her hot date. *Fair compensation for tonight's complete FUBAR, right?* It was a rare occurrence to not get what she wanted. It stung, more than she'd ever let on.

The warrior must never give in or give up.

Chapter Four

"No man is an island." — *John Donne*

In the piano bar, she surveyed the room. No blond men. And she was running late. Had he stood her up? *Fuck.* Messed with twice in one night. It just couldn't be happening. Was she losing her touch? Was twenty-seven getting old?

She went up to the bar and slipped onto a stool. Checked her reflection in the mirror, overcome by doubt. No way. She looked the same. His loss.

"What can I get you, gorgeous?" the bartender asked, his appreciative smile speaking volumes.

"A Coors Light and a cheeseburger with the works," she said without hesitation, her stomach rumbling to punctuate her point.

"I'll have the same."

She turned in surprise to find Will sitting down beside her.

"Hey, you." She gave him a speculative look and reached out to touch the sexy dimple exposed on his chin. "Nice, you shaved off the beard. Told you a handsome mug was hiding underneath all that stubble."

He rubbed at his chin. "Going to take some getting used to. It feels naked." He accepted the beer from the waiter and clinked glasses with hers, leaning forward to whisper in her ear, "Thanks for the heads-up. I didn't feel like sitting in a Manila police station all night when my invite didn't check out."

"Yeah, that'd be a bummer. Almost as much as what happened to me." She took a sip of her beer. "Missed out on a great opportunity tonight. This guy came along and cockblocked the governor's son from giving me a tour of the country's private antiquities. Like I needed that. I've always taken care of myself and always will. I didn't learn karate for nothing. I got the moves, baby. Just let him try something."

Will's eyes flew open with outrage. "Marcus Salang has a terrible reputation with women. I'd give that guy who blocked him my best regards and hearty thanks."

She ignored his dismissal of the guy responsible for her loss, focusing instead on her disappointment. Guys just didn't get it—a strong woman could take care of herself. "I didn't even get to see the famous sword. That sucks big time."

"Forget about it. It was for your own good."

"Really! I thought you of all people would understand how much I wanted—uh—to see it." *Not ever going to admit she'd been there to nab it.* "You disappoint me, Will," she said with a pout. She looked around the nearly deserted bar, but the blond stranger was still absent. She fiddled with a lock of the wig, wrapping it around a finger. It didn't feel silky like her own hair. And it wasn't nearly as exciting as her own bright shade.

"Can't say I like the wig much. Red's far more your color. Besides, gives fair warning to anyone thinking you're going to be an easy target."

She gave him a poke on his impossibly hard biceps for the impertinence.

"It goes as it's meant to go, beautiful. At least I'm not in jail tonight. That's worth a toast."

"Maybe. Might teach you some humility, though, sitting in a Manila jail cell." She smiled to soften the blow.

"It's not my lack of humility that's the problem, beautiful."

Their cheeseburgers arrived and she dived in. "I'm starving."

"So, what's the plan for tomorrow?" he asked, dabbing at a bit of ketchup on her lip with his napkin. She thanked him with an appreciative glance and swallowed the last of her burger.

"So good. Yeah, we've got an appointment at nine a.m. with the police captain."

"Then we'd better get some sleep," he said with a yawn.

"What's up? You're usually ready to howl all night long. Thought you might like to play a hand of poker before turning in?" she taunted. Maybe this night could be saved yet.

"Are we on for tonight, then?" Interest flared bright in his eyes.

"Ha. You're going to lose! Your clothes, that is."

"Phhttt. You're going down, beautiful. I'm a hell of a poker player. You head on up to your room and check on that knurly cat of yours. I've got a couple of calls to make. Then be prepared to lose – it all." He grinned wickedly at her, his voice deep and rumbly.

"JK's not knurly! He's all sweet-smelling and shiny now. Not a tangle in sight."

"Whatever you say." He chuckled, picking up his cell phone. "He'll always be a tyke to me. Albeit a lucky one – hanging on to you."

Lacey flipped him the bird and headed for the elevator. She'd show him. Add a few extra layers of clothing, just in case, though. Stay prepared. She smiled, enjoying the thrill of anticipation, when the bell dinged indicating her floor. Stepping off, she rummaged around in her bag for the door key, keeping one eye alert for trouble.

The hallway was quiet. Maybe too quiet. The little hairs on her neck rose when she inserted the key card into the door. Her intuition kicked in on opening the door, getting a definite sense of someone having been in her room. Was it just the maid, or something more ominous? A faint odor hung in the air, eluding her.

She glanced around the room. Nothing appeared disturbed. But the disquiet lingered. She was all too aware that her personal interest of seeking treasure others wanted, just as fiercely, could be downright dangerous. Her throat tightened. Where was JR?

He came bouncing across the carpet at that moment and she scooped him up, hugging him tightly. He squirmed in her arms. She loosened her grip and ruffled his fur.

What's that on the bed?

Stunned, she stared at the gleaming object disbelievingly, then padded barefoot over to it. She put JR down on the floor.

Fuck. It can't be. Can it?

The Tiger's Sword rested on the bedcover, its curved blade gleaming under the low light thrown by the side table lamp. A katana of great magnificence, its squared hilt was long enough for a two-handed grip and its blade was at least seventy centimeters long. *Unbelievable, really.* She blinked several times. *A mirage?*

She took a few steps closer, reached out a hand to touch its brilliant sheen and ran a finger down over the gold inlay of its grip. Carefully, of course, its well-honed sharp edge cool under her touch. Without a doubt. The real McCoy.

How on earth had it gotten there? She glanced around again, suddenly worried that someone was going to jump her from behind and reclaim it. She sat on a chair beside the bed, starring at it, her body thrumming with the strangest sensation. Who had done this? Who even knew she wanted it? The only name that came to mind was Will, but no way — that was impossible. Or was it? He had been acting oddly earlier, wanting to go to bed so soon, before she had deliberately enticed him into playing poker.

She chewed on her bottom lip, considering. She'd met a man at the event, taller, blonder, blue eyes, a much bigger flirt than even Playboy Will.

No.

Fucking.

Way.

She got up, heart racing. She picked up the sword, hefting it with both hands, stomped across the room to the locked adjoining door between their suites, banged on his door with her foot.

"Open up!" she called through the closed door. "I need to talk to you!"

He did. Stood there in a blond wig minus the contacts and the shoes with the lifts, a grin as wide as the ocean they'd just crossed plastered all over his handsome mug.

Goddamn it all to hell!

She thrust the sword at his broad chest, enjoying watching his eyes widen as she brought it close enough to make contact. "You bastard! You did this! You set me up!" She kept pretending to stab him with it as he laughingly backed up. Wincing at the continued onslaught, he finally put his hands up in mock surrender.

"So, arrest me," he said with no apology whatsoever in his tone. "You've always talked about having a samurai sword, so I made it happen. Tit for tat, Miss Cameron. Think back on all the practical jokes you've played on me. Setting me up time and again. I think you can handle having the cards turned just this once."

"I should run you through with it! You played me!" But the words were losing their sting. *I've used Will outrageously at times. No denying that.* And she did have the sword, further softening the blow. She lowered the blade, to point it at the floor.

"We need to take the sword to the plane. Right now," she urged.

"All taken care of. Jack's on his way up to remove it and hide it while we try to find its rightful owners." He pulled off the wig and tossed it on a table. Ran his hands through his dark hair.

"Way ahead of you, buddy," she crowed. "After a thorough records check, I'm now the temporary owner. No strings attached." She caught him slowly shaking his head at her, like she thought she was trying to get away with something. "And no—I did not cheat."

"You'd better not have," he said, pursing his lips.

"Why didn't Jack fly with us today?" she asked. Jack Brody was Will's closest ally and operations manager. His right-hand man, especially when he was out of the country.

"Wanted you all to myself," Will said with a mock grin before adding something that rang truer, "Plus, he had to take a later flight. Family stuff."

"What's he going to carry it in?"

"A gigantic hulking oboe case." He gave a half-laugh.

"Well, you guys are in fine playing form, I'll give you that." She laid the sword back down on the bed, imagining its history. The warrior hands that had held it, depended on it, dead and gone now, only their exploits left to leave a mark on the world.

Now that she'd calmed down, her mind pictured for just a moment meeting the golden-haired stranger in the bar for a wild night of nothing but pure sex. The best kind. No commitments to foul a girl up. It was hard to believe Will was that guy. And yet, maybe not. *Look how successful he is in attracting female admirers at all those charity balls he attends for the sake of the family business.* Though he seemed to get too much pleasure from the hook-ups for it to be much of a sacrifice.

She slanted her eyes at him, observing the newly uncovered chiseled jawline. *Hmm.* Who knew what had been hiding behind it all this time? There was something special about a man with a fresh shave. Too bad Will was her friend and not someone to jump straight into bed with. Like right now. Her blood heated, visualizing celebrating the day's victory with a big man. And at least now she knew she wasn't losing her touch, since the guy could hardly show up in the bar to meet her if he didn't exist. Though, if he'd kept up the charade, they just might be in bed together right now. *And just how will that go?* Her breath caught in her throat, fantasizing Will's eyes smoldering with desire when she slid off her gown and stood before him. Him taking her in his strong arms and kissing her until the world dropped away. Kissing his way down her body...

He shook his head, laughing out loud, the sound traveling across her skin, adding a heightened awareness of just how much she wanted him, right then. "The look on your face was priceless. Wish I had a picture for posterity."

"You know, if you'd only stayed in character tonight and met me in the bar—" She ran her tongue over her lips absently, her mind focusing on the loss.

"What are you saying? I could have carried the charade further? Had your hot little bod pressed against mine in my bed right now?" The look he gave scorched her, made her mouth dry right out. She could not look away, their glances locking for a second, electricity arcing between them.

He moved first, crashing his lips down on hers. Not a friend kiss, but a man's kiss, a kiss that shook her to the core, woke up nerve endings, flooding her panties with liquid heat. He ran his hands down over her body, drawing her in closer. His kiss deepened. He used his tongue to slip around hers, devouring her.

The desk phone rang. Harsh. Insistent. Entirely unwelcome.

"Damn it." Will took a step backward, his tone roughened, his face flushed dark with emotion.

She watched him stomp across the floor to answer it, her heart in her throat. What had just happened?

There was too much going on in her body to follow the conversation. She took a couple of deep breaths to steady herself. Her best friend had morphed into the hottest guy on the planet right in plain view, scaring her, challenging her, making her want more. She couldn't think of one bit of warrior code to cover this moment, to make sense of it.

He hung up, scrubbing a hand over his face. Was it shaking or had she imagined it? Because *she* was shaken, right to the core. *Get it together, Lacey, it was just a kiss after all. Yeah? Really. You call that just a kiss. Like the Rocky Mountains are just puny hills.* No wonder he had women dropping at his feet. Her knees were like rubber, barely holding her upright.

"What a drink?"

"Definitely."

She walked a few steps on those unsteady legs, settling on the nearest chair and tucking her legs up under her body. "Nice suite," she said. Lame, but it was all she had.

He poured them both a Coors Light from the minibar into tall frosty glasses. "Nicer than mine."

"We can always share," he said with a leer as he handed her a drink. He appeared to have regained his composure quicker than her. Her body was still trembling inside.

"Not on your life. Last time we had to share a bed in the desert—ha—remember what happened? That damn scorpion crawled up under the mosquito netting and nearly ended one of us."

Will had been such a gentleman too, giving her more than her fair share of space when circumstances had conspired against them. Good thing considering what had just happened. She quickly ignored a slice of regret.

If there was one thing she treasured, it was her friends, and nothing, not this newfound lust, not the urging of well-meaning Ringers who thought they should hook up, no, nothing, nada was going to get in the way of her and Will staying friends. She planned to spend her life in the pursuit of the dream. And it did not, could not, include the husband, the white picket fence, and the one-point-seven children. Because, with her family affliction, it could only lead to heartache. No, best to stay her badass self. That she could deal with. That she understood. No disappointments that way. *Ah, I have one bit of wisdom for this moment of time. A warrior stays true to his course. Knows his limits.*

"You handled it well." Will joined her, sitting down across from her and sprawling out, long legs with those powerful thighs spread wide. Such a man's man. All big bones and his own warrior attitude to spare. And yet, she'd seen him comfortable in any setting. From elite parties to special ops, he was more than capable. Some woman would be damned lucky one day. She suppressed a deep twinge of regret that it could never be her.

"It's what I do." She took a long pull on her beer, enjoying the tang of the flavored hops. She could drink a keg all by her lonesome tonight, all kidding aside. She'd never been thirstier. Kissing Will had opened up a chasm of need she had to tamp down with all her might, just to stay sane and do the right thing.

"And you do it very well." He looked at her, his intense dark brown eyes with their golden highlights promising so much. She ignored the direct hit to her libido. *Tonight has to be a fluke, right?* He'd gone out of his way to fool her and that had fucked her up. Things would settle down. They always did.

A sharp rap on wood came.

"That'll be Jack." Will put down his drink and got up. He crossed to the entrance, checked the peephole, then opened the door to let the visitor inside.

"Hey, good buddy." Jack trooped in carrying the awkward oboe case.

"Hey, yourself," Jack said, his expression exasperated. A normally calm man, tonight his dark eyes flashed with annoyance, his military-style brown hair standing to full attention, his body language defensive. He was a younger, taller, sturdier Tom Cruise. Will's brother-in-arms.

"Do you have any idea how damned annoying it is to carry this godforsaken thing around? So, where is it?" Jack swiveled his head, glancing about. He gave Lacey a smile, his expression changing to one of keen interest when he took in her dress. Or lack thereof.

"Ah, great dress, gorgeous. But I like the red hair better." His eyes smoldering, he licked his lips, annoyance obviously forgotten for the moment. Will gave him a frown for free.

Lacey sighed. With all the shenanigans, she'd forgotten she still had the wig on. *Men. Don't want to bed you but don't want anyone else to either.* A sliver of doubt crept in if this even rang true anymore, after what had just happened between them. "Thanks. The sword's on my bed," she remarked.

She got up and the two men followed her into the bedroom. She swayed her hips just for the pure joy of it. Though she couldn't have either of them, it didn't hurt to torture them. *Remind them who's boss.*

"Nice," Jack said as he laid the black oboe case alongside the sword. He snapped open the case's hinges, exposing the midnight-blue velvet inside and the deep impression reserved for the priceless relic. Lacey picked up the sword, giving Will a narrow-eyed look. "I can't believe the stunt you pulled off, buster." She carefully tucked the sword into the cut-out slot, then pulled the built-in Velcro sections over it to secure it in place.

She gave the sword one last admiring glance before Jack closed the musician's carrying case and picked it up to head for the jet.

"Clever camouflage," Will said.

"Easy for you to say. You don't have to haul this sucker all over hell's half-acre," Jack grumbled.

"Sorry. Seemed a brilliant idea at the time," Will said while he watched his friend struggle out of the door lugging the massive case.

"Yeah, I can just see how sorry you are. Well, you owe me this time. Nice to see you, Lacey. Make sure this guy takes you out to some nice places while you're here in Manila," Jack said with another appreciative grin her way and hurried off as fast at his burden would allow.

"Guess I'd better buy him a big bottle of his favorite and very expensive Scotch."

"His tastes run almost as expensive as yours, eh?" she teased.

"And he liked your dress almost as much as I do. So yeah—he's got great, very expensive tastes in liquor and women."

"Just doing my job. Keeping the male of the species off-balance," she quipped. Her cell phone buzzed. She checked the number. "Excuse me, gotta take this."

"Hey, Lacey, I need FaceTime with you." A picture of her gorgeous writer friend filled her mind. Lots of thick honey-blonde hair groomed into perfect waves, and wonderfully expressive green eyes, with the low-pitched sultry voice to match. *Shame she's always tied up writing her stories. She should live at least one hot romance a year if she was going to write about them, right?*

"What's up, Rebecca, you sound out of breath?" Lacey asked as she grabbed her laptop case, took out her computer and opened it on her lap. She booted it up and clicked into the app. Rebecca's gorgeous face filled the screen, her hair bunched in a messy topknot and half falling down. Her attire would not win her any awards either — a faded sweatshirt with the Winnipeg Jets' hockey team logo across the front. And were those potato chip crumbs stuck to the front of her shirt? Not her writer friend's usual polished image.

"Is Will there? I'd like a man's opinion too." Rebecca's voice was all breathy. At least that hadn't changed.

"Ah, yeah. Join me," she said impulsively, looking at Will and patting the spot beside her on the bed.

"Sorry for interrupting your evening, guys, but I'm on a tight deadline for the final edits for my romance novel and I need your help. It comes down to how far I should go with this — as in, have I gone too far? Is it too over the top? Or too clinical? I think I'm losing perspective. I've been working all night on it and all my brain cells have vacated for parts unknown."

"O — kay," Lacey said. *This should prove interesting. A sex scene.* Something brand-new for her friend, who had been busy pursuing the suspense genre, last she knew.

"Fire away, Rebecca. We're both listening," Will added, sitting close to Lacey on the end of the bed, facing the computer screen. He filled the space at her side with his presence, his male scent marking her, his body heat searing so close. But she couldn't have moved if her life depended on it, taking a deep appreciative breath of his cologne, with its undertones of intoxicating musk. Very stirring. She was totally alive, just like the moments during the shark attack. Was it not knowing the outcome that created that sense?

"Okay. Here goes. The hero's talking to the heroine. Keep in mind that it's a historical novel and written in first person." Rebecca stopped to take a deep breath and began to read.

"'Like a goddess rising from beneath the waves, ye are, lass,' he murmured as I waded over to stand in front of him, enjoying the sensation of moving languidly through the water. He reached out a hand and cupped my sex, slipped a finger along the slit, feeling the slipperiness that eased from me constantly in his presence. I arched against the invasion and he pushed one long, thick finger up inside me while he leaned forward and took a nipple between his lips to suck it long and hard. It sent shards of pleasure lancing through me, centering on my throbbing core. I moaned. I felt about to explode and I almost climbed up his body in my need to have him inside me. I settled my legs around his waist, giving him full access to my open cleft.'"

Rebecca took another deep breath as Lacey and Will both stared riveted at the screen, the air around Lacey seeming to vibrate with some wild electricity.

"It goes on, 'His huge cock pressed against my swollen sex and slipped inside. With a mighty thrust, he pushed deeper into me, driving himself right to the hilt. I felt myself stretch widely to accommodate him and my back arched as I thrust up against him, wanting to accept all of his glorious cock.'"

She stopped abruptly, staring at the screen. "Oh, I see part of the problem now! I used the word 'cock' twice and the word 'need'. Not allowed. So, what do you think?"

"Ah, works really well, Rebecca, if you're trying to set e-readers on fire," Will deadpanned, his voice strained.

"So, you think it's not too clinical? That readers will get it—you know—get the hots themselves? Apparently, that's what's supposed to happen, according to the one-page primer I got from the publisher."

"Oh yeah, you got that part down pat," Will said in a low growl. Lacey couldn't even raise her eyes to look at him—she just didn't trust herself in the moment.

"Lacey?" Rebecca asked, chewing on her thumbnail in her concentration.

"Works for me. Damn hot, girlfriend. Well done. But I thought you were writing a *Da Vinci Code* kind of thriller?"

"Thanks, guys, for helping. I owe you. I need this one for the money and experience, Lacey, that's why. I need to stretch my boundaries too." Rebecca laughed at the innuendo. "Catch you later."

"Anytime," Lacey said automatically as she took a deep breath to still her racing heart. She was flustered. She *never* got flustered. And it was all Rebecca's fault, reminding her of what she was missing out on. *Damn it all to hell.*

"Well, that was interesting." Will cleared his throat. He got up, his back to her, and retrieved their glasses abandoned on the dresser. "Want another?"

"It's tempting, but I'd better not. We've got an early wake-up call." She could not afford to take the chance of drinking more, loosening up around Will, causing more havoc this night. They'd shared friend kisses on the cheek before, but never something so intimate, so amazing. *Christ, Lacey, get your mind off it.*

He nodded, not turning around. "Sleep well, beautiful. We'll do the poker thing another night," he said over his shoulder, then quietly closed the door to his adjoining suite behind him.

She pulled off the wig and prepared for bed, her overheated skin tingling and driving her to distraction. This whole situation was so unfair. She slipped under the covers, wishing she could release the pressure mounting inside. She swallowed hard. *Should have brought my vibrator.*

Will was moving around in the next room. *Who knew my best friend was so damn hot? When did that happen?* She dreamed of throwing open the connecting door and flinging herself at him totally naked so there would be no mistaking her intentions. Just one night—hell, just one hour would help. But she couldn't take a chance of losing her best-friend status by having sex. Even if it looked to be mind-blowing sex. She sighed, too antsy to sleep. *A warm bath. Yes.* She got up and padded to the bathroom, turned on the faucet and adjusted the temperature, then sat on the side of the tub, waiting for it to fill. She eased down into the water, praying it would work a miracle and relax her.

Thirty minutes later, she drained the tub. She padded back to her bedroom and turned on the television set, determined to watch a movie, but her mind kept drifting away from the story. Voices next door. *Will must be watching TV too.* She sighed, got up and retrieved a cold bottle of water from the fridge. *Going to be a long night, girlfriend.*

Her buzzing phone woke her. Groggy from lack of sleep, she forced her eyes open and groaned. Seven a.m. *Time to get up. Feed and entertain JR. Drink a gallon or two of coffee.*

She was ready to roll an hour later, showered, body hyped up on caffeine. A light rap on her door alerted her to company.

"Ready, beautiful?" Will asked, looking all freshly showered and scrumptious.

"Yup, as good as it's going to get today after a night of lousy sleep," she grumbled picking up her bag containing all her essentials for the day.

"That's a shame. I can sleep anywhere, anytime. Military training assists with that." Will took the carryall from her and placed it over one broad shoulder, pretending to grimace at the weight.

"Lucky you. You recommending I join up just so I can learn to sleep on a dime?" His happy smugness grated.

"Lacey, the military would toss you out on your ear. Either that, or you'd tell them to go to hell first time they told your sweet ass what to do," he said with a soft chuckle.

She grinned sheepishly. *Sweet ass, eh?* "Yeah, I guess, I'm not known for kowtowing to anyone."

"Kowtowing? Hell, you couldn't take an order if your life depended on it, which brings me to an important point. Today, you're going to learn a new skill."

"What new skill?" she asked, narrowing her eyes as she locked figurative horns with him.

"Letting me take the lead — run the interview — or at least until we see how things are. You watch for tells and the lies."

She rolled her eyes. "I know how to run an interview. One of my specialties."

"I know — you're damn good at it — but we're venturing into enemy territory. No reason for these guys to trust us. We're not from their country and we have an agenda. They may not appreciate that we want to get at the truth. They might even be under the impression that a noble lie is better for these babes-in-the-woods Canadians. Just sayin', be prepared. You don't know exactly what quagmire you might be stepping into."

"Okay, Daddy, I hear you. But damn it, I know all this! I read up on their culture already, duh."

"Lacey, Lacey, Lacey." He shook his head, his eyes grim. "I'm not playing around here. I will abort this mission if you pull any shenanigans."

"It's not yours to abort, buddy. But okay, I hear you. I'll be good. Promise." She crossed her fingers over her heart for emphasis, giving him her most sincere expression. He had a valid point and she would try her best. After all, he was the one doing her a favor. And she was a professional, long past worrying about who got to the answers first. He could go for it. Mano on mano with the lieutenant, if that was what it took. She had her own strengths and, knowing that she could see the truth of things, she'd go in with confidence, learn all she needed to in no time, without saying a darn word. *Well, maybe. Depends on what's called for.*

He nodded in satisfaction. "Okay then, let's go."

Chapter Five

"Once we realize that imperfect understanding is the human condition there is no shame in being wrong, only in failing to correct our mistakes." — *George Soros*

Thirty minutes later, they pulled up in front of the Manila Police Station, one of eleven community stations in the city. Will leaned forward to pay the driver provided by his business connections. *Best way to ensure safe travel.* The man twisted around in the front seat to collect the fare, his expression amiable, and his hand outstretched.

"There's a nice fat tip in it if you wait for us and keep the air conditioning cranked." Will counted the pesos into the man's hand. Much as he wanted to rent a car and drive himself, this made more sense. The streets of Manila were choked with vehicles and parking was a nightmare. Lots of cash would oil the way. "We might have some other spots we'll need to visit today. Can you free up the time?"

The man nodded. "Of course. I will wait for you and keep the meter running, yes?"

"Yes." Will nodded.

He opened the taxi door for Lacey and the swamp of humidity that was downtown Manila saturated his skin. Thank goodness, the air was still breathable. By noon they'd be in an unrelenting sauna, air conditioning the only lifeline and darn near essential to duck the toxic fumes. He wasn't acclimatized and he didn't want to be the one catching hell from Lacey if she didn't have cool air blowing across all that exposed flesh. He shut the image down, feeling his groin threaten to tighten. *Last fucking thing I need, walking into a Manila police station with a hard-on.*

Last night had been torturous enough. He didn't require a repeat of that performance to remind him how much his body would enjoy jumping into bed with her. Anytime. That amazing, fucking-un-believable kiss haunted him, lingered. Made him want so much more from her. Hell, he wanted all of her. But she'd always made it abundantly clear that he was only a friend. That insane moment with her writer friend — priceless. He couldn't even have chanced turning around as he'd vacated her bedroom or she'd have seen first-hand his interest, imagining fucking her into submission until she realized what they could have together. Everything.

But breathing in her sweet vanilla fragrance heightened by the saturated air was not helping one little bit as they walked side-by-side into the police station. He couldn't help but notice how her sleeveless yellow sundress exposed her dimpled knees and a few inches of her sleek tan thighs. He wasn't the only one. Every male head swiveled their way. She strode confidently across the floor, the low heels he approved of her wearing in the field clicking on the tile as they approached the counter.

"William Thornton and Lacey Cameron. We're here to see Lieutenant Jomar Versoza. We have an appointment at nine. We're a little early," he explained to the uniformed man who gave them a slight frown and a thorough check-over. Apparently, they passed muster, because he pointed at the array of empty chairs down one side of the room. If it wasn't for a half-dozen uniformed police officers not hiding the fact they were watching them, the station would be vacant. *Maybe no crime this early in the morning?* He doubted that. Going after the drug cartels and dealers was the country's main focus now, leaving few resources for anything else. All courtesy of the president.

"Please have a seat. He'll be with you shortly." The clerk went back to click-clacking away on his computer keyboard.

Will put his hand on Lacey's lower back to direct her. He remained standing while she slid onto the plastic chair, her exposed thighs drawing even more interest. He sighed.

"Sit down, you're making me nervous." Lacey tucked a stray curl back into place. She'd piled the shiny mass up on her head this morning, a smart move in the heat. Except it left her delicate swan-like neck and creamy shoulders bare. He swallowed, watching the tiny heartbeat in her throat flutter just under the fragile gold chain of her necklace. He shifted his vision away and focused instead on frowning out of the window at the busy street, checking that their taxi was still waiting at the curb.

Lacey stirred at his side, leaned over to whisper in his ear. "Okay, I've got an idea. I'm going to act as your fiancée. I think it will help ease things — you know, with all the macho stuff that goes on in these places."

"What?" His stomach clenched.

"William Thornton?" a strong male voice inquired. Will swung around to see a uniformed man standing stiffly before them, taller than the other officers in the room. He wore a blue shirt with darker blue pants and sported a red and gold insignia on his shirt front, the official logo of the Manila Police Department. The man looked vaguely familiar and he frowned again. *Where do I know this guy from?*

"Yes." Will gave him a quizzical look.

"I'm Lieutenant Jomar Versoza." The officer offered Will his hand.

Lacey stood. "I'm Lacey Cameron, the fiancée." She laid her slender hand on Will's arm, giving him a wide, happy smile from her lovely, upturned face. If only it were true. How was he going to break down her defenses? One brick at a time, if that was what it took to dismantle them.

"Miss Cameron, congratulations are in order then. You are one lucky man, William Thornton." The lieutenant took her hand and gave it a brief shake. "Please, come with me."

Will directed Lacey to walk ahead of him so he could watch her back and they followed the man down the hall and into his office.

The drab beige walls of the crowded office were lined with framed photographs of police field actions. Drug busts, community events, shaking hands with dignitaries. Standard stuff. The desk was filled with precarious stacks of file folders, leaving barely enough room for the desk computer and keyboard. The filing cabinet had suffered the same fate and stood resigned to its heavy load in one corner of the room.

The lieutenant leaned forward in his office chair and tented his hands on the desk, his dark eyes intense and probing. "Perhaps you don't remember me, Lieutenant Colonel Thornton, but I remember you. I was trained by your joint operations with the US army a number of years ago."

"I thought you looked familiar," Will said.

Lacey gave him an interested look but remained silent.

"Are you still with your unit?"

"No, I went on from there to a couple of tours of duty with the JTF 2s in Iraq and Afghanistan."

The man's dark eyebrows rose upward as the information impacted. Normally Will wouldn't have mentioned the elite Special Operations Forces unit of the Canadian military, but it just might assist Lacey in her investigation. And the sooner they got to the bottom of things, the better.

"Ah, counter-terrorism activities, direct action, hostage rescue, personnel recovery and foreign internal defense. Quite the résumé," Versoza said, respect lining his tone as he ticked off their mandate.

Lacey gave Will another look. He could almost see the wheels turning.

"Yes, the army kept me busy."

"Have you left the military?" Versoza asked, pursing his lips, his eyes watchful.

"No, just between tours." Will needed time to sort out his life. Maybe he was done with the military, maybe not. At the very least he was going to straighten out their family munitions business now that he was home.

He ignored the recoil in his brain at the situation developing between him and his father, Will's insistence on their dropping the lucrative area having caused a firestorm of a reaction.

"Good. Don't like to see a good man with your abilities set aside. What can I do for you today?"

"We're here to learn all we can about Daniel Wright's mugging and murder," Will said smoothly. "We're here on behalf of his sister, Megan Wright. Lacey's a good friend of Megan's." No way would he discuss Lacey's PI involvement until he learned the lie of the land.

The man's face tightened almost imperceptibly. "Ah, I believe all was revealed in the report filed by the officers that investigated. Flashing all the money around is the obvious motive as none was found on the body. A terrible incident." He nodded at Lacey. "I'm very sorry for your friend's loss."

"Thank you. Do you have a suspect in custody yet?" she asked.

"No." He cleared his throat. "And the chances of finding who did this heinous crime are slim, I'm sorry to say. I'm not certain if you're aware, but most of our current resources are being directed to our war on drugs for the foreseeable future."

"That's unfortunate, but I am aware of the current political climate. How did you ID the body?"

"What do you mean?"

"He'd been shot in the face, right?"

"Yes, well, he still had his driver's license on him. The thief only took the money. He must have been interrupted and had to run away, considering the black-market value of such an item."

"Do you mind if we speak with the officers who are working the case?" Will asked.

"I would like to say yes, but unfortunately they are no longer with us. Valdez was transferred. It was already in progress before he worked the case. And Marcos has left the department—a family illness." The lieutenant shrugged, scratching the side of his nose and partially covering his mouth with his hand. *A tell. The man's covering something up.* "But everything they found out, they put in the file. I'll have one of the officers make you a copy, if that would help?"

"Yes. I'd appreciate that," Will said. The lieutenant picked up his phone and made a quick call, asking for the copy to be prepared.

Will snuck a glance at Lacey. She gave him an innocent look. *What's she thinking?* What he wouldn't give to see inside that brilliant brain for a couple of minutes. Figure out what made her tick and come up with the exact right game plan to win her over. He wanted more kisses like the one they'd shared last night. He understood alcoholics now—one drink was too much, a thousand not enough.

"Would you take some advice if I offer it?" Versoza asked, choosing his words carefully, his hands back to being tented on his desk.

"I can't promise you that. But I will take whatever you have to say under advisement."

"Fair enough. My best advice to you both is to leave Manila—go home. Tell your friend all that can be done is being done, and I assure you that's true. I give you my personal guarantee we're doing our best to bring the killer or killers to justice, even though it's proving an almost impossible task."

"You would have no objection to our visiting the mortuary?"

"To pick up the man's ashes? That should be done by his wife's family. And a copy of the coroner's report has been placed in the file we're preparing for you. All there is to know is inside the file. You have my word on it," Versoza said. He rubbed the side of his nose again.

Another tell. Definitely hiding something.

"I see. Well, we shouldn't take up any more of your time, lieutenant. I appreciate your seeing us and having the report prepared for us."

"You're most welcome. I hope it assures his sister that we're doing all we can to bring his killers to justice."

"Yes. I can see that," Lacey said amiably enough.

Versoza gave her a look, pursing his lips.

A quick knock on the office door and it opened. A young police officer came in with the promised file and handed it to his captain, then about-faced and left.

Lieutenant Versoza stood up, handing the file over to Will. "I hope you take my advice and go home — let us take care of this. Manila's not the safest place for tourists right now, especially with such a beautiful woman at your side. It draws too much attention. And…" He now seemed to be choosing his words even more carefully, as if needing to tread a very thin line. "Your digging into this particular case — stirring things up — you can be sure it will get noticed. And not in a good way."

Will sensed Lacey's shifting mood without looking at her, fidgeting in the chair.

The man continued, "With the drug war going on, I sincerely believe it is in your best interests to just go home. I can't say it any plainer than that." He nodded with grave concern.

Will stood up and Lacey followed his lead. Another round of handshakes and they were out on the street. He kept his eyes on the traffic, scanning the area. A kamikaze motorbike rider raced by, packages of food piled high in the carrier, narrowly missing the back of their taxi. Just a daily occurrence in the overcrowded streets of Manila.

He opened the back door of the taxi, ushering her inside. Putting a finger to his lips, he alerted her to say nothing. She gave him a slight nod. Unfortunately, sitting beside her with her delectable fragrance floating all around him and her warm curvy body so close, he could reach out and touch her — not exactly conducive to his staying calm.

"Where do you want me to take you now?" the taxi driver asked, looking in the rearview mirror and locking gazes with Will.

"Give me a minute." He opened the file. He ran his forefinger down the page, checking. Lacey sat quietly and watched his actions for a moment. Then she took his hand, her warm fingers tantalizing, sending a message to his brain that she could grasp any part of him she wanted. Anytime. She pointed at the top of the page he was scanning, indicating the location of the mugging, then traced her finger over to a tourist feature close by.

He made a quick decision. If he didn't do this much at least, Lacey would just go out and do it on her own, a far worse scenario. And now he was concerned. Versoza was lying, touching his nose and hiding his mouth. All classic signs. And Lacey knew that as well, being a 'liedar' expert, having taught him all she knew on the subject. Hell, she was even an expert at spotting micro-expressions, flashes of falsehood that appeared on a person's face when they told a lie. An amazing feat — most people needed to see a still-action video or photograph to spot them. Lacey could do it in real time.

"Take us to the Malate Church." Lacey was right. It was close enough to where Danny Wright had been mugged that they could walk to the spot from the church and check with the neighbors to see if anyone had seen anything. And it was daylight. Safest time to visit. If they weren't followed.

Chapter Six

"Of all the wild beasts of land or sea, the wildest is woman."
— Menander of Athens

Lacey chewed on her bottom lip. *Not that unexpected that Versoza lied.* People lied at least once every ten minutes in conversation, according to the latest studies. *Mostly to make others feel better, of course — who wants to know their ass looks big in their new jeans, anyway?* Social lying was the glue keeping civilization intact.

But the bigger question remained — was the lie about the officers being unavailable for them to speak with on Danny's case other-focused, to protect someone else, or self-focused, to give the lieutenant an advantage? When she'd gone for training in this fascinating area, she'd found herself to be a natural lie wizard, able to detect lies above the eightieth percentile. That had since edged up with training to over ninety percent of the time, unlike the general population's dismal record of around fifty percent. Blame evolution. *With our ancestors living in close quarters, lying didn't occur very often, but if it did, you'd better lie damn good if you wanted to stay in the tribe.* So, most people weren't good at spotting lies, but damn good at creating them. *Ha.* She was good at both.

Which made the fiasco with Will all the more alarming. How had she missed the ruse? Was she losing it? And having him sitting beside her and being all alpha male today — not helping, not one bit. Of course, she had taught him all he knew on the subject of catching people lying and how to cover things up, so maybe that was it. She'd taught him too much. She took a deep breath, enjoying the clean citrus with its underlying tones of musk emanating from the man. *So near and yet so damn far. And all Will.* She tapped her toe on the taxi floor, considered her options.

"Do you want me to wait again?" the taxi driver asked, turning around in his seat. Will laid a tidy sum of pesos in his outstretched hand. The man smiled, nodding at the amount of money creasing his palm.

"Yes. We won't be long. There's an even bigger tip in it if you wait."

"Thank you, I will wait." Of course he would. Sometimes Will appeared too generous, not having grown up short of funds like she and Lily had, and not seeming to appreciate his good fortune nearly enough, throwing hard-earned cash around like it meant nothing to him. Maybe that was the point — he hadn't liked how it was earned, if Lacey remembered the conversation on the plane correctly.

They exited the cab, standing on the street for a moment to avoid suspicion, admiring the fourteenth-century baroque-style church that fronted a park.

Beyond the park, the sparkling blue waters of Manila Bay beckoned.

They strolled casually around the church, then, as soon as they were out of sight of the cab, headed off at a fast clip down a side-street in the opposite direction from Manila Bay. Lacey's heart rate increased with every step. The quicker they checked this out, the better. After Versoza's warning, a clock was now ticking off the minutes they would be allowed to remain in Manila unchallenged. Even though he'd been careful, she hadn't missed that his warning was sincere, that someone higher up was taking a personal interest in the case. And she hadn't missed that he was lying about nearly everything else.

The street narrowed to wide enough for only two pedestrians abreast by the time they reached the location of Danny's mugging a few minutes later. There wasn't much to see, really. Just a few closed steel doors rusted with age on the dismal alleyway. *What was Danny doing back there? Odd place for a tourist to visit*, Lacey thought, noting the condoms lying discarded in the alleyway, unless he had proclivities he hadn't shared with his sister. After all, in Manila, he could just have paid a bar fine and taken the girl or 'ladyboy' back to his hotel. *Common enough practice.*

"What next?" she asked, biting on a fingernail.

"Knocking on back doors doesn't seem all that wise, but we could go around to the front and see if any of the places are open for business. It's kind of early for this sort of establishment — at least in the States. Maybe we'll get lucky."

"Yes. I've got Danny's photo on my phone. We can show it around."

"Okay, but remember to stay on guard. Not the best part of town, but tourists are necessary to their enterprise, so we should be safe enough."

"Not to worry, I'm always watching," she assured him. She punched him lightly in the biceps, giving him a cheeky grin. "And I have the added advantage of having the famous Wall with me for window dressing."

"Just don't be taking advantage," he teased. "I've got a price tag attached for being your man candy."

"More than willing to pay it, sir," she quipped back.

A busy street confronted them just around the corner, a surprise for eleven in the morning, people jostling on the sidewalk and women standing outside a large bar aptly named the Dollhouse, judging by the size of the petite women, looking for business. *Oh, this'll be fun.* She hitched up her imaginary big-girl panties and followed Will inside.

The inside of the establishment was nicer than the outside suggested, all shiny chrome surfaces and plush burgundy furnishings. Waitresses dressed in cute skirts and halter tops served drinks, while miniscule thongs appeared the norm for the half-dozen women swaying to the music on the stage.

As the women caught sight of Will, a slight pandemonium erupted as a few of the 'waitresses' flashed their smiles and their tits while the women on stage stepped up their game by adding a few smooth dance moves to their swaying, even using a forefinger to entice him forward. *Just. Fucking. Great. All jiggling breasts and tight asses.*

Lacey sighed. Will gave her a look, flashing her a smile too. "What? Just doing my duty here. We need their cooperation, right?"

She followed him to a round bar table near the stage and plunked down. At least no one was pole dancing. Lacey rolled her eyes, catching sight of the pole gleaming silver and tall right smack-dab near the edge of the stage. If a dancer chose to avail herself of it, Lacey would have the perfect view of her va-jay-jay. Problem was, so would Will.

"You are so *guapo*. I am horny. You horny?" A girl sidled up to their table, letting go with the super-sweet compliments, her eyes and smile addressed to Will. This was going *so* well.

Another young girl—hell, they all looked underage in this place, though Lacey was fairly certain it was just an illusion caused by good lighting—jockeyed the woman away and asked for their drink order.

"I'll have a beer. How about you, beautiful?" Will asked, returning the young girl's smile. *Is Smiling 101 taught in school, for heaven's sake?* Lacey ground her teeth together, hoping she could locate a dentist in Manila if she needed one in a rush. She moved her head back and forth in an effort to loosen the tension in her jaw.

"Just bottled water, thanks." Lacey pasted on a fake smile in a futile effort to fit in. She was ten years older, five inches taller and ten pounds heavier than any other woman in the room. Not to mention the curly red hair. Everyone else had shiny dark waterfalls cascading down their bodies and around their doll-like faces. And those damn sweet smiles. Well, except for the dour, heavy-set *mamasan* seated in a corner watching proceedings and no doubt in charge of collecting the bar fines when a man asked to take a girl home 'as his girlfriend'.

The second girl, a nubile young thing a decade shy of Lacey's advancing age, gave her a sweet smile. At least she shared her favors.

When the waitress left to fix their drink order, the first beauty moved in and whispered something in Will's ear, her dark hair swaying forward and caressing the side of his face. He laughed out loud, a generous sound that grated further on Lacey's stretched nerves. She fidgeted in her chair. Their server came back with their drinks and set them down. Will dug out some pesos and paid her, nodding his thanks. The female grinned at the size of her tip.

"Relax. She was just letting me know her price." She locked eyes with him.

"And what is the going rate for a home visit from the Dollhouse?"

"My prospective new girlfriend would cost a thousand pesos. About seventy-two dollars Canadian. Pretty good rate, eh?" He laughed again, removed the white napkin wrapped around the neck of his beer and took a swig.

"So, are we going to do what we came here to do?" she queried, toying with the napkin, folding and refolding it accordion-style on the tabletop.

"We need cooperation to make this work." His handsome mug lit up with a broad smile. "And I have just the thing." He got up and pulled a long chain attached to a bell, making it clang loudly. Lacey frowned. Then caught the significance. Above the bar a sign read, *Ring the bell and all the ladies receive a free drink.*

"And I imagine you pay for that privilege?" she asked, unable to keep the grumpiness from invading her tone.

"Of course. Relax, this will be fun." He sat and leaned over, kissing her lips. The action brought him close, too close, his warm lips pressed to hers then sliding across the sensitive surface. Heat radiated and continued down her body, pooling in her core. What the hell? She took a deep breath in an effort to ratchet down her feelings. *Why in God's name did he have to kiss me like that and remind me of last night's amazing one? Here, of all places, when there's nothing I can do about it?* Though maybe jumping his bones might not be as frowned upon as, say, doing it in the local library…

Before she could demand an explanation for the kiss or take any action, they swarmed. From everywhere, nubile semi-clad bodies surrounded them in a split second. Well, make that surrounded Will. Lacey was elbowed aside. Two women even had the audacity to perch on his knees, one running her long slender claws — ah, fingers — through his hair. He lapped it up, grinning like a damn Cheshire cat, his big arms easily holding the small bodies of the squirming women busily vying for his attention. *Just when you think you know everything about somebody, they completely stump you and act like a goddamn fool.*

She tapped her toes under the table, wishing she had not worn practical shoes eyeing their fuck-me shoes. This was worse than that time in Cairo when that belly dancer had taken a liking to Will and insisted on dancing pretty much on his lap all night, shaking her ample lady bits.

When the commotion finally died down, the *mamasan* waddled over, her eyes sharp with interest, her mouth stretched in a smile.

"You Canadian?" the woman asked, pursing her lips.

"Yes, from the heart of our great nation—the Canadian prairies—specifically the city of Winnipeg in the province of Manitoba."

She nodded. "You need new girlfriend?" She peered over at Lacey, the insinuation clear that she could do better by him.

"Perhaps I could be enticed. But I need information first. There was a young man killed outside this bar a week ago. A tourist named Daniel Wright. I'm paying a reward for anyone who knows anything—saw anything that can help me understand what happened to my friend."

She narrowed her eyes. "How much?"

"Ten thousand pesos."

Her eyes widened. "Just for information? Not if the info also leads to the killer?"

Shrewd woman. She understood crime-stopper rules.

"Yes, just for info."

"I'll check around for you. Do you have a photo?"

Lacey dug out her phone and found the photo, handing it over. The woman moved away to speak with the girls, Lacey's phone displayed in the palm of her beefy hand. Lacey recognized a few of the overheard snippets of conversation being spoken in Tagalog, second language for most in the Philippines and the first for over a quarter of the population.

"You do know they're going to take full advantage of this and everyone will have an answer conned up in a heartbeat?" she asked Will.

"Probably, but someone might know something. Only way is to play Go Fish."

Lacey's lips still tingled and her lower extremities burned with excess heat, along with her seething brain. *I need to get laid. Soon. Before I embarrass myself.*

No one moved to take Will up on his offer, though a few of the women snuck a quick peek at him. A few minutes later the *mamasan* dropped her phone off with a shrug. "No one has seen him."

Dumbfounded that she'd called it wrong, Lacey frowned, looking over at Will. He didn't seem concerned in the least. In fact, he appeared to be entirely enjoying himself, nodding his head to the beat of the horribly lame music. She rolled her eyes. *Men.*

A young woman, perhaps a few years older than most, sidled up to their table. "You want best girl in Dollhouse just for you, handsome man? Only fifty dollah — US." She bent over Will, her full, high breasts complementing her trim ass as she whispered something in his ear. She probably even had that exact seven-to-ten waist-to-hip ratio that men were said to adore in their prospective mates.

Though Lacey strained to hear what the annoying woman murmured, she couldn't pick up anything much through the red haze obscuring her vision. This was the last fucking straw.

Will nodded, his interest, obvious by his expression, dumbfounding her. "Yes. Whatever you want. You're exactly the girlfriend experience we've been looking for."

The woman pointed over at Lacey. "You? Only twenty dollah more," she said with a shit-eating grin.

Lacey was instantly insulted, frowning as the woman endowed Will with yet another smile as she turned back to him when Lacey didn't answer her inquiry right away. She couldn't or she'd explode. *Why am I worth less? An irrational thought — but really, talk about sexist.* But more importantly, was Will into this? She'd never seen him so self-satisfied, as though he more than enjoyed women giving the impression that the sun rose and set with him.

The woman pranced off. Lacey rubbed the side of her face. She'd gritted her teeth so hard her jaw was screaming in protest.

"She's gone to get her street clothes on," Will said. "I had no idea this would be so easy and the women so darn nice to complete strangers." His smug expression did her in.

"What you need is a bib."

"What?"

"You're drooling all over the floor, lover boy."

His eyes met hers, his expression alight with good humor, not insulted at all by the insinuation. "This will be fun. When in Rome, right?"

Something clicked in her mind like one side of a Rubik's cube becoming all one color. She made certain her thoughts stayed hidden, keeping the pout in place. Clever, she'd give him that. But damn him for making her forget how calm and collected she normally was at sleuthing out information. She didn't need a man for that. Ha, she'd taught him all he knew on the subject. *Time for me to take the bit out of your mouth and take the lead, Mr. William James Thornton III.*

A few minutes later and the trio walked out of the bar together. As soon as they hit the street, the young woman spoke up. "How far to the hotel?"

"We have a car waiting. Come on," Lacey said, enjoying the look of surprise now covering Will's face before she took the woman's arm and strode off.

Will was quiet as they walked the few blocks back to the vehicle. *Not so funny now, eh?* She glanced at the woman. *Hmm. Very pretty. This will be fun. How far can I go with this before Will tries to shut it down?* She could handle it any way it went, of course. *Experimenting in university's going to pay off dividends now.*

Will opened the door of the taxi and ushered them both inside. The driver gave him a wide grin of approval and a thumbs-up sign, then sped off in a toxic cloud of unburned fuel, the blue haze adding another layer of pollution. She fairly itched for a shower.

"What's your name?" Lacey asked the young woman tucked in between her and Will. Her street clothes consisted of a short white gauzy sundress that complemented her dark coloring to perfection, her dark hair flowing around her pretty face.

"Nina."

"I'm Lacey."

"Is the hotel far?" Nina asked.

"No, not far. Perhaps we can pay for you to stay the entire night?" Lacey asked, giving Will a questioning look.

"Uh, yeah, that's fine," Will said, his brows knitted, remaining silent for the ride back to the hotel. Lacey chatted brightly with Nina until the taxi came to a stop.

Will paid off the driver. They went into the hotel and up the elevator to their floor.

"Nice," Nina said as she walked into Will's suite and glanced around. JR opened one sleepy eye to check them out, then went back to napping, curling up in a tighter ball. *Smart cat.*

"Would you like something to drink, Nina?" Lacey asked, nodding at Will to act as bartender.

"Sure, white wine." The woman settled down on the sofa, looking quite at home. Her English had improved dramatically in the taxi.

"Make that two glasses," Lacey instructed. She turned back to the woman. "How do you like working at the Dollhouse?"

Nina shrugged. "It's okay, I guess. It helps me send money to my family."

"Of course."

Will approached and handed them their wine.

"Thanks," Nina murmured, giving him a sweet smile. Lacey added her own smile to the mix, keeping her expression neutral. Will's dark eyebrows rose, nearly meeting his hairline.

"Have you worked there long? Had a few 'girlfriend' experiences?" Lacey asked.

"Yes, and I would very much like to be the girlfriend to such a handsome man as Mr. Willie."

"Hmm. Can't say I see the attraction—but when in Rome, right?" Lacey said with a shrug, smiling and taking a long swallow of her wine. Nina did the same.

"Okay if I take a shower?" Nina asked, setting her empty wine glass down.

"Of course. Follow me. I need one too." It was too much fun to watch Will's expression as she ushered her charge into his bathroom.

Will let out a whoosh of air. What the fuck? Was Lacey into this? *More importantly, what am I going to do?* The stolen kiss still burned on his lips. She'd seemed so willing when he'd kissed her last night. Maybe he'd misread the signals? The fact that he had leaned over and kissed her again was a surprise in itself, though that he could blame on her for responding to his advances last night. Then a sword and a novelist had gotten in the way. Regret stirred. *Maybe I should have met her in the bar as Michael and discovered where that would lead us? What if that was my only chance to be with her? No.* He shook his head, warring within himself. That wouldn't be right. Damn it all to hell, things were getting complicated. Not that that woman had ever been easy. Keep to the game plan, work on showing her that he was her best bet — that was his golden ticket.

The sound of the water running droned on for some time. He downed two straight Scotches before the tap was turned off.

The women pranced into the room, both dressed in towels. *What the fuck?*

"Would you like to freshen up as well, lover boy?" Lacey asked, her beautiful emerald eyes as sparkling as the gems they were named after.

"No, I'm fine." He cleared his throat. Much as he wanted Lacey, he wanted her all to himself, not as part of a scene. Actually, never as part of a scene.

But before he could come up with the right words to stop it and save face, Lacey gave him a look that he recognized spelled trouble and moved closer to their guest, slipping her slender fingers behind the woman's head and bending down to capture her lips in a long, lingering kiss.

His mouth went as dry as sand and his heart hammered so loudly he was certain everyone in the bloody hotel could hear it. He stood like a fool, mesmerized by watching two beautiful women kiss passionately. And not just any simple kiss, but a full-on lip lock. Complete with accompanying moans that sent his blood rushing away from his brain to parts even more appreciative of the amazing display and unconcerned about proper decorum. *Fuck, not now.*

"Ah, ladies, I think —"

"You want to join in, Mr. Willie?" Nina asked, turning her kiss-reddened lips his way. Lacey ran her tongue over her own pretty lips and gave a gentle sigh. The spectacular picture they made would be burned into his brain for a lifetime. *Damn it*. That was not what he wanted. He wanted Lacey all to himself.

"You have such sweet lips, Nina. What kind of lip cream do you use?"

"Fuck the lip cream, Lacey. Time to break this up," he growled, fisting his hands at his sides.

"Excuse me? Did you just insult us? And after we're all primed and prepared to see to your every imagined scenario of a three-way? William James Thornton, you disappoint me."

Yeah, he was certifiably crazy all right. Just about every other full-blooded male in existence would be chomping at the bit to get some of this action. Time to 'fess up. He took a deep breath. "Lacey, I think you might have gotten the wrong impression. Nina's here to give us some information on the case. That's all I'm paying her for. She knows something about Daniel Wright and everything else was just a cover."

"Oh, why didn't you just say so up front, lover? I had no idea you were doing this on the cheap, and only paying for information and not more delicious after-hours pursuits."

He pressed his lips together, his gut roiling. *One. Two. Three…* Even counting to ten like his first and only therapist had recommended brought no relief. Or maybe it did — he hadn't ranted and raved a denial. *A man has his pride.* Though the way Lacey was acting, it would shred into tatters if he wasn't careful.

"Will's not being cheap, Lacey. I would throw in any extras you want for the same generous amount he's already offered. It would be my pleasure. I hear Canadian men are wonderful lovers. Very generous in every way, if you catch my drift."

"Uh, I'm right here." He resented being spoken over.

"Yes, so you are, aren't you, standing right here in all your glory. Even if it's all covered up at the moment. You need to relax, like you suggested would help me earlier at the bar." Lacey's expressive eyes sent daggers his way. *Oh shit.*

"Damn it, Lacey, I was doing all this for you."

"Don't do me any favors. I can handle this all on my own, thank you very much!"

"Oh, really. You seemed to need me there to sort things out. I was the one that got the goods for you. Nina's here to share what she knows."

She turned to their visitor, her lips pursed, hands on hips. "Your assessment is quite correct about most Canadian men, Nina. Others buy fancy sport cars to compensate."

"Now, that's just hitting below the belt. You know I had the car foisted on me by dear old Dad to impress his buddies," he said through gritted teeth.

Lacey shrugged.

A fine red haze obscured his vision, his blood near the boil. He gritted his teeth to keep from saying something he would no doubt later regret. Or be *made* to regret was more like it. *Damn. Complicated. Gorgeous woman.* She would be the death of him. Guaranteed. But he wouldn't have it any other way. She excited him, made him want more.

He locked eyes with her and tried to send a mental message to stand down. She glared back, not giving an inch. Okay, he was up to bat, then.

"Isn't there something in that warrior tome of yours about knowing that looking beyond oneself to care for others is the ultimate goal? That self-improvement is crucial to helping said others on their own journeys? And that thou shall not give your best friend so much grief that he has a fuckin' heart attack?"

"Well played, Mr. Thornton."

"We aim to please, Miss Cameron."

She gave a snort.

She looked better, though. He caught a glimpse of a twinkle in her amazing eyes before she turned away to address Nina. "Sorry, but I'm on a bit of a tight schedule. Please, tell me what you know about Danny Wright's mugging and murder." The investigator in Lacey surfaced as she pressed Nina for the truth.

"Danny did come into the bar that night."

Lacey's eyes widened. "You saw him?"

"He was throwing money around. Won a lot of money gambling at a place he liked to frequent—I forget the name. He left for a few minutes and I heard a couple of shots."

"Did anyone call the police after the shots were fired?" Will was wishing Lacey would go put on a dress so he could concentrate. Just a flimsy towel covered her, exposing creamy shoulders and toned thighs. Even a hint of the tops of her well-rounded breasts made his mouth water.

Nina nodded emphatically. "I was in the alley taking a smoke break when the body was picked up. I caught a glimpse when the sheet fell away. He'd been shot in the face—it was horrible." She shuddered. "I was with another girl, Layla, but she won't talk. Scared. We were warned to stay quiet by the *mamasan*. Not sure why exactly, because that's all there was to see. But that's why I had to cover my tracks." Nina pressed her lips together. "I hope I did it well enough. Everyone thinks my English is deplorable, so hopefully they won't suspect. I do it to make the customers feel more comfortable. It works. I get better tips."

"It's brave of you to come forward," Lacey said.

Nina shrugged. "I liked Danny. He was generous to me. Kinder than a lot of the men. A real gentleman, if you know what I mean. Though a couple of the other dancers complained about his treatment of them, I never saw anything but good behavior on his part. I'd like to help in some small way if I can. Maybe you can find out who did this?"

"I'm going to try," Lacey promised. "Anyone else see anything?"

"Not sure. Nobody's talking much about it. Oh, but he did say he had powerful friends. Bragged about it. I never saw any evidence of it. He always came in alone."

"Well, that's very helpful, Nina. Thanks for stepping forward. Now, if you'll excuse me, I want to get dressed. And Will, could you order another driver? We need to see the coroner and visit the mortuary ASAP."

Will let out a deep breath, glad the fireworks were over. She'd never taken his antics so seriously before. And that was the problem. He wanted her to start taking life more seriously. Start taking *him* more seriously. Being a playboy for his brother's charities had given him a reputation he wanted to step away from.

He paid Nina and escorted to a cab, heading back to his suite a few minutes later.

Lacey was already dressed and ready to go when he opened the door.

"You're a bad girl for playing me." He suppressed a smile.

"Duh, Will, you know better than to try to pull anything over on me. Of course I knew, lover boy. Even you aren't that big a playboy. Unless I'm mistaken?" she asked, her round innocent eyes with their deep pools of liquid quicksilver locking with his.

"Hell, no!" he sputtered. "I have no intention of heading down that path. Ever. Okay, but you can't say that I didn't get you last night, Miss Smarty Pants."

"Maybe," she teased, sashaying away from him.

"Damn right, I did," he grumbled, holding the door open for her. "Well, at least now we have a motive for Danny's mugging. Throwing money around can get you killed in any number of places."

"But why shoot him in the face? Seems kind of extreme," she asked.

"Yeah." *Like they were trying to hide his identity.*

Minutes later, they were in the back of the taxi. Their new driver drove the streets of Manila like a speed demon with a reckless disregard for anything, dodging trikes and cars as if on the Indie 500 racetrack. It sent Lacey careening into him. Her warm shoulder pressed to his, arousing the keen interest of his groin, giving him a repeat performance of the night before. Surreptitiously adjusting himself, he tried keeping his mind focused on the view from the car window, barely allowing himself to breathe in her delicious fragrance. *Torture.* It was downright torture. And he wouldn't give up one precious second of it.

But he needed some distance to clear his head. *Figure out a new game plan.* Surely if she'd been attracted to a blond Will, she'd be attracted to a dark-haired Will? He just needed to be patient. Soon he'd have his life on a better track. Atone for his family's missteps in the past. Then he would have something substantial to offer a woman.

Will paid the driver to wait, ushering Lacey into the facility. A caustic odor of strong chemicals permeated the air, assaulting his nostrils, a stark reminder of what went on in the place. Many people couldn't afford to bury their loved ones immediately, needing to hold public events like skimming off poker games to raise the necessary cash to have them released to their care. Hence the urgency to embalm the body for longer storage. Hell, even then they only got five years in a cement slot in a row of temporary grave sites in aboveground storage until more money would be demanded or the body forcibly removed and the slot given to another family. Their only recourse was to pay a sum each year. Not possible for poor families, which most Filipinos were.

"Yes, can I help you?" a harried-looking middle-aged man responded to the tinkle of the bell over the door. *No angel will be getting their wings today.* The dismal space they stood in with its drab green walls and dusty-looking furniture wasn't reassuring. The man, dressed in a blood-spattered white lab coat and latex gloves, didn't offer his hand, but stood waiting impatiently, his mood obvious from his tense body language.

"Yes, we're here about Daniel Wright."

"Daniel Wright?" he queried, a frown creasing the skin of his forehead, drawing attention to the sallowness of his complexion, a likely hazard of his occupation. Then his expression smoothed. "Yes, you're the wife? Here to pick up his ashes? Come with me."

"Ah, no, I'm not his wife."

The man stopped in his tracks. Waited.

"I'm Lacey Cameron and this is Will Thornton, my fiancé. We're here to see what you can tell us about the case I'm investigating for a friend, Megan Wright. Daniel Wright — her brother — was mugged and killed not far from here," Lacey said.

The man's face tightened, his eyes glinting suspiciously. "It would be better if you talked to the police working the case. They should be the ones answering your questions." The man crossed his arms over his chest.

Standard defensive tactic. Not planning on being very helpful.

Lacey gave him a coy smile, moving in closer to the man.

"I was wondering who came in to identify the body. I would like to know their name and address to offer my condolences. Also, I wish to give some money to the family to help them with expenses. Do what I can to help, if you know what I mean." She gave him an innocent look, meant to disarm, touching his shoulder. Will gritted his teeth, prepared to spring into action at a moment's notice.

The man's face relaxed at Lacey just wanting a name and address. Or more likely it was the mention of cash and the attention of a beautiful woman who needed to put on the brakes about demonstrating this kind of brazen behavior if she knew what was good for her.

"I would also like to offer some financial assistance to your fine establishment, perhaps a fund set up for people unable to pay the full cost of burial," Will smoothly added. He wanted this ended. *Now.*

"Yes, and how many others would you care to help?" The guy's eyes gleamed with even keener interest. *Obviously hoping to skim some off the top. Good.*

"Let's say enough for another ten families to buy their loved ones who are without resources a proper burial. I'll leave it in your capable hands to choose who's most in need of the help."

"That is generous. Let me check my files." He left the room, leaving them alone.

"Damn it, Will, I had this," Lacey muttered into his ear, shaking her head in annoyance.

"I want to help out as well. And a fund for the families is a small matter." Why was she so rattled today? She had never minded his help, financial or otherwise, in the past.

"You must know not all of this money will pass into the right hands, right?"

"That's why I upped the compensation. To make certain some does." He shrugged. "You can't please God without being acquainted with the devil, Lacey."

"What the hell's that supposed to mean?"

They were again interrupted before he could answer, the man back with a piece of paper clutched in his hands, a smile on his face.

"I have the address of the wife's sister. She identified the body. I'm sure she would be more than pleased with any offers of help on your part. And it's generous of you, Mr. Thornton, to set up a fund for the unfortunate people unable to afford proper burials for their loved ones. I will personally see to its administration."

"Thank you. My people will be in touch." Will stepped forward and offered the man cash 'just to get him started', promising more in the future. They made the exchange of one kind of paper for another, Lacey hiding her disapproval. Barely.

Chapter Seven

"All warfare is based on deception." — *Sun Tzu*

"I'm going to see Athena Marcos by myself. No ifs or buts about it," Lacey said through gritted teeth as they made the awaiting taxi. She'd had enough, more than enough. She knew the game through and through, had had years of study and practice.

"Lacey—"

"No, Will, you're going overboard here. This is my investigation. You're interfering with how I do things and I want it stopped."

"What? I'm just trying to make it easier for you. Keep you safe."

She let out a deep sigh. "I'll be perfectly safe grilling Athena. She's another woman, for heaven's sake! Have you forgotten my expertise at karate?"

He pursed his lips and rubbed his chin, giving her a steely-eyed glance, then stood down, surprising her, though his expression remained grim. "I need to be dropped off at the hotel first, then."

"Fine."

At the hotel, he paid the driver, ignoring her instant frown. "Take the lady where she needs to go and see her back here when she's finished," he instructed him. The man nodded once.

"I won't say be careful, because I want to keep my head on my shoulders. But stay well, beautiful."

She stood down herself at his caring words as he opened the taxi door, preparing to disembark. "Don't worry about me. I've got my big-girl panties on."

"Hardly," he chucked, turning back. "Don't forget I've seen how small your underwear is. A red lace G-string still hanging from that moose antler back at Casey's place comes to mind."

"Yeah, seemed as safe a place as any to keep it," she quipped back, smiling at the fond memory of hanging them on the one-antlered beastie to celebrate Casey getting Soapy's Gold.

The driver sped off and her last glimpse of Will was of him standing on the sidewalk watching her leave. *Phew.* She settled back in the seat, relieved to finally be getting some time to get her head straight. The man was driving her crazy! And why does he have to smell so darn good, anyway?

Disembarking yet again a short time later, the air quality growing more dismal by the ticking hour, she walked up to the front door of the small, squat family dwelling. If it was this steamy in June, how hard would typhoon season, lurking just around the corner, be? She didn't intend to find out, needing to get to the bottom of this case pronto. Though maybe being forced indoors by a monster storm with her partner in crime might not be half bad. Especially if all technology was unavailable, leaving them time to get more acquainted. *Hmm.* Her body stirred, alive to the possibilities after last night's kiss. She'd nearly laughed aloud at his horrified expression when he watched her kiss Nina. She'd just managed to hold it in, not wanting Athena to think her a loony tune for giggling out of the blue. He was so darn predictable.

"Yes?" An attractive young woman opened the door, her dark hair pulled up into a high ponytail, her Bambi-like brown eyes registering surprise as she took in Lacey standing on her doorstep. *Perhaps she was expecting someone else?* She was wearing pink sweats that barely contained the goodies — not the casual ones either, but the sparkly bedazzled kind.

"Athena Marcos?" Lacey asked.

She nodded silently and waited.

"I'm here about Angel Marcos-Wright — your sister?"

"Yes, she's my sister." The woman's tone and expression shifted, a certain wariness replacing her open posture.

"I'm here to offer my condolences at the loss of your brother-in-law, Daniel Wright. And to offer any assistance I can to your family," Lacey said. "Like taking his ashes back to the States for the widow, if that would help ease things."

The woman gave a slight frown, eyed her with speculation, then opened the door farther, letting her pass by. She indicated a spot to sit in the tiny living room, a formal space that didn't appear much used, like a parlor in days past.

"Can I get you anything to drink? I have water and soda." The woman appeared more neutral in her assessment now, obviously prepared to listen.

"I could use some water. It's been a long, hot day so far." She gave her hostess a smile, pressing her hand to her forehead as if under stress.

Athena snorted. "Better get used to that if you intend to stay in Manila long."

"I guess I'd better, eh?"

"I'll be right back," Athena said, giving a full view of the word *Juicy* printed with sparkles on the ass of her sweats as she exited.

Lacey sat, tapping her toe. She glanced around the room, trying to sniff out anything out of the ordinary. Nothing unusual to be seen. She hoped to get more from Athena. *Time to go to work.*

Athena came back with two glasses of water in plastic orange tumblers.

"Thanks," Lacey said, taking a sip of the tepid water and setting the glass down. "Nice place you have here."

Athena raised her eyebrows. "You're kidding, right? It's a dump. I'm so out of here soon as I find the money."

"Really?" Lacey replied, chewing on her bottom lip. "Where would you like to live?"

Her hostess narrowed her eyes at her. "Anywhere better. But housing's outrageously expensive in the good parts of the city. So, you want to know about Danny? Did someone send you here from the insurance company?"

"No, I'm just here on behalf of his sister. She's so broken up about his death she couldn't come. And we've been friends for years, so I volunteered. Anything you can share, though, I will tell her in the utmost confidence. She just needs to know, understand? She's grieving—"

"About Daniel? You know he was an asshole, right?"

Lacey sat back, shocked at the anger behind the words. "I find that hard to believe. Danny was a good guy. At least when I dated him in high school."

"You dated him? Then you should know." Athena's mouth thinned into a straight line.

"Ahh, actually, I don't know." *The warrior listens first, then decides.*

"The way he treated my sister. It wasn't right." She shook her head, her eyes filling with unexpected tears.

Lacey told herself to relax — being angry would only torch the situation. She needed to understand what was going on. She thrust down her basic need to defend Danny, searching for this woman's truth.

"Why don't you tell me why you think that?"

"I just don't think that — I know that."

"How?"

"He often disrespected her. Threatened to take away her son Mathew if she didn't go along with his wishes. Didn't even bother to bring her to Manila his last trip. He deserved what he got."

Lacey swallowed hard. But the woman didn't seem to realize she was incriminating her own sister with her words, giving the widow even more motive to get rid of her husband.

"Kind of harsh, isn't that, Athena? To wish him dead?"

"He hit her. Did you know that?"

"No, I'm sorry. I wasn't aware." Whether or not the abuse had actually happened, Athena believed it to be true, which surprised Lacey. Something was more amiss here than she'd expected.

Athena swallowed hard, chewing her bottom lip. She covered her mouth with her hand. "Okay, maybe he didn't deserve to die, but he wasn't exactly a prince among men."

"Did you know him well? Are you certain it was his body you saw in the morgue? Could you be mistaken? He was shot through the face, after all." Lacey swallowed, uncomfortable with her last statement. It still felt surreal to her, someone of her own generation dying — murdered and gone, just like that.

"Yeah, it was him." She didn't look Lacey in the eyes as she made the flat statement.

"You are absolutely certain? Because we have another witness who's raising doubts that it was his body in the morgue. And she knew him quite well," she lied, fishing more with her gut feeling than with the actual facts. She needed to be certain the body was Danny's, and, with it already cremated and its extreme facial destruction meaning any photos of it were useless for identification purposes, she had few options open to her.

"What witness?" Athena asked, her expression instantly worried.

"You know it's a felony to lie, right? That it will get you into all sorts of trouble. If someone is leaning on you to say this, to commit perjury, now is the time to speak up. Before it goes any further."

Athena pressed her lips together, her eyes worried.

"I can help you, Athena, if someone is pressuring you or your family." Lacey's tone was the perfect blend of conciliatory and concerned.

"No." Athena shook her head. "It was Danny in the morgue, I'm certain. I know my own brother-in-law. You're just trying to confuse me."

Lacey let out a small sigh of frustration. "Do you know where Danny liked to gamble? He was flush with money from a recent win that night—the apparent motive for his murder."

"Club Ten was a favorite place."

"How about his ashes? Do you want me to pick them up and deliver them?"

"Why would she want them?" she shrugged. "After he mistreated her. And the answer to your question is no, not yet. They want money first. But yeah, we should collect the ashes. You want to do that—be my guest."

"Okay, here's what I am prepared to do. You come with me to the mortuary and we retrieve the ashes together. I'll pay what it costs to release them. Then I will deliver them to your sister. Does that work for you?"

"Sure, if you're paying, but I prefer you pick them up yourself. I'll make the call to authorize it," she said with a sly smile.

* * * *

Will's cell phone buzzed. He sat on Lacey's bed, trailing a toy mouse on a string for JR, waiting for word of Lacey. He'd gotten some paperwork done, but found himself struggling to focus, thinking about that amazing kiss they'd shared. Knowing he wanted as many as he could get. ASAP.

"Will," he said into the phone, still dangling the stuffed toy for the over-zealous kitten.

"I need to see you. But not at the station. Meet me tonight at the café on the corner of Amorsolo and Roosevelt. After midnight. And come alone," Lieutenant Versoza said, his voice terse with warning.

"Sure, what's up?"

"Can't talk now." He hung up before Will could protest.

Now what?

Chapter Eight

"Oh! What a tangled web we weave, when first we practise to deceive." — Sir Walter Scott

Had Danny really changed that much since high school? Sure, they'd only dated a couple of times, but there had been no evidence of violence. She wouldn't have dated him at all if that were the case. Especially since her own father — well, she wasn't going there. All the way back to the hotel, Lacey racked her brain for answers. How were they were going to prove a hundred percent it was Danny's body cremated at the morgue? Though that was looking more and more possible, with the motive of stolen money.

But Athena wasn't the most reliable witness. She was hiding something — that was also clear. The puzzle was still missing too many pieces. Lacey shook her head, frustrated by the lack of answers.

The taxi stopped and she picked up the small urn purchased at the mortuary for the ashes, Athena having eased the way with the promised phone call. She swallowed hard. The container's appearance was unsettling, a permanent reminder of the finality of Danny's death for Megan and her family.

She entered the hotel, urn in hand, and hurried across the marble floor to the reception area. She was about to ask the desk clerk for information on the swimming and gym facilities, intending to work off some of her frustration, when a woman's voice cut through her thoughts. She spun around.

"Will, hello, it's me, Porsha."

Lacey caught Will looking at her, and she gave him back one of her own specialties, an eyebrow arched with derision. The woman quickly moved in on him with an expression of what could only be called idol worship, giving him a smile of pure simpering silliness. *Now what?*

"Porsha, what are you doing here?"

To his credit, he did sound dumbfounded. While he greeted the woman, Lacey gave her a thorough check. *Hmm.* Sleek dark hair cut to show off great cheekbones, timeless red lipstick applied to full lips, dark glasses framing perfect eye makeup, and clothes that covered yet showed off an excellent figure. Very good at the sexy librarian look. Too good. She was working some kind of angle. *And it better not be Will. My best bud's off-limits to interloping skanks.*

"I've come to see you. After what we shared the other night, I knew I needed to get to know you better, and that it just couldn't wait. What you did—nearly took my breath away. An experience I will never forget," she gushed.

Experience? What is she talking about?

Will beckoned Lacey to join them. She stood her ground, quite prepared to make the introductions awkward, then relented with a loud sigh when he gave her a look of desperation, running a hand over the back of his neck, his tell for stress.

"Ah, Porsha, this is Lacey Cameron, a close friend of mine. Lacey, this is Porsha Evans, a reporter for *Maclean's* magazine."

"Nice to meet you," the woman said.

Liar. Lacey held out her arm, shaking the reporter's hand, the bones crunching together quite satisfactorily. The woman winced and pulled out of her grasp. "Likewise. So, you're on a story?" Lacey asked.

"Partly."

What other part is there?

"I don't know if Will shared what happened?" Porsha said.

"No, he didn't." She clipped her words.

"It was nothing anyone else wouldn't have done in the same circumstances, and with the same training," Will said, his tone subdued.

"Do tell," Lacey said.

"He didn't share that he saved a man's life?" Porsha asked, holding the trump card. The woman flickered a glance at Lacey, then looked up at Will, her eyes filling with admiration. "The man's going to pull through. Did you know that? I wanted to share that with you in case you were unaware. One of the reasons I'm here."

And the other reason?

"I needed to see you in the worst way, so please forgive my just showing up. My editor's been hounding me about the story after he found out about your heroism. It was in the *Winnipeg Free Press* yesterday morning. It's timely, Will, and the story needs to be told. People need more heroes, now, more than ever."

"I'm not a hero. Just a guy," Will said.

"I beg to differ. What you did — running right up and giving the man CPR with no thought of any danger you might be in? Well, I say you're a hero. And I think the rest of the country will agree, too. I want to share that with our readers, plus the story of your heroism overseas. How you won the Star of Military Valour multiple times — more than any other soldier in Afghanistan. The story could not be more opportune with what just happened. Please, I just need a few minutes of your time. I'm now on a tight deadline, thanks to your recent valor." She gave off smiles reminiscent of Lacey's recent experience in the Dollhouse.

Skank.

"Let me take that for you," Will said, reaching for the urn Lacey held at her side.

"I've got it," Lacey said, refusing to give it up. She leaned in close to him, mouthing for his ears only, "You stink of cheap perfume, lover boy."

Before she could turn away, he reached for her and pulled her in tight for a full-body hug, almost as if he was rubbing himself up against her. Leaning down, he whispered in her ear, "I smell much better now, eh? Branded yours." His warm breath left a trail of destruction in its wake down the side of her neck. Oh yeah, definitely one of her erogenous zones. Her body tingled with the sensation, wanting more while anger still played havoc with her emotions. Rollercoaster rides were overrated.

"Let me go."

A clearing of a throat nearby suggested someone else was uncomfortable with the intimate display. *Ha. Hopefully that too-good-to-be-true reporter.*

"Not till you say I smell good."

"I will not!" she cried. He kept his arms firmly in place, not allowing her any leverage for escape. The urn had ended up behind his back, held by only one hand in the brouhaha, and she was worried about dropping it.

"Will, the urn is slipping from my fingers."

He quickly let her go at the urgent tone in her voice.

She endowed him with the widest grin of victory, wishing her body had not enjoyed the vertical wrestling quite so much. Heat still flooded her, suggesting all systems were waving him in for a horizontal tango.

"I'll leave you two to talk. I have places to be." Lacey hurried away, not bothering to say goodbye to the reporter. In the elevator, she set the urn down carefully and took out her phone for a quick search to see what the hell was going on. *Oh.* She played the video of Will working on the elderly man. Twice. *What was that skank doing with my Will?*

Without giving it any more thought, she dialed the number. She needed more answers.

"Marcus Salang."

"Hi, Marcus, it's Anne Cameron from the Governor's Ball."

"Ah, Miss Anne, how lovely to hear your voice." The oil fairly dripped on her even over the phone.

"Yours as well. I was on my own tonight, and had this epiphany that you too might be at a loose end, and might have the time to show me your Club Ten that I've been hearing so much about?"

"What a charming idea, and your timing could not be more perfect. I have a recent acquisition you might find interesting. I'll send a limo for you. And it would be my supreme pleasure to show you whatever else you'd like to see of mine."

Just the club, buddy. "Great, I'll be there shortly."

She leaned down and picked up the urn. A thrill raced down her spine. Perfect. It was exactly the invitation she needed. A chance to check out Club Ten, where Danny had most likely won the money.

* * * *

Porsha wasted no time. As soon as their beers were delivered in the small, intimate lounge off the lobby, she got right down to demonstrating her wordsmith ability with her opening bid.

"How many billionaires shoulder a rifle? Or spend sleepless nights ducking shells and shrapnel and machine gun bullets? How many of them are killed or wounded in battle defending their country's interests? That is what makes you unique, Will. What people will want to know about and understand. Why a man fights when he doesn't have to." Her voice rang with sincerity, her words designed to tug at his heart. She was good. Very good.

Did she know about his family's interests? How one of his father's businesses supplied munitions? That the family's fortune had been built on the blood of dead men? It went against all Will stood for.

"Why should only a poor man's son fight? We all have an obligation," he said, going back to the beginning. What had started him on the journey, the idealism that had driven him to enlist, seemed long ago, a past life.

"A lot of people would argue with you about that. How many politicians' sons and daughters are sent to the front lines? Lots of times in history, the rich have bought their freedom from service. Paid for another body to replace their own. I'm not saying it's right. I'm only pointing it out."

"A journalist's job."

"Yes, it is." She ran her fingers around the rim of her beer glass.

"Coming home from the war, seeing the devastation that it brings to fellow soldiers, it changes a man," he ventured.

"I can only imagine," Porsha said, taking a sip of her beer. "How are you coping?"

He pressed his lips together. "I cope fine. I'm one of the lucky few. Lots of help for me to transition back to being a productive member of society." He didn't mention his father's edict to just get over himself and get down to business.

"Just because you have all that doesn't mean it's not hard. You still went through the same emotional experience as other soldiers," she said, pointing out the flaw in his reasoning.

"I have other ways of coping with the resources I have at my disposal. Ways that most soldiers can only imagine. I'm going to make a meaningful difference and that helps a great deal — gives me purpose."

"Yes?" she asked, prompting him to say more, her dark eyes locked with his, the intensity in their intelligent depths working on him. It was tempting — to share his new passion. Was this the right time?

"Helping run the family's businesses keeps me busy."

"And yet here you are in Manila helping a friend with a problem. How long have you known Lacey Cameron?"

"Lacey? A few years."

"Where did you two meet?"

He laughed. "Now that's a story."

"Do tell." Porsha leaned forward in her chair, elbows on the table, chin propped in her hands.

He snorted, giving her a half-grin. "You're good."

"So I've been told. But I'd rather hear about you and Lacey. She didn't seem too happy about my arrival earlier."

"Well, Lacey is used to getting her own way. And she does have a lot on her mind. Her friend was murdered right here in Manila a few days ago."

"Really? That does suck. How did it happen? And where?"

He filled her in on the details. What did it matter? It was all on record.

"That's an unusual job for a woman. Private investigator."

"Lacey's an unusual woman."

"I can see that." Porsha leaned back in her chair and took another sip of her beer.

"Okay, so we met at university when I transferred there for my final semester. I stepped on her tail." He laughed aloud at the memory.

"Her tail?" Porsha looked disbelievingly at him.

"Yeah, it's true. The Brass Ringers—the sorority she and her classmates started together—were hosting a Halloween party at the Hub, the student bar on campus. She was dressed as a mermaid with a long flowing tail, one of the Disney characters, I think. Well, look at me—I wasn't nicknamed the Wall when I played college football for nothing — and I stepped on that train and tore it clear off. Turned her costume into a mini-skirt. Well, all hell broke loose," he said, chuckling again, reliving the fond memory. She had legs that didn't quit. "And I got a slug in the jaw for my trouble. Lacey's true Irish."

Will checked his iPhone. It was buzzing importantly with an incoming text message from Lacey's unique ringtone. *What the hell?*

"Sorry, I gotta go."

"Is something wrong?"

"No, no, it's fine. Just some business that needs immediate action."

"You still owe me."

"What?"

"You're hiding something, Will, and I intend to find out what it is. Best if you tell me first. I can work with that."

"Oh, yeah, later."

"I'm holding you to it," she said with a small smile that didn't quite reach her big brown eyes.

"Excuse me." He made himself walk at a normal speed from the lounge. *Goddamn it, Lacey, what have you got yourself into this time?*

* * * *

"I thought it was just down the street," Lacey said to the uniformed driver of the limousine. The side alley they'd just turned into wasn't familiar. Was this a mistake? But being the governor's son, the guy had to be careful, right? She pushed her worry aside. She was a Canadian citizen and he could hardly make her disappear. But then Danny was dead or missing. Of course, there was no connection. No indication the pair had ever met. So far. But Nina had mentioned something about an important friend. Perhaps Marcus Salang was the mystery guy? She'd need to dig deeper for that connection when she'd finished up with Salang tonight.

She texted Will. Reluctantly. But she needed to follow procedure or he'd get in an even bigger snit. She took a date-stamped photo of the sign over the door that read 'Club Ten' in glowing neon, for extra insurance. The low-riding building, in repetitive golden hues created from a mosaic of iron-stamped twelve-inch tiled squares, had an air of gaudy mystery about it, like most public places in Manila.

Stepping out of the limo, the hot night air making even the thin fabric of the spaghetti-strapped dress uncomfortable, she walked past the driver. He gave her a slight bow before opening the club's steel door for her.

She murmured her thanks and strolled inside, her purse swinging on her shoulder by a sturdy gold chain, reassuring her with the items it held. Mace, a sturdy pen for poking eyes out, and her fav, a law-enforcement-grade Taser — fully charged. The club's dance music was not overwhelmingly loud, which was refreshing, though the rhythmic beat of the bass music coursed through her, adding to her apprehension.

A pair of ubiquitous bouncer types greeted her, thick arms crossed over well-muscled chests and abs, enhanced by tight black T-shirts. Handy for averting trouble in any club or bar.

"I'm here to see Marcus Salang," she said.

The men gave her a thorough look up and down, taking in her short blue swing dress and matching stiletto heels, obviously impressed with her appearance.

"Lucky man," one said, nodding his head for emphasis at his partner.

"Where may I find him?" she prompted.

"I think he's been waiting for a woman like you all his life. I know I have, sugar," his partner said, his dark eyes glowing with intent.

"Excuse me. I'm not near sweet enough for that nickname — more like the hard-as-nails kind," she said, narrowing her eyes at him for a quick steely-eyed perusal.

"Maybe," he said with a grin and a shrug. "But why should just the rich pundits get all the good-looking women? It's worth a try, right?"

A noise of someone clearing their throat behind them made the pair straighten up and become silent.

The new man, who must have been the official greeter or host, gave the twin bouncers a look of disgust, beckoning her to follow him into the club. "Right this way, ma'am."

She trooped along behind the man, taking in her surroundings. Half club, half gambling hall.

"I hope you will forgive the men. They grow bored with their roles and sometimes forget who they are. And who they work for."

"They're both employed by Marcus Salang?"

"Everyone here is. He owns many businesses in Manila. Very rich, very powerful family."

"Nice gig if you can get it." *Rich doesn't necessarily mean better.* Though in Will's case, it proved true. His father, not so much. The man had been hard on Will growing up. No wonder he'd escaped to Iraq and Afghanistan, even with their harrowing costs. She hadn't really given the matter a lot of thought since he got back, but it dawned on her now that she was sometimes a bit dense about the big picture. Too caught up in proving something to a world that had always made her feel second-best. Maybe that needed to change? She swallowed hard. Here she was again doing the exact opposite of what he instructed — heading out on her own. *But I did send a text. And I won't be hamstrung by any man. Not even Will.*

"Yes, it is." The man's response interrupted her uncomfortable thoughts, but he did not sound envious of his employer, gesturing toward an alcove hidden from view by other patrons. "Mr. Salang awaits you."

"Thank you." Was she supposed to tip him? But the man vanished before she could dig a few bills from her purse.

She took in the labyrinth set apart from the larger room by obscuring screens. The murals were cheerfully painted, colorful images depicting an age long past of happy costumed peasants busy stacking grain and dancing. *Nice.* She straightened her shoulders and walked into the maze. It was darker inside, but not cramped. Through the screens, she could see the others moving around and hear the shouts of glee when someone won at craps. Safe enough. She patted her purse, enjoying what she had tucked inside.

"Ah, Anne, the goddess from the palace. Have a seat, sugar."

Lacey gave him a level look, minus a smile. *Not that damn sugar again.* What was it about this crew? Probably hoped to have women melting all over them. The man was alone, giving the impression of the big bad wolf about to pounce. Good thing she was no sheep.

"Marcus," she said, taking the seat, not the one he offered — his lap — but the chair a couple of feet away.

"You hurt my feelings, sugar." Apparently, he didn't get the significance of a woman's sigh.

"Sitting on you might hurt more of your anatomy than just your feelings," she said tartly, adding, "And don't call me sugar. I never melt, and that's a promise."

He gave a huge belly laugh. "You're a spitfire. I like that — matches your red hair. I like it much better than the brown, by the way."

"So, your man was just saying your family has a financial stake in a lot of businesses in the Philippines."

"Yes." He answered with pride. "We help out the people of our fine country by assisting them in many ways."

I'll just bet they are pleased at all the 'assistance.' But maybe she should be giving him the benefit of the doubt, not knowing all the facts? Nah, her gut said he was a user, not a builder, and it was seldom wrong. And since when did throwing money around atone for the kind of things his government was known for pulling?

A waiter appeared at her elbow. "What would you like to drink, miss?"

"A bottle of water, please." Less opportunity for tampering. She wouldn't put a roofie past this sleazeball.

Marcus swung his arms outward making a gesture of generosity. "You can choose anything you want to drink. Come, think bigger. Bring us a bottle of the finest champagne," he directed the waiter, who nodded and exited to do his bidding.

The waiter was back almost immediately, obviously a prepared kind of guy, deftly pulling the cork from the

January Bain

magnum of champagne. He poured two glasses and handed one to her.

"Thanks," she said. He bowed and left them alone without having brought her any water.

Marcus picked up the other glass and leaned forward to clink glasses with hers. "What shall we toast?" she asked.

"To the beginnings of a new friendship," he said, swallowing the glassful.

"To friendship." She took a sip and set the glass down.

"Drink up. There's plenty more where that came from."

"Thanks, but I seldom partake of libations," she lied through her teeth. Drinking was one of her hobbies. She enjoyed trying liquors from all around the globe.

"Really? You have no idea what you're missing." He smacked his lips and poured himself a second glass.

He swallowed half of that, then sat back in his chair and gave her a calculated look. "So, Miss not-so-sweet Cameron, what are you doing in our fine city?"

Funny guy. She pursed her lips. "Just the usual touristy stuff."

"Like going to police stations and mortuaries?"

Her heart skipped a beat. "Why do you ask what you already know?" she countered.

"I like to take the measure of a person in my town. Check out their veracity."

"My town. Where are we—Dodge City, 1870?" She gave a snort.

"You're not an open book. That simple fact alone makes you far more interesting than most beautiful women I've had the pleasure of meeting."

She snorted again. "Plus, you're hoping your compliments will soften me up."

"Perhaps."

"I'm just here in Manila trying to help a friend find out what happened to her brother." No point in hiding it now. He obviously had his resources. And it wasn't as if it affected him at all. "Did you ever meet him? He liked to gamble and apparently won a lot of money that night. It was the motive for his killing, far as we know."

"Danny Wright was murdered by a mugger looking to rob him. Not wise to flash all that money. That seems abundantly clear from the television news. And no, I did not meet him personally. Though, when I saw the news report, I recognized him."

"I need to be certain. His sister worries that his wife might be involved in his death. For the money. He took out a number of life insurance policies in the past year." Which reminded her she needed to get back to Vegas and talk to the wife soon.

"Hmm."

He appeared surprised at that information.

"Well, that's always a possibility. A woman scorned is a force to be reckoned with."

"Perhaps. But I have another theory." Something made her want to knock that smug look right off his smarmy face. And she was prepared for this.

"Yes?" he prompted.

"I think it's all a scam. That Danny Wright's not dead. That this whole setup is so he can collect the money himself. That he and his wife are both in on it. And the wife's sister who identified the body is also involved." *The warrior is always one step ahead of his enemies, leads with a good offense.* And this bit was custom-built to provoke a reaction. Of course, this was entirely a theory out of left field, meant to disarm, and she had little faith in it. More likely the wife and sister had arranged to have him killed. She could have gone with that one, but this one would most likely hit harder. Tarnish reputations.

"And that's easy enough to do in the Philippines where documents are a dime a dozen." He drank another glass of the champagne, smacking his lips with satisfaction. *Ugh.*

"Exactly."

"Perhaps," he said, rubbing the back of his neck. He looked far less pleased now, his eyes narrowed in thought, a darkness lurking behind the enlarged pupils. Was it only the mud slung at his countrymen behind the tell? Or had she hit a nerve?

"Well, whatever the situation is, I'm hoping to know soon. His sister is grieving his death and it would be nice to be able to give her good news that it's all a scam. But if he's dead, I want to confirm it for her. Then I'll be on my way."

"You have documents that say he's dead, right? A police report that confirms it. And his ashes. What else do you need? Who has made you think otherwise?" Marcus asked, his tone icy.

"No one," she said, with a dismissive wave of her hand. "Just a feeling. I'm most likely wrong about it. You know, women's intuition and all that." She backpedaled, worried about Nina all of a sudden. She took another sip of the champagne to hide her fluster. She needed to dig a little more on this sleazeball.

"Yes, women's intuition. It often gets females in trouble. You don't want to be stirring up a hornet's nest for nothing and making spurious comments in my country about false documentation."

"Please accept my apologies about that." So maybe that was it? He didn't like that part of her angle. She took a longer sip of the champagne and found she'd finished it.

Marcus refilled her glass.

"So, do you like to dance, Miss Cameron?"

"Not really," she lied again. The last thing she wanted was this creep's hands planted on her bod. She was only here doing her job. "You said you had something interesting to share with me? A recent acquisition," she prompted.

"Ah yes, the acquisition."

She nodded. "It sounds intriguing. What is it?"

"It's not here, of course, but at my mansion. Safer. It's a very rare find."

"Do you have a photo?" she asked. *Yeah right.* No way in hell was she going anywhere with him.

"Of course." He pulled out his phone and brought up the proper screen, thumping through the camera's photo roll.

"Ah, here we go." He turned the camera's screen to face her. She glanced at the photo and this time her heart stopped. The Rose of Cairo. A jewel of impeccable beauty. A pink diamond of incalculable worth. A stone she would give her eye teeth to obtain.

"It's beautiful. Incredible. Congratulations." Easy to gush. The image sank deep into her subconscious while she peered at it, with tentacles of desire rising to greet it.

"Yes. It will be the centerpiece of my collection," he boasted, his eyes shiny with hubris.

The guy must go through money like water. How can he afford such treasure? Even being the governor's son has to have some fiscal limits, right?

Her phone rang. *Right on cue.* She answered. "Yes, of course, I'll be right there." Lacey got up. It really was time to exit stage right. She had what she needed.

"You're going somewhere?" he gave her a surprised look. "I thought you might like to see the Rose of Cairo tonight?"

"Sorry, I can't. My cat JR's escaped from his room and I need to find him. Perhaps a raincheck?"

He frowned, not bothering to hide his disappointment laced with anger. He was not a man to turn down lightly.

"Please accept my thanks for the champagne," she said, offering her hand to her host. He accepted it and pulled it up to his lips, though it seemed more of an automatic gesture than the last time. He kissed it briefly and let go.

"If you must, you must."

"I'm sorry, I must."

"I'll be in touch," Marcus shot back. "Soon."

"Please do." *Politeness wins Brownie points.* She walked away, pleased with her evening's work. She exited the club, stepping back into the limo. At the hotel, she tipped the driver and hurried up to her room. *Game on.* She had major sleuthing to accomplish now that she had a suspect.

Will banged on the adjoining suite door about five seconds later, his face livid with emotion when she opened up. All alpha male and commanding-looking. What was his problem?

"What did I say about you going off on your own while we're here?"

"That you didn't advise it." Oops, so that was it. He was pissed she'd slightly broken her promise she'd made on the jet. What had she said exactly? *A warrior will say whatever it takes to get the job done. At least, this warrior will.*

"You promised me, Lacey. That you wouldn't go off alone. And at this time of night. I've been worried sick. I promised the Ringers I'd take care of you. Is that all your word's worth?"

A frisson of guilt struck. "Yeah, well, you were a tad occupied with that reporter ska — woman." She quickly self-corrected the perfect word choice. "Besides, I had it covered," she shot back. "I don't go to places like that without a backup system. My trusty mace and Taser, and my spectacular karate moves." She made her point, impulsively demonstrating a perfect Bruce Lee-esque kick of her right foot into the air, ignoring the fact she had a dress on. Ladylikeness. Not her forte or her concern. She spun around at the end of the move with a flourish, enjoying her dress fluttering out around her, giving a satisfying display of her red lace panties. Her signature color, and the only color she ever wore in underwear. It was that or commando.

"I could flatten his ass in a heartbeat. What's your problem with all this? You're hovering like I don't have my shit together. You know better. I've always held my own in the past. Even rescuing your sweet ass in the Coast Mountains when we were investigating Slumach's Gold, if you've conveniently forgotten." It wasn't like this friendship was only one-sided. She'd pulled her fair weight, too. Like going for help when he'd broken his leg climbing. *Time for a reality check.*

"And you thought that made it okay? That I would not worry about your hanging out with that sleazeball? Nice kick, by the way." A corner of his mouth quirked up for a split second when he complimented her kick. *Ha.*

"Will, we've been through this before. I need space. And this is what I do. I work at finding out the truth of things. Megan needs my help and I can sense I'm getting closer to knowing what really happened." Excitement flared, reminding her of the thrill of the hunt. If curiosity was a virtue, she'd be nominated for sainthood.

"To quote Jack Nicolson from *A Few Good Men*, you can't handle the truth. At least, not my truth."

"What does that mean?" Confused, she crossed her arms over her chest. Nothing annoyed her more than this kind of conversation. Too personal.

He scrubbed a hand over his face, apparently considering his next words. The silence hung between them. JR came over and rubbed against her shins and she reached down to pick him up for a hug.

"I don't know what I mean. I had just hoped for more from you."

Well played. This sucked big time, feeling like the bad guy. *I gotta get this circus back on track.*

"So, I've got some hopefully quick research to do, but then, maybe we could do something together? Something fun?" A quick memory of the big hug in the lobby followed by the sizzling kiss of the night before gave her an idea.

"Like what?" He gave her a piercing look, watching her pet JR.

"Well, you still haven't given me a chance to win that Bose system."

His eyes lit up like a wildfire racing across the Canadian prairies. "You are so going down, baby!"

"Give me an hour and come a-knocking."

He gave a huge wolfish grin. "You can count on it."

She set JR down and hurried to boot up her laptop. *Work first. Play later.*

Hmm. She raced through the images taken at Club Ten on the computer screen, fingers flying across the keys, searching for any proof that Danny and Marcus had ever been seen together.

* * * *

Will punched the number in the elevator for the lobby, late for his appointment with the lieutenant. He had just enough time to fit it in. What did Versoza want? Most likely intending to pass on some titbit of info. His mind went back to what mattered most to him. *Lacey.* Who had hurt her so badly that she was now a virtual fortress against letting a man get too close? Was it her father? Had he hurt her mother in some way, and that was why she was so damn confusing all the time? He needed to know more, but he could hardly ask her. She'd throw up a defense as strong as Fort Knox.

He shook his head. Understanding how a woman thought, especially one as mercurial as Lacey, was never going to be his strong suit. Who was she tonight? Looking at him with those big doe eyes, sex-kitteny and guilty as charged for all of thirty seconds before exhibiting that amazing karate move. The picture of her in her red lace panties was now burned into his retinas for all eternity. He imagined easing them off her sweet ass with his teeth. *Get your mind off sex and back on business.* He stepped off the elevator and exited the hotel, determined to do just that. Not going to be easy with a promised game of strip poker enticing all his senses. Oh fuck, was this going to be *the* night? The one where at least all physical borders were stripped away? Maybe leading to stripping off some personal ones?

The hot, muggy Manila night surrounded him, adding another layer of discomfort. By the time he reached the restaurant for the meeting with the lieutenant, he was as antsy as humanly possible without self-combusting. He'd far prefer to be back in the hotel, downing a few Scotches to settle his nerves.

Through the café window, he could see Versoza waiting at a table inside. The man looked nervous. *Now what?*

Will nodded at the man and slid into the booth opposite him.

"You look like you want to chew someone's head off. Hope it's not mine," Versoza said.

"Sorry I'm late. Nah, women. For the life of me I can't understand them. One minute one way, another completely different."

Versoza snorted. "I'd rather take on an army of invading zombies than try to understand a female brain. Any female in particular getting to you?" A small grin accompanied the question. Will suspected Versoza knew exactly what woman he was talking about. His pretend fiancée. *What I wouldn't do to make that a real thing.*

"Doesn't matter. I'll sort it. You called me. What's up?"

"Are you planning to leave Manila soon?"

"We have to be back in the States by Saturday. In two days. A friend is getting married and we're standing up for them as witnesses. Why do you ask?"

"I saw that video of you saving that old man's life."

That surprised him. "Really? The world is overly connected these days, I'm afraid."

"Maybe. But I found it rather touching—well, I wanted to warn you."

"Warn me?"

"There are things at play here that you would be best advised to leave alone."

"You already said that at the station. You'll have to do better than that, Lieutenant Versoza. I'm a man who doesn't scare easily."

"Jomar, please." The man ran a hand over his clipped dark hair.

The waitress came up, holding a pot of coffee. "What can I get you?"

"Just coffee."

She turned his white ceramic cup right way up and poured Will a cupful. "Cream?"

"No thanks."

She left and Will glanced around. The other patrons were all involved in their own discussions, the noise levels ebbing and flowing in a steady drone. No one seemed interested in him and the lieutenant.

"This case has been attracting some unusual attention," Jomar said tentatively.

"Yeah?" Will took a sip of the strong hot coffee. "How so?"

The man looked out of the window at the pedestrians passing by, his eyes dark and his body tense.

"I only tell you this because something makes me feel I owe it to you. You're one of the good guys. Manila, it's not the place for you or that female friend of yours."

Will remained silent, waiting.

"This case, it goes all the way up the political channels to the top." Jomar shook his head, pursing his lips. "Dangerous for you to stay much longer in this country."

"Can you give me a name, at least? Who's running interference?"

Jomar licked his lips nervously. "I can tell you this. The governor's office called. Asked that we discontinue our efforts to find the killer or killers. Invoked diplomatic privilege. Apparently, this case is now tied to national security."

"Really?" *What in the hell could Daniel Wright have had to do with national security? A two-bit gambler who treated prostitutes better than his own wife?* Still, the man deserved justice.

"So, please, go home. See your friends get married. Be smart. Manila is too dangerous for you now. Daniel Wright was a victim of a mugging gone wrong."

"Do you think someone in power ran amok and killed him for the cash? Or was he involved in something more? Damn it, if you suspect who killed Daniel, I have a right to know. His wife, his family, his friends, Lacey — we all have a right to know who killed him."

"That may be so." The man shook his head. "But I doubt we will ever find out who killed him. All the tracks of the killer are long gone, covered up by masters of the sleight of hand. Jack the Ripper could not have hidden his identity better."

"Fuck! That's just wrong, you know that."

Jomar sighed. "Of course I do. But I want to stay alive. You go home, you're safe. My coming here tonight has put my family at risk. I only did it because I respect you, Will, a fellow soldier. But I have to go. There's nothing more to be said. But I urge you, go home and take that beautiful woman with you. Make beautiful babies together." He got up and threw a couple of bills down on the tabletop.

"I thank you, Jomar, soldier to soldier. You're a good man. Call me if there is ever anything I can do for you." It wasn't much, but it was all Will could think to say.

"There is one thing you can do. If anything happens to me, please, help my family." He pulled out a white business card with some information scribbled in ink on the back and handed it to him. "My address and home phone number."

Will nodded, a chill coming over him. Jomar was worried. Suddenly, finding out the answers to Daniel Wright's death came under a new light. Was it really worth it to put Lacey at risk? *No, definitely not.* "Of course. You have my word."

"Thank you." The man hurried past the other diners and out of the café, only pausing at the doorway long enough to be certain his way was clear before vanishing into the night.

Will sighed, then drank the last of his coffee. Lacey wasn't going to want to hear this, but it was time to go home. ASAP. Nothing more could be learned in Manila if no one was talking. Not if the murder was being covered up by the authorities.

Chapter Nine

"Real generosity towards the future lies in giving all to the present." — Albert Camus

What is taking Will so long? Lacey paced the hotel room, the promised hour having come and gone. She didn't know where he'd gotten to, which ratcheted up the tension. Even the bath she'd had after giving Megan an update on Danny's case, and talked with Rebecca and Casey to assure them they'd be home in plenty of time for the festivities, hadn't relaxed her.

A moment of clarity and she stopped pacing, visualizing her next move. She usually preferred to talk in person, but with the wedding in two days, she needed answers before leaving Manila. Something told her it might be harder to come back to the country than not. Everywhere they turned, they were warned it was too dangerous — that they should leave. How much of it was bluff, and how much was real? Hard to say. The

PI business was dangerous, but getting to the truth was more than worth it. At least, it had been in the past.

She sat back down and logged onto FaceTime, sending off a request. *Ding.* One minute later, it was answered. She explained what she needed to Megan. Lacey signed off, then went back to waiting. The minutes slipped by and she was about to give it up for the night. Maybe the woman was at work and couldn't get away? She checked the time on her phone. A couple of minutes to midnight. With Manila nine hours ahead of Vegas, it was three in the afternoon in sin city. She hoped the woman worked the night shift and was available.

Finally, another *ding* resounded in the hotel room.

"Angel Marcos?" Lacey answered the request, staring at the computer screen. The woman was very pretty, a baby-doll type. Dark glossy hair enhanced with thick bangs surrounded a well-made-up face with bright red lipstick and expertly lined and shadowed eyes. Perfect for a hostess in a Las Vegas casino. *Bet she gets good tips.*

"Yes, I'm Angel Marcos-Wright," she said, the expression in her eyes cautious. "Megan said you'd call."

"I'm Lacey Cameron. I'm in Manila investigating your husband's death."

"I know who you are. What do you want from me?"

The sweet doll face tightened with emotion. Fear. Why was she afraid?

"I'm sorry for your loss. I knew Danny in school."

The woman's expression softened. "Thank you. You're helping the insurance companies prove my husband is dead, right? I need to get that money released—soon—and they are really slow about it. I don't think they believe me, but I know nothing about what happened to Danny. He went to Manila on his own. Left me at home."

Hmm. "Why was that?"

"What?"

"Why did he leave you in the States? Didn't you usually go with him?"

"I don't know. He just wouldn't take me. Something about his needing to do some business and that he wasn't staying very long anyway." She licked her lips and glanced away to the right and up slightly. Lying.

"His ashes have been released and I was planning to bring them to you in a few days."

"Okay. That should help with proof for the insurance company, right?"

"Yeah." A truly sad widow. *Fuck.* Could she really have arranged to have her husband killed from the States? It hardly seemed credible, but what else could it be? If so, the sister was most likely in on it.

A child's high-pitched voice called out from close by. "Mommy, Mommy!"

"I have to go. My son needs me."

"Of course. I'll be in touch."

The image on screen blinked to black.

Lacey took up her cell phone from the bed where she'd set up her office and brought up the sister's cell phone number.

It rang a few times. *Please, please pick up.*

"Hello," Athena said, speaking loudly to be heard over the music of a band and conversations in the background suggesting she wasn't at home.

"Athena, it's Lacey Cameron, I was just talking with your sister, Angel."

"Is she okay?"

"Yeah, she's fine. I was hoping to speak with you again? Clear up a couple of points?"

"I told you all I know." As sweet as ever.

"It won't take long, I promise." *Just long enough to find out if you were directly involved in Danny's death. What I wouldn't do for some sodium pentothal in my PI kit.* Angel's fear had to be coming from somewhere, and most likely from the worry about being discovered as part of a scheme to do away with the husband and collect the money. Megan was probably on the right track. Angel Marcos-Wright was looking guilty as sin.

"Okay." A big sigh to convey the sense of being put upon. Now, if Will had called, Lacey was certain the conversation would have gone much differently. "I'm at Club Ten. You know where it is?"

She hesitated for a moment, swallowing against the bile rising in her throat, but time and the need for the truth pressed harder than upsetting Will. "Okay, sure, I'll be there soon."

"Just a sec." Her voice and all other noise disappeared for a few seconds as if she'd put her hand over the phone for privacy, before she came back on. "Everyone's decided to leave anyway. Meet you at my place."

Much better.

Lacey picked up the folder Versoza had copied at the police station for them and stuffed the files she'd been studying back inside, alongside the ones Megan had given her. The autopsy photos slipped out and she picked them up. The two photos included were rudimentary, copied onto flimsy paper, making them blurry with the limited pixels available in the printer. She swallowed hard, bile rising in her throat again. It was time to take a look. One was a closeup of the gunshot wounds to the face, impossible to make out anything except the gore.

The image sickened her, her stomach roiling in horror at what had happened to her friend. She got up, stumbled off the bed and raced to the bathroom, throwing up the contents of her stomach into the toilet. She picked up a towel and wiped her mouth with a shaking hand.

Lacey straightened up, catching a reflection of her face. The stark truth visible in her eyes stared back at her. Danny was dead, no matter who'd done it or who'd arranged it. *And I won't stop until I have justice for Danny*, she promised the woman in the mirror.

She went back to the bed and slumped down. She was about to stuff the photos back inside the folder when an odd pattern caught her attention on the second photo. Danny's upper torso with his hands laid out on his chest, one on top of the other, exposed his right hand to the camera. She looked closer, ignoring the horror of the ruined face this time. Five small dots, nearly invisible but a definite pattern, in the web between the thumb and forefinger — an international symbol. Her breath quickened and her mind whirled, full of questions.

She dressed quickly in jeans and a T-shirt. *Time to go to work.*

Fifteen minutes later Lacey ordered the taxi driver to stay put and strode up to Athena's house and knocked.

The young woman answered it, not looking overly pleased to see her.

"May I come in?" Lacey asked briskly.

"Sure," Athena said, shrugging with indifference. She was still dressed for going clubbing, her bright orange dress stretched and having no choice but to conform to her ample curves. Her thick dark hair was tucked into a twist at the top of her head, her makeup choices bright as well.

The house looked much the same. A woman's expensive leather jacket hung from the back of one of the living room chairs.

"Nice, is the jacket new?" Lacey asked, keeping her expression innocent.

"Yeah, I got a raise." She gestured for Lacey to sit down and did likewise, tucking her feet under her body and pulling a throw from the back of the sofa to fold over her legs. She pursed her lips, giving Lacey a direct look. "So, what do you need to know?"

"As I said, I was talking with your sister Angel earlier tonight," Lacey began, trying to keep her distaste for the experience from coloring her words.

"You're taking the ashes to her, right? As proof of his death?"

It stung that Athena didn't even mention her brother-in-law by name. "Yes, Danny's ashes are going home with me. Did you know Danny had been in jail?"

Athena frowned, caught off-guard. "Jail? Here in Manila?" she asked.

"Don't know for certain. But somewhere, maybe the States. The symbol for being in jail is international. Did Angel ever say anything about it?"

"Symbol?" Athena looked confused.

"You ID'd his body, right? And with his face" — she swallowed hard at the memory, bile threatening to rise again — "not visible, how did you know it was him? Did he have a tattoo or something else to identify him?" If the grieving sister-in-law mentioned it now, Lacey would catch the lie in her eyes, marking her as an accomplice.

"I just knew it was him." Athena dismissed Lacey's concerns, though Lacey could see the wheels turning. No doubt Athena would be checking up on that detail ASAP, asking for the coroner's report, filling in her sister. "Besides, they had his wallet, right? Who else could it be?"

"You got to wonder why the killer didn't take the wallet too," Lacey mused. She frowned. Something just wasn't adding up. Especially if Athena didn't even know about the tattoo. But if Danny wasn't dead, where was he?

"Duh. He was most likely interrupted and ran away without it. He got all that money, after all," Athena said. She looked away as she spoke, chewing on a thumbnail. *Liar.*

"Damn!" she said, looking down at her torn nail. "Now I need a manicure. Is that all? I need to get to bed. I gotta work in the morning, unlike some."

"Don't worry, sweetheart, I'm working right now."

Lacey's words spoken with pure conviction startled the woman. They locked eyes for a split second. Athena looked away first.

"Are you sure you don't want to amend your statement? Come clean? If you had anything to do with my friend's death, I will hunt you down. That I promise."

"Get out of my house!" Athena screeched, not taking to the threat at all well.

"Did you and Angel arrange things?" Lacey pressed.

"Arrange what things?" Athena looked confused again with the thrust from another angle.

"Arrange for someone to kill Danny? Were you so upset by the way he treated your sister that you decided to kill him? Is that what happened?" Lacey deliberately softened her tone. "Or maybe it was self-defense? Was that it? Did he attack you?"

"No! Nothing happened! Get out! Now!" She threw off the blanket and stood up, pointed with an accusing finger at the doorway, her body shaking with indignation.

The woman believed what she was saying. *Telling the truth. Now.*

"I know you didn't like him," Lacey said. "I'm sorry if I upset you. I just need to get at the truth. Danny was a good friend of mine. He deserves justice. And, for what it's worth, I do believe you that you had nothing to do with his death."

The woman said nothing, her rage evaporating as her shoulders slumped. "I have nothing more to say to you. Please leave."

"If you think of anything else, don't hesitate to call me. I'll be in town for another day, but that's it."

"You should go home," Athena said, biting her bottom lip. "You're going to find nothing but trouble if you keep pushing."

"What kind of trouble?"

"Things are not always what they seem," she said, her eyes darkening with some kind of inner torment.

"What are you hiding, Athena?" Lacey asked quietly. Her heart lurched, banging against her chest wall. Would the woman come clean?

"Nothing. I have nothing more to say to you."

"Okay, but be warned, I won't be able to help you in the future if you're hiding something. I'm sure the authorities around here take as dim a view as we do in our country of being an accessory to a crime."

Athena shook her head, her lips pressed tightly together. Lacey had no choice but to leave.

Stepping in the taxi a few minutes later, she drummed her fingernails on her handbag. The tattoo. *Time to do some more research then talk to the wife again.* With less than twenty-four hours until they had to leave, she had to step up her game. Get the answers.

* * * *

Will let himself into his room, trying to be quiet to avoid waking Lacey, as much as he wanted to after the invite. She needed her rest and tomorrow, first thing, he was taking her home. No objections allowed. He crept to the connecting door and listened. *Good. She must be asleep.*

He fired up his computer and checked his email. He'd let work issues drift while he was in Manila and he needed to catch up. His phone dinged while he was dealing with business. He glanced at the number. Porsha.

"Hi," he said.

"I was wondering if you have time for a drink?"

"Not really. Why?"

"I was looking into Daniel Wright's murder and I have some information for you."

Will sighed. But if it would help Lacey…

"Okay, the bar in five."

"Good. I'll be there."

He shut the laptop lid and got up. Two minutes later, he entered the hotel's lounge area and spotted the reporter at a table. She must have called from the bar — she had her things spread out on the tabletop.

"Hey, Will," she said, looking up from her work as he slid into a chair.

"What have you found out?" he asked. He shook his head at the barkeep to indicate he didn't need anything.

"Get right to it, eh?" she said with a snort. "Did you know that Danny liked to gamble?"

"Yeah, so?"

"Did you know who he'd been spotted with a few times?"

"Okay, I'll bite."

"Marcus Salang, the governor's son. Apparently, they liked to gamble together. They seemed to be interacting in a recent video posted on YouTube by one of the players. Took some digging to find it. It had been deleted."

Porsha looked pleased with herself as she swung the laptop around so that he could view the video himself. He pressed Play and watched the twenty-one second clip. The images did reveal Marcus Salang and Daniel Wright gambling at the same table and making a couple of comments that made them both laugh. So, that must be what the important official didn't want exposed. Must be the governor, then, putting pressure on the police. Hardly a crime for the pair of young men to be gambling together, but, knowing politicians, even the hint of a scandal sent them into hyperdrive. The lieutenant was overreacting if he thought this placed them in the path of extreme danger. Will took a deep breath. The information was welcome.

"If they did have the same interests, perhaps it's just coincidence they were in the same place at the same time?"

"Maybe." She shrugged. "But they seemed quite friendly. And, since I got you here—"

So, it was just a ploy to continue the earlier interview. "What do you want to know?" he asked bluntly. He disliked games. Well, except maybe with Lacey. He had enjoyed the karate move, relishing the image of the hot red panties. He'd missed out on a game of strip poker tonight, letting her sleep. A huge twinge of regret at that mishap overcame him, making him sigh aloud.

"I've done some more digging," she said, giving him a bright reporter smile, ignoring the sigh.

Of course you have.

"And I noticed that you have been traveling to Afghanistan a lot. It seemed odd to me, considering your war record. I mean, you'd think that's the last place you'd want to visit. So, what is it you're not telling me, Will? Why do you make so many trips there? I've documented at least one a week for the past few months."

A headache threatened. He frowned at the reporter. The timing wasn't right to unveil his plans. The press getting hold of it might jeopardize delicate negotiations.

"Sorry, I didn't mean to upset you, but I did think it strange. And it is my job to get at the truth."

"It's not that. It's just a bit soon for all this to come to light. I'm not ready." He ran his hand over his hair and rubbed the back of his neck.

"And you're afraid that, as a reporter, I can't keep my mouth shut."

He snorted. "Duh."

She laughed. She had a nice laugh. Unusual in a woman, a deep belly laugh.

He joined in, the sound infectious.

The laughter died as he caught sight of Lacey walking up to their table.

"Well, I see I've interrupted a moment." The tart sound of her voice filled his mind.

"Lacey. I thought you were asleep," he said. She was all frowny and adorable in jeans and a snug blue T-shirt. The game of strip poker loomed in his mind. She was awake after all.

"Yeah, well, I had work to do. No time to sleep."

"Would you care to join us?" Porsha asked, purring.

"No, I was just getting a cheeseburger and heading back to my room." She carried a white Styrofoam container in her hands as proof.

"I'll join you." Will got up.

"No need. Enjoy yourself. Jolly Roger needs me. You just go ahead, living up to his name!" Lacey snapped and hurried away.

"Excuse me," he said to a confused-looking Porsha and raced after his friend, catching her at the elevator. He hopped inside as she pressed on the Close button with a stabbing motion of her forefinger.

She ignored him as the glass and chrome box headed back upstairs, stopping at their floor. The fragrance of the charred burger emanating from the container made his stomach rumble loudly in complaint, but she just gave him a level look. "Get your own. You can afford it," she said, exiting the elevator and striding to her hotel door in one smooth, very huffy move.

They reached the door at the exact same time. She fumbled with her package and the room key, dropping the card in the process.

"Damn it!"

"Here, let me help." He bent down and picked up the plastic device.

"I don't need help," she fumed, tapping her toes as she waited for him to insert the card.

"There you go," he said and followed her in before she could slam the door in his face. He took in the room.

The bed was strewn with papers and her electronics. *Yeah, still at work.* He'd misread this entirely.

"I'm taking you home in the morning," he said, tossing the key card onto the narrow tabletop near the door.

"Like hell! I need the day. I'm on to something," she said, turning around and facing him square-on, glaring at him.

"What?"

"I went face-to-face with the grieving widow tonight, and she's anything but grieving. She's fearful of something as well. Then I went and saw the sweet sister Athena, and she was less than forthright. And, did you know Danny had a tattoo on his hand? The international symbol of five dots, representing he'd been in jail?"

"And did you know that Porsha has some Club Ten footage and Marcus Salang and Danny appear to have known each other?"

"Duh! I found it already, Einstein." Lacey snorted.

"We're going home for the wedding in the morning and that's that. And what in the hell were you thinking going out on your own again tonight? Didn't we just have an altercation over that very thing? Have you forgotten all that so soon?"

"You weren't available. What do you expect me to do?" She had set the food down and now crossed her arms over her chest, pushing the rounded globes of her breasts higher. She looked really good in a T-shirt, too good. And the jeans accented her gorgeous curves. He liked to see her dressed so simply. She didn't need any artifice with her beauty.

"Okay. I'll give you that."

"Where have you been? Talking with that reporter all this time?"

"Porsha? Hell no, I had an appointment with our police friend, Lieutenant Versoza. He gave me some information about the case."

"And?" Lacey sat down and opened the container with the food. She took half of the huge burger and placed it on a napkin, then handed it to him.

He took it and sat down opposite her, gulping it down in a few bites. She laughed, the sweetest sound in the world at that moment to him, then polished off her own piece.

"Go ahead, have the fries," she said, shaking her head. "You were going to tell me about the lieutenant's info?" He relaxed. The old Lacey was back.

"Well," he began over a mouthful of fries. They'd shared food so many times together that it added some much-needed normalcy. "He was saying the investigation's been quashed by higher-ups. He's worried. Warned me again to drop it." The promise to look after his family came back to him, sending a shiver of worry through him. But the extremeness of the man's worry just wasn't adding up. A minor scandal at best. *Why all this cloak-and-dagger stuff?*

"That all?"

"Yeah, he didn't stay long. Hurried away, saying he didn't want anyone to know that he'd talked to me."

"This case is beyond baffling." Lacey shook her head. He reached over and wiped a drop of mayonnaise from her bottom lip. A tortured memory popped up, making him want to kiss her, feel her soft warmth against his.

"You mentioned a tattoo?" he asked, forcing his thoughts back to the case, shifting in his seat.

"There's the thing—it's a prison type. And it turns out he was in jail for a short stretch, just a few weeks. Hard to believe he'd bother getting a tattoo."

"Hmm, that's odd, but not unheard of." He'd finished the fries and he got up, throwing the container into the wastebasket.

Lacey moved to the bed and began collecting her strewn papers and electronics.

"We need to see someone who has seen Danny lately, someone who can verify the tattoo. Do you think it's too late to go and see Nina? Check it out."

He checked the bedside clock. "Two a.m. She might be busy with a client. And it's not the best part of town to be roaming around in the middle of the night. Besides, you should get some sleep. We're going home in the morning."

"No! I thought we'd decided to give it one more day. The wedding's going to take up so much time. I need to settle this. Now. Otherwise, we'll just have to come back. Besides, we still have a game of poker to play. I'm up for an all-nighter, if you are."

He let out a long breath, the carrot working all too well. "Okay, beautiful. Then can we go home? I have your word on it?"

"Yes," she said, reluctance obvious in her tone. "I promise."

"Let's go." Filled with purpose, he directed her out of the room, into the elevator, hired a driver and had her back at the Dollhouse in twenty-one minutes flat.

The party appeared in full swing when Will escorted his charge inside. People lounging at the doorway, women roaming the room or sitting with men at small tables, even a pole dancer doing a floor show while the stage was crowded with swaying, dancing women. He caught Lacey's tight expression and pointed out a table as far as possible from the pole or stage.

"Let's head over there," he whispered loudly in her ear. The driving beat of the music annoyed him. Though the food had helped, his head still ached. Time to find Nina, sleuth out what Lacey needed and get the hell back to the hotel.

He spied the large *mamasan* doing business a few tables away, a male patron handing her a few bills that she placed in a small metal box resting on the tabletop. Will nodded at the woman when she looked up and caught sight of him and Lacey. It took a moment, but recognition flared in her expression and she nodded back, obviously remembering his generosity from his last visit, because a wide smile of greeting accompanied the nod. *Good.* At least it was status quo in the bar.

"What do you want to drink?" the hostess asked. It was hard to hear in the din of the room and she leaned in closer for his order. Awkwardly close. Her top was too small and her skirt too short for Will's comfort, not wanting a repeat of the last performance at the Dollhouse. No way was he giving Lacey any more ammunition. He'd had quite enough of the drama in Manila. Maybe the wedding activities would offer some better times with her. Didn't women love a wedding? At least it would give her a break and her being a bridesmaid and his being a groomsman meant time together on the dance floor.

"A bottle of beer. What about you?" He reached out and nudged Lacey's bare arm. She swung her head around, checking out the room — most likely trying to spot Nina through the thick crowd — and said, "Sure, a beer's fine."

"Two beers. Coors Light, if you have it. Oh, and is Nina working tonight?"

"I think she's here somewhere."

"Thanks. There's a big tip in it if you tell her we'd like to see her again."

The pretty young girl looked from Will to Lacey, seeming to be assessing exactly how large a tip. Will pulled a few bills from his pocket and handed them over to her. "There's more if you get her to come to our table right away. We're kind of in a hurry."

"Okay." She hurried away on her errand.

"I don't see her anywhere." Lacey turned back from studying the crowd, worry darkening the bright green of her eyes.

"She might be in the back," he said.

"I hope she's okay." Lacey chewed on her thumbnail. The waitress came back with their beers wrapped in white napkins. Will pulled out a few more bills from his pants pocket and laid them on her tray.

She leaned over and whispered in his ear, "Nina's not here right now. Who else could I ask to take care of you?"

He racked his brain. Who had Nina said had also known Daniel Wright? "Layla, is she available?"

"Maybe. I will check."

He ignored the beer while Lacey took a sip of hers. A few minutes later, a young woman hurried over, giving him a wide smile of greeting.

"You want to party?" she asked, glancing coyly up at him through thick black eyelashes.

"Please, sit down. Would you like something to drink, Layla?"

She sidled onto a stool. "Champagne, please." *Standard issue.*

"Of course." He raised a hand to alert the waitress, who hurried back from hovering nearby. *Money, the world's only international language.*

He waited until the bottle of their finest champagne arrived and the ceremony of opening and pouring it was concluded to allow for a triple rate before picking up his glass and toasting the occasion.

"Cheers," he said. The woman downed the glassful, licking her lips suggestively in the process.

"So, you're a friend of Nina's?" Lacey asked, leaning forward onto the tabletop now that she had her quarry in sight.

"Yes, I know her." The woman's expression remained calm, suggesting she was unworried about her co-worker.

"We enjoyed her last time. How is she? I was surprised she wasn't here tonight."

Layla shrugged. "She wasn't feeling well. That time of the month, you know. No matter. I take good care of you. Very good care of you. You forget all about Nina."

"Fine. Did you ever take good care of Daniel Wright?" Lacey pressed.

"Danny? The man who was killed?" she asked, confusion clear in her dark brown eyes. "I know nothing about him." She swung her mane of hair around to partially cover her face.

"But you did see him from time to time?"

"Maybe. I have lots of boyfriends."

Will poured the girl another glass of the bubbly brew. "We just really liked her and hoped she was doing well," he said.

"Nina's nice."

"But you did have dates with Danny, right?" Lacey asked, sipping at her beer and pretending nonchalance.

"Sometimes. He was a generous man. He liked two girlfriends together."

"Yeah, I liked him too," Lacey said. "He was a friend of mine."

"When was the last time you had a date with Danny?" Will asked Layla.

"I don't know. A while. Why?"

"I wanted to know if Danny had any tattoos?" Lacey asked.

"Tattoos?" Layla swung her hair back from her face. "That's what you ask?"

"Please. It's important." Will leaned over and handed her a thick stash of bills. The girl's eyes grew wider.

She looked around nervously, then took them and stashed them in her halter top. "What kind of tattoo are you looking for?"

"One on his hands."

"Hands? Maybe."

Lacey dug a photo out from her purse. "Like this one." She handed it to the girl.

Layla shook her head. "Dots. Maybe. I don't know. I can't say for certain." She shrugged. "I didn't stare at his hands, if you know what I mean." She waggled her eyebrows suggestively.

"Think about it for a minute. Try visualizing him. Close your eyes. That may help you," Will said.

Layla complied, closing her eyes for a few seconds. "Sorry, I'm not certain. Is it important?"

"Just something we're following up on," Lacey said.

"Who are you?" The girl's eyes narrowed further. "Are you with the police?"

"No. Just friends."

The woman finished her second glass of champagne. "You want to go now? I'm very good. Better than Nina. You pay me more — you see."

"No. We just wanted to talk."

The woman's expression became confused. "I thought you wanted girlfriend?"

"Maybe next time," Will promised. "But enjoy your champagne." He got up and took Lacey's arm. *Time to go home.*

Chapter Ten

"The best laid schemes o' mice an' men..." – *Robert Burns*

"We need to confirm this. Because if that wasn't Danny's body, then what's going on here?" Lacey said as she stepped into the taxi. Will climbed in behind her and she turned to face him to watch his reaction.

"I have no idea what the deal is. Maybe he got that tattoo at the last minute as some kind of a lark. Who knows?"

"No way, that's not Danny." She shook her head while the driver sped through the traffic, honking his horn zealously at every perceived infraction of the rules. He added choice swear words for good measure. *God, Manila's such a loud place. How's a girl to think straight?*

"The tattoo makes no sense, okay? I'm beginning to wonder if it was Daniel Wright's body."

"Then whose was it and where is Danny?" Hope rose in her chest. Maybe her friend was still alive. "Maybe he felt threatened, went into hiding, set this whole thing up to hide the facts?"

"But why? He could have just gone home. He's an American with an American passport. Besides, what kind of trouble could he possibly be in that would make him want to fake his own death and leave his wife and child behind? And why on earth would the authorities care this much?"

"I don't know. But I can't let this go. I need to get at the truth, for Megan's sake."

"God, Lacey, you don't make it easy for me to keep you safe."

She stiffened her spine. "I have to come back, Will. Surely you see that."

He stayed silent, looking out of the side widow of the taxi.

"I'll just come back by myself," she warned.

Still he was silent. She laid her hand on his leg. The strong thigh muscle rigid under her hand, she pressed her palm against the warmth. "Please, Will. I can't let this rest."

"If I promise to bring you back, will you come home with me in the morning? I've arranged for the jet to be cleared for take-off at nine."

She took a deep breath. "Okay, but soon as the wedding is over, we come back, right? You can manage a few more days away?"

"I'll have to. I can't have you roaming the Philippines alone. Can you just imagine the havoc for the locals after unleashing Lacey Cameron, PI Extraordinaire on them?"

He said the words lightly, but underneath his concern thundered.

"I'm holding you to your word then." She squeezed his thigh. He reached over and pulled her hand off his leg to put it back down on her lap.

"I'm a man of my word," he said, steel edging his tone.

"And I'm not?" she said, filling with righteous anger. Never had he acted so strangely. Will was changing. And she wasn't sure she liked it, not one little bit.

"No, Lacey, you're not living by the same creed I am. You run off half-cocked on your own agenda and let others slide through the shit stream it causes. It's two steps forward, one step back with you."

"I do not!" *I'm not that bad, am I?* Like she had a choice. She had to work this case. Had to get at the truth.

He went silent again. Damn it, Danny's case was causing so many problems. Fine. The silent treatment it was. *Two can play that stupid game.* But the loss of control bothered her more than she cared to admit.

At the hotel, they went their separate ways. Ten minutes later she climbed into bed and fell into the coma-like sleep of righteous exhaustion. So much for a fun all-nighter playing poker.

Dimly she could hear voices. One raised, harsh and demanding, one frightened and trying to appease. She came up through the layers of consciousness, trying to make out the words. A sound of a body hitting the floor. She pulled the blankets over her head. No, Daddy! Stop it! She clamped her hands over her ears to make the terror go away, her body shaking uncontrollably. He was at it again, hurting Mommy. And she was helpless to stop it, helpless to make her daddy stop hurting her mommy.

"Lacey! Wake up! You're having a nightmare. You're safe and sound with me, beautiful." She awoke with a start to Will shaking her gently.

"What?" Groggy, she stared up at him, pushing up through the layers of fear and panic. *I'm safe with Will in Manila.*

"You were having a nightmare. Screaming loudly. I'm sorry, but I had to wake you or security would be at the door. Most likely they'll be breaking it down shortly."

"Oh." She was grateful he'd woken her. She'd had that particular nightmare more than enough times. She glanced over at the clock — 4:55. Yeah, right on time.

It was then she realized he was naked. Completely. Never had she seen Will naked, without at least a pair of swim shorts or boxers on. She swallowed hard. She slept naked when not in the field and sharing a tent with others. *One more thing in common.*

He looked good. Damn good, even if he was frowning from worry. And the endearing pillow hair, combined with his warm spice and his fresh-from-bed fragrance, made her mouth go instantly dry. God, he smelled so good she had the overwhelming urge to lean forward and take a bite right out of him, nuzzle in close and not let go. She chewed desperately on a thumbnail, any sacrifice to keep her oral fixation at bay.

"Want to tell me about it? You know you can tell me anything, beautiful. You're safe with me. You were shouting something about your father." His glance drifted from the thumbnail she was avidly chewing to the quick, up into her eyes. She watched his Adam's apple move up and down as he swallowed. His brown eyes were dark pools of liquid in the dim light from the radio clock on the dresser. The sound of it ticking mimicked her own heartbeat, quicker than normal. *Will.* He was always there when she needed him. A blur of images from the past flew across her mind's eye. Will at her side, marching into the unknown on so many fabulous adventures with her. Helping keep them both entertained with easy banter and quick answers to her sharp barbs. *Best friend in all the world.*

"Really? Sorry, guess I've been so focused on this case it's affecting my sleep." She dismissed the dream. No biggie. It had happened before and would happen again. It was the nature of the beast that was her father.

"You weren't dreaming about the case, beautiful." He ran his hand over the back of his neck, the movement making his washboard stomach ripple. He watched her intently for a few seconds before glancing away to say, "I think your unconscious mind's trying to make you confront something in the past. Something important. Maybe something that can help you move forward?"

"What? It was just a dream, handsome. Nothing more. Nothing I want to dwell on. And I thought it was you who suggested I move at too fast a rate as it is?" she teased lightly. The dream had receded into the mists where it belonged. And she had this awesome male exemplar sitting naked on her bed. *Riveting. Impossible to ignore.*

She let the blanket slip to her waist. She caught the flare of lust in his eyes before he swallowed and looked away again.

"You might want to cover up. I'm a man as well as your best friend."

"I'm counting on that. A warrior appreciates gifts offered and doesn't count teeth, to paraphrase the gift horse analogy."

"Well, Miss Cameron, you have a lovely set — of teeth." A wicked grin accompanied his words.

"I'm counting on it." She reached for him then.

"Lacey, you're vulnerable right now. It wouldn't be — "

"I want you. Right now. If you're not up to it, just say so. But I think the timing is exactly right." *Make me forget. Give me what I want. Just for one night.* She pushed all other thoughts right out of her mind, her lust making it easy.

His expression shifted, the passion exploding behind his eyes visible even in the low light. He took her mouth, his hands moving lightning-fast to grasp her shoulders, drawing her to his hard, bare chest. She fell into the moment, greedy for pleasure, let her naked breasts press against his. Yes. She parted her lips, his tongue thrusting into her mouth, tasting her. She fell into the kiss head first, a breathless tumble making her off-kilter and dizzy. *Never felt like this before. So. Right.*

He moaned, whispered against her mouth, his warm and spicy breath making her tingle all over. "Lacey, oh my God, I've wanted this. Dreamed of this for so long. It's always been you, beautiful. Always you."

His words flowed over her, into her. Yes, of course. Why had she not seen it before? All those times he'd come to her. Helped her.

She pressed her open mouth to the firm flesh of his shoulder, breathing him in, sucking on him, wanting to consume him. All of him. Her ears filled with the roaring of her own blood, her body throbbing with instant need, instant connection. A heavy liquid weight filled her belly, demanding attention.

"I want you," she whispered against his heart, the steady beat of it under her cheek as she pressed her head to his chest.

"Oh, my beautiful woman. You're sure?" His voice broke slightly, his emotions appearing to get the better of him. She shattered at the sound.

She reached up and laid a trembling hand on his face. He nibbled at her fingers, sending waves of pleasure dancing across her heated flesh. Her body surrendered to it, craving the feel of his skin, his muscles, his bones. She slid her hands down his body, seeking the solid warmth of him.

"I've never been more certain of anything in my life." *A warrior knows when to let go. When the time has passed for holding back.*

The craving turned into action, the fire in her belly taking over, pushing her over the edge. He responded by tearing off the covers, exposing her nakedness.

"I want to kiss you all over," he whispered. "I want this time — our first time — to be the best. To last."

His words were beyond romantic. Beyond anything she could have imagined. She responded by lying back against the sheets, inviting his caresses. His kisses. His questing hands. *Please. Be mine.*

She shivered involuntarily, his hands finding her breasts. He palmed them, his skillful fingers rolling the pebbled nipples between them, making her gasp, her breath ragged.

"You like that?" he said, his tone light and teasing. His hot mouth replaced his hand, and he sucked. Hard. Then harder. She arched off the bed, the throbbing growing, stealing all her control. Heat pooled in her center, making her voice quiver.

"Oh yes!"

"And this?" He kissed his way down her body, nibbling at her hot flesh, caressing each curve and square inch of her, drowning her in passion.

"Oh, God, you're bad. You're *so* good. Don't stop. Ever."

184

A wicked grin accompanied his reaching the apex of her body, pushing her thighs wide apart. She fell into a maelstrom of sensation, with him busy licking avidly at her swollen, needy flesh and finding all her hidden, sensitive places that begged for his full attention.

Her fingers fisted the sheets while he sucked greedily on her. Pushed her to the brink, out of control, needing release. The sharp odor of sex filled her nostrils as she gasped for breath. The room vanished, passion crashing into her, sending her reeling into the abyss.

"Please, please—" she whimpered, lost to the sensation as wave after wave of her climax sluiced through her, pushing her hard. "I'm coming—"

He obliged. Licking and nibbling, making her shudder when the sensation became almost unbearable, too intense.

"Amazing. You taste like honey." He gave her no time to recover, crawling up her body, perhaps needing to claim her again.

"I'm protected. On the pill," she just had to time to whisper breathlessly before he nodded and slid into her without preamble, using his fingers to separate the slick folds, pushing himself into her inch by inch until he was balls-deep. Her walls stretched to accommodate the wanted invasion, the necessary invasion. The connection fired her blood, his cock solid and huge, pressing against her, the length and tightness binding them. She wrapped her legs around his waist and squeezed hard, urging him on.

He slid his hands into her hair, fisting it tightly, thrusting himself into her, over and over until the sensation of their being separate began to blur. Vanish. His eyes bored into hers and she was unable to look away, mesmerized, the connection intimate and mind-blowing. She stared into those pools of deep water, drowning in them, yearning for truth. Seeking the answers. Then knowing the answers. *Yes.*

She writhed against him, a creature out of control, wanting him to invade all the parts of her. To feel everything. She let him in, past all her defenses, into the depths of her soul. She reached for him with both hands, feverishly sought the hard muscles of his back, his ass, drew him to her, wanting him to ravish her flesh, make them one. And he did, the very air, thick and sweet, making her drunk with each breath.

At the height of her pleasure, when she could no longer hold anything back, his heat flooded into her, invading her, her body thirsty as if she'd been lost in the desert all her life.

"Oh, Will," she whispered, the throes of orgasm sending her reeling. He held on to her still, letting her ride the endless waves, before finally collapsing onto her, his limbs trembling with exhaustion.

It took long moments to feel the bed solid under her again. He held her tight, her head resting against his broad shoulder. She knew she would never be the same. How was what she'd experienced even possible? It was all too much, scarier than facing Lily, scarier than being broad-sided by the shark, for this was unknown, uncharted and unexpected territory.

The next thought made her worry all the more, her mind clearing a bit. *What have I done?* This was Will, her best friend, and she had thrown herself at him, pretty much begged him for sex. No man could turn that down. What would happen now? There could be no going back to exactly the way they were. No way. No how. Fear prickled at the edges of her mind.

She went to pull away, wanting to turn back the clock, to run away, but he only eased her back, sliding her onto her side and spooning against her.

"Hush, go to sleep, my precious love. It meant just as much to me — maybe more. We'll talk tomorrow. Sleep now. Let things take care of themselves." And she did, after a time, his words and tone reassuring. She slid into a dreamless, embracing, comforting void, satiated and exhausted beyond belief, filled with a sense of wonder at the discovery and still stirred to the depths of her soul.

The alarm going off startled her awake. She was alone. The events of the night came flooding back, filling her mind with wonder. She looked at the closed door between their two suites. Had it really happened? It seemed too over-the-top to be believed. But concrete evidence proved it had. *Now what happens? God, no time to worry about it right now.* She was running late.

She rushed around the hotel suite, showering and packing, constantly stepping around the rambunctious JR, who thought it was all about playtime. Then she stopped short. *Friends with benefits.* She liked the sound of that. *Will that work with Will? Oh crap, what about Lily?* They'd let their lust take them over. It was so unlike her. She prided herself on her independence and self-control, at least with the male species.

A knock on the joining suite door interrupted and she moved to answer it.

"Good morning, handsome," she said, biting at her lower lip. She was suddenly off-kilter, her mind a battlefield of worry. There were too many ramifications for their hooking up, and it was far too early in the morning for such a profound dilemma.

"Morning, beautiful," he said. A look of pleasure than vulnerability crossed his face. He bent down and kissed her, an almost chaste kiss on the cheek.

"I know you can do better than that!" she said, the minx inside unable to be thwarted, making her reach up and slide a hand behind his head, drawing him in close. His tantalizing fresh-from-the-shower fragrance washed over her, and she let her fingers pause in the thick hair, feeling each silky strand slide against her sensitive fingertips.

He kissed her then, a firm press of warm lips sliding against hers. *Nice.*

"How are you?" he asked, tracing a tender finger down her cheek.

"I'm good. All packed," she said brightly to hide her worries. Hiding things — that she was a pro at. Years of intensive training. *Besides, it couldn't have been that good, right?* But memory said it had been that. And more.

"Good. The jet's fueled and ready for us."

"About last night —"

"Let's talk once we're up in the air. We're running late."

"Uh, sure." She swallowed her disappointment, reaching down and scooping up JR, preparing to exit the room.

The taxi ride to the airport remained quiet. She tried to gauge Will's mood with furtive glances his way, but his cool expression wasn't up to sharing. Maybe he was still tired? Both of them were running on a couple of hours' sleep. Hardly enough. She was barely functioning, still caught in a kind of lustful haze tinged with worry.

Soon Will had the Learjet pointed for home and she breathed a sigh of relief. Time spent with her friends would lighten things. Thank goodness she could count on them, if not herself.

She intended to stay awake and keep Will company, have that important discussion, but she suddenly woke up and found they were setting down at the Richardson airport in Winnipeg. Stretching, she glanced over at Will smoothly and efficiently going through the necessary protocols to safely land the jet. The man was good at every darn thing. Her body throbbed at the reawakening memory of how good he had been last night. So damn good. *Got to let that go.*

"Nice flying," she said, swallowing hard.

"Thanks. You snore, you know."

"I do not snore. Must have been JR. He was sleeping too." She petted his silky fur, looking forward to settling him into his new home. *Lily is going to love JR, though probably not me so much, if she finds out about last night.* She'd have to work hard to keep it from her. Her twin was too good at reading her.

"Can't blame it on JR, beautiful. I know what I heard."

"Better get your hearing checked then. It's off."

"Yeah, right."

She waited while he set the Learjet down and taxied over to the Thornton family's private hangar. When the sounds of the high-pitched motor died away, she unbuckled her seatbelt.

"Are you going to share your findings about the tattoo with your friend Megan?" Will asked, unbuckling the harness that strapped him in.

"No, I don't want to give her false hope, just in case. I mean, he could still be dead. However, time to do a skip trace on him. This might have turned into a missing person case, instead of a murder investigation. And skip tracing—definitely my specialty. You know I once had a client that had multiple IDs, but he kept the same phone number? Idiot. All I had to do was run a single reverse search on Google. Hardly earned my money on that one. And easy enough to run a reverse photo of him on Google's comprehensive reverse image search or on TinEye. If he's alive, I'll find him."

"I have no doubt you will. You're good at your job. About last night—"

"Don't worry. I won't hold you to it."

"Hold me to what?"

"I did enjoy our 'friends with benefits' scenario very much," she said, smiling at the memory of how fantastic they had been together. Far too good together. Regret colored her world, difficult to shake off.

"You think that's all this is? Is that all it was to you?" Will scowled.

"That's not so little," she snorted. "Do you know how many people I know that would give anything to have such a hook-up? And I know you, Will. You like to play the field. If 'friends with benefits' is too much of a commitment, I understand." She shrugged to let him know she would not be offended. She'd let him off the hook, even though her stomach churned at the idea, but, for Lily's sake, it was for the best. Will would just drive a wedge between them.

But he didn't respond to her magnanimous blessing, going all steely-eyed and cold. He got up from the captain's chair and exited the plane, leaving her to trail along, snuggling JR in her arms. *What? He must be a relic from the Stone Age not to appreciate what I have to offer, right?*

Hurrying to the hangar, her mind ablaze, the ground beneath her feet less certain, she nearly smacked into her friend Casey.

"Casey! What are you doing here?" Casey looked every inch the woman about to get married, her white-blonde hair recently conditioned and trimmed, styled for a change into soft waves instead of the requisite messy braid designed for field work and her lifelong passion of digging up old bones. And right beside the bride-to-be were Lily and Rebecca. Lily was the mirror image of Lacey, while Rebecca looked gorgeous as ever.

"We came to pick you up, silly," Casey said, hugging her. JR hissed a warning at being squeezed between them and Casey scooped him up, making a fuss over him.

"Thanks for coming, guys." She embraced each of them in turn. Reaching Lily, she gave her such a big bear hug her twin finally pulled away, asking, "Everything all right, sis?"

"Yeah, sure. Just an exhausting, emotional trip."

"How's the investigation going on Danny?" Lily asked, her green eyes concerned.

"I'll fill you in later. I just want to have some fun now. What have y'all got planned?"

"Oh, don't you worry," Rebecca chimed in. "It's going to be nonstop fun right up until the honeymoon!"

Casey playfully punched Rebecca's upper arm. "It's not going to stop then! The honeymoon's going to be fun too."

"Oops, didn't mean it the way it came out." Rebecca laughed.

Lacey breathed a deep sigh of relief. The Ringers were in fine form. For forty-eight hours, she could relax. Just as soon as she checked in with the grieving widow.

An hour later, sitting at her computer in the condo she and Lily shared in a trendy downtown loft in Winnipeg's Osbourne Village, she sent off a FaceTime request to said widow. While she waited for a response, she absently played with JR, the memory and lust of the night before pressing up against her. Will's arms around her, holding her close, his body all commanding and so unbelievably hot. Worst of all, just so damn right for her. How to deal with that? And the overwhelming guilt about Lily? She knew she was impulsive—at least, everyone accused her of it—but she must have lost her damn mind in Manila to have taken such a chance.

"What do you think?"

Lacey spun around at her sister's voice. She took in the sight of her identical twin dressed in a short, sequined midnight-blue number that set off her red mane to perfection, and gave her two thumbs-up. "What's the occasion?"

"The social's tonight," Lily looked exasperated. "Did you forget?"

"Sorry. My mind's been on this case." Lacey pulled the hair off her neck and bunched the thick mass together, tugging the curls through one of the elastic ties she kept on the desktop to keep it out of the way.

"Well, I've got to go and help the crew set up before the party. Don't be too long, okay?"

Lacey chewed on her bottom lip to hide her discomfort. "I'll catch up with you soon." She was keeping one eye on the computer screen and at that second Angel Marcos-Wright's face popped online. Maybe she should have gone to Vegas in person, but time was in short supply. She'd have to make the best of it.

"Hi, Angel," Lacey said, giving the woman a smile to hide the professional scrutiny. "I'm back in the States now and I thought I should check in."

The widow's demeanor screamed of nervousness. She wouldn't meet Lacey's eyes and she kept looking around as if she expected the boogie man to jump out any second. *Guilt?*

"Will you be bringing me the ashes soon?" she asked, adding accusingly, "You promised."

"I can't for a couple of days. One of my close friends is getting married and I'm in the wedding party." Lacey glanced over at the urn supposedly holding Danny's ashes she'd brought from the airport.

"I need them."

"Of course, the wedding's tomorrow and I'll be able to deliver them after. Okay?"

The woman gave a sigh. "Guess it will have to be."

"There's one other thing I was wondering. It's about Danny. Did he have any tattoos?"

Angel swallowed, began picking at a fingernail, not looking at the camera. "Yeah, sure, who doesn't these days? Why?"

"Could you describe his tattoos?"

"He had a small one on his upper back of a pair of dice. Oh, and one on his hand. Weird, just five small dots. He got that one in prison. Some kind of sympathy for the plight of prisoners kind of thing." She closed her eyes during the recital. An obvious lie.

So, the sister had called and warned her, meaning she had to have checked with the morgue and now Angel's pants were about to burst into flames for telling such a whopper.

"Are you aware of the penalty for a false insurance claim? You would do hefty prison time and your son would be put into the foster system. Is that what you want?"

The woman's face imploded, tearing up. "I'm not lying. Danny's gone and we're all alone here, trying to deal with so much stuff because of it. I get overwhelmed is all." The woman dabbed carefully at the tears in the corners of her eyes about to ruin her expertly applied makeup. "I have to go to work. Please, if you can't come right away, send the ashes by express. Okay?"

"I'll see you get them," Lacey promised before Angel's image vanished from the screen.

A knock at the door startled her. She got up and crossed the floor. Peeping through the eyehole in the door, she checked out her visitor — Will carrying the massive oboe case. She opened the door, needing to hide her uncertainty behind bravado. *A warrior stands their ground.* "So, you're hand-delivering it. Nice of you. Bet Jack appreciated it. He wasn't too happy carting that thing around the Philippines."

"I aim to serve, m' lady," he said with a grin.

"What's gotten you in such a good mood?" she asked, taking the awkward case from him and setting it down. Considering earlier, this was a bit out of left field. *Ha, and men think women are mercurial in nature.*

"You'll never guess who I'm partnered with for the wedding?"

"Lily, I think." The reminder didn't sit well with her, driving the guilt home. Being on good terms with her sister was written in her personal code of conduct, right up there with 'thou shall not deliberately hurt or harm any innocent creature, large or small.'

"No. Try again."

Damn, he looked good. Too good. Dressed in casual clothes, his jeans hanging off his trim hips, white shirt opened at the neck exposing healthy, tan flesh, the freshly showered fragrance of cleanliness surrounding him. She wanted nothing more than to throw herself into his arms and have a repeat performance. Check to see if it really had been that fantastic. Her insides clenched tight with the need, with pure frustration. It was only the image of Lily dressed for the celebration party that kept her glued to the carpet, unable to move.

"Rebecca? Miranda? Elin? Ava? Tessa?"

Will shook his head, unable to hide a grin as she mentioned every sorority member of the Brass Ringers, who all, of course, had been chosen as bridesmaids. Thank goodness he'd remembered his promise to handle her with kid gloves until he got at what was bothering her. He'd gotten over her stupid suggestion of friends-with-benefits. That was just Lacey being careful. What had happened to them last night would take time to sort through, no doubt. But as far as he was concerned, the deal had been cemented. She'd listen to him more now, he was certain. Would stay in touch and be safer. No two people could connect like they had last night and not change for the better. *Thank you, God.*

"Well, tell me already!" she said, obviously exasperated. He stared at Lacey, hands on curvy hips, giving him the look that always melted something deep inside him. The look that said, 'you've got two seconds, buddy, to provide what I need or I'm gonna go ballistic on your ass.'

"You, beautiful. We're partnered."

"Hmm. I think we'd better get that fixed. We're not a good match."

"Now you've just hurt my feelings," he teased. "And how come we're not a good match, pray tell?"

"Because we're not!"

"Well, that certainly helps explain things. Maybe if we practiced some dance steps, we could be a good match." Before she could scoot away, he reached out and tugged her stiff body close to his.

"Stop that!"

"Why?" he asked, swinging her into a two-step, humming a rhythm.

"You can't carry a tune," she said, though she managed a few steps in sync with his.

"Better than you." He blithely ignored her words. This side of Lacey he knew well, found comfort in. "You suck on karaoke nights."

"I do not!" she argued.

"Yeah, you do." He swung her into a deep dip, and when her eyes flew open and locked with his, he pulled her close and kissed her, thoroughly kissed her, enjoying the sensation of her full, warm lips gliding over his. He felt the moment she caught fire, her heart pounding so fast that a beat pulsed against the side of her neck when he slid his lips down to kiss the soft skin of her throat.

"Lacey, my darling," he murmured, his cock thickening with anticipation. Lust, overriding lust, coursed under his skin, heated and seared, made his need for her abundantly clear.

"No, not here. We can't do that to her."

"What are you talking about? Do what to whom?" Confused, he quit kissing her to look her in the eyes. Those amazing pools of green shone with emotion that struck his core.

"You know."

"No, I don't know."

"Lily."

"*Lily?* What has this got to do with her?"

"You mean you don't know? That Lily has a thing for you?"

"I really like Lily, but it's never gone further. Is this what your reluctance is about? You're worried about hurting your sister? Was the nightmare part of that?"

"Yes—no. I don't know what I know anymore." She pulled away, crossed her arms over her chest.

Oh boy. Classic Lacey avoidance move. "There's nothing between your sister and me except friendship."

"Fine. But I should get back to work. And I've got to get ready for the party."

Exasperated, he ran his hands through his hair. "What's really going on? I know you're attracted to me. Last night in Manila—beyond amazing. Is it because I left you alone? I got a phone call and didn't want to disturb you."

"Who from? That reporter?"

"No. Just business."

"Anyway—" She looked pointedly at the door. "I'm running late."

"Fine. I'll get out of your hair. You're welcome, for the sword." And before she could answer he stalked to the door, yanked it open and left.

Chapter Eleven

"We dance around in a ring and suppose, but the secret sits in the middle and knows." — Robert Frost

The last thing she wanted to do was to talk about the cause of her nightmares. And that would be Will's next deduction and line of questioning, no doubt. She wasn't going there. Not now, not ever.

Damn it, of all the times to have to put on a happy face and go to a party. But this was Casey and Truman and they deserved her best efforts. So, thirty minutes later, gussied up in a silver sheath and four-inch heels, she hopped in a cab.

The venue the bridal pair had chosen for the stag and shower, a purely Manitoban tradition where both sexes celebrated together instead of apart, was a private ballroom at the Hotel Fort Garry. Memories of the night the Ringers had converged on the supposedly haunted room 202 ran through her mind, making her oddly nostalgic. *The first Ringer to get married — kind of a big deal, the end of an era.* She pulled herself together, paid the driver and hurried inside. *Running late as usual.*

She looked around after a chorus of hugs from her friends brightened her mood. No Will. She had wanted to thank him properly for the sword. She sighed. Now that too would have to wait. She didn't like the feeling of being off her game, one step behind. *I'm supposed to blaze the trail, not be playing catch-up.* Her mind burned with emotions she had to curtail.

She accepted a celebratory glass of champagne from a passing waiter and took a few sips, huddled with her sorority sisters.

"How was Manila?" Rebecca asked. "Bring me any tourist brochures?"

"I'm sorry. I forgot. But I have to go back after the wedding—new developments in Danny's case—so I promise, I'll pick up some then." Rebecca's writing thrived on exotic locales and all her friends pitched in to bring her fodder.

"What new developments?" Rebecca asked over her glass of bubbly.

"It's complicated, and I don't want to get into it tonight, but things just aren't adding up."

Her phone buzzed with an incoming text. She glanced at it. Will. Her heart rate immediately increased ten-fold.

Sorry, something's come up. Can't make the party. Tell Casey I'll make it up to her. W.

"Shoot," she said aloud, deflating in an instant.
"What is it?"
"Will can't make the party."

"Will's certainly busy these days," Miranda said. She was the group's paranormal researcher. Her face sharpened as her lips twisted into a look of speculation.

"That was certainly something, his rescuing that elderly man from the accident," Rebecca said. "The *Maclean's* reporter, Porsha Evans, has written some really nice things about him lately. He's a real hero."

"Yeah, well, he'd better get his ass home for the wedding. Without him, the pictures are going to be all lopsided. And no one else could fit into the Wall's tux!" Miranda said with a chuckle.

Lacey looked around the venue, sipping her drink, looking for anything to keep her mind off Will's absence. The slide show of the bride's and groom's lives showcased larger-than-life on a gigantic white screen in one corner was not the usual happy family moments of dogs and pools, but toddler Casey at digging sites for her future position at the U of M, and Truman pointing out unusual features at Roslyn Castle in the British Isles. The auction of donated goods to raise money for the pair's favorite charity — the Siloam Mission, Winnipeg's homeless shelter where all the Ringers volunteered to serve meals — was set up on one long table against the far wall, reminding her of obligations.

"Excuse me, girls, I need to buy raffle tickets." She scooted across the floor to the small table where an older woman sat selling the tickets off a long roll of colorful ticker tape with the message Admit One printed on each numbered entry. Essential fare for any social in Manitoba.

She bought a long ream of them, pulling them apart along the dotted fold-here lines while perusing the row of fabulous prizes. *A three-day vacation at Disneyland. Not too shabby, guys.* She threw a few in the brown paper sacks taped to each possible prize then went back and stuffed more of the tickets into the fantasyland sack for good measure. *Who doesn't love Mickey Mouse, eh? There. Duty fulfilled.*

She stood still for a moment, her mind working on the puzzle of Danny. It made her miss the approach of the woman who was suddenly right in her face.

"Lacey, I see you got home all right," Porsha said.

"I didn't know you knew Casey and Truman well enough to come to their social."

"Will mentioned there was always room for one more." She gave a graceful shrug, à la sexy librarian as per usual, with the unnecessary black-rimmed glasses pointing out her gorgeous eyes.

"Will's a generous guy." Lacey succeeded in mostly keeping the words sounding positive.

"Actually, I was hoping I could talk with you about him. Get more insight into his character. I know you're a good friend of his. He speaks highly of you."

"I'll just bet. But I don't have time right now. This is a big night for my friends, so if you'll excuse me —"

"Another time, then?"

Yeah, right. "Ahh, I'm tied up for the foreseeable future. Excuse me." Lacey stomped away.

The rest of the evening unfolded better and at midnight Lacey was able to slip away from the party and head back to her condo. The next day would entail hours of being tied up with the wedding and she still had an ongoing investigation that was driving her crazy. And where the fuck was Will?

* * * *

Will set the Bell-Boeing 609 Tilt-Rotor helicopter down near the compound, his thoughts grim. Where he was, deep inside Afghanistan, the area was far too rocky for the Learjet, meaning he'd be making multiple trips before this day was through, across the border and into the relative safety of the new compound in Pakistan. At least it was away from the worst of the war zones and kept the children closer to home for their parents to visit when they could. Whatever it took.

The thundering sounds of bombs exploding in the distance squeezed his heart into a tighter fist. Could he get everyone out in time? God, even if he wasn't going to heaven, he'd go through hell for these children. They had been through so much, and just as he was getting the place up and running too. *Fucking unfair.*

"Will! Thank God, you're here!" Jack rushed up to him as soon as he strode through the main gate. The man had already bunched a group of the children together and were now herding them toward the helicopter. Those without limbs were assisted by those with. The distant mortar fire screamed disapproval. A couple of the smaller children wept quietly, and the big tears streaming down tiny faces made his heart squeeze tight all over again. The crying children were being comforted by older siblings, but most of them were stoic, far too used to war. Somehow, that made it even worse.

They assisted the children into the belly of the copter, side by side, wasting no energy on talking. As soon as the space was filled, Will yanked the compartment door closed on the side of the helicopter, securing it. *Precious cargo inside.*

"I'll be back within the hour."

Jack nodded and slapped him on the back. "We'll be waiting, buddy."

* * * *

Lacey woke after a few hours of sleep with a plan. *Get through the wedding, then head back to Manila. With or without Will.*

She checked the time. Hair appointment at ten. Photos at one. Wedding at three. Just like Casey to have it all set up like a military maneuver. *But why haven't I heard from Will? You'd think he could have spared a few minutes.*

The morning marched by, and all too soon the Ringers were gathered at the familiar United Church in River Heights, the church the bride's side of the wedding party had attended for years. Lacey stood near the rectory door, furtively watching the wedding guests file in and sit down at the highbacked, uber-uncomfortable wooden pews, watching hawk-like for a sign of her errant groomsman—any sign.

The house of worship featured the stained-glass rendition of the Last Supper behind the altar where soon Casey and Truman would offer up their forever vows. *So romantic, if I wasn't so on edge. And all this in a matter of minutes.* Lacey pressed her lips together, the storm that had been building the past few hours threatening to explode and incinerate everyone present. Where the fuck was he? She was the only bridesmaid without a partner and it hit harder than anyone could imagine.

* * * *

Lacey checked the time on her Air Canada ticket, unable to keep her legs still. Restless, she tapped them continually on the tiled floor of the airport waiting room. Boarding would be called any moment, and still, she hadn't heard anything. Not a fuckin' word. Soon she'd be out of cell phone range. Was he safe? Once she knew that, then she could rage on. But until then, she worried. And she hated worrying. Anger and guilt, now those emotions she understood all too well.

"I'm sure he's fine. Something big must have come up. Don't worry. Soon as we know anything, I'll text you," Lily said. She didn't even need to ask what was on her twin's mind. Everyone was concerned. So unlike Will. Leaving the country with no word since. Hell, he'd always been the stable one, whereas she had *always* been told she was a bit headstrong and impulsive. *But for heaven's sake, how else am I supposed to get things done?*

"Yeah, well, it is what it is, right?" The words meant nothing and yet it was a phrase people said. Her body pulsed but then she realized it was her phone set to vibrate. *Incoming text.*

She fumbled the phone and finally read the message.

Please forgive me, something came up. See u soon. W.

"Yeah, he's fine," she said, compressing her lips together so tightly her teeth began to ache. She rubbed at her jawline and down the side of her neck to ease the tension.

"Does he say what happened?"

"No. But I don't care." Will was safe. Now she could let out the frustration that was eating at her stomach lining. The helpless shame she had felt partner-less at the wedding—just about the worst thing ever. "He can go to Hades for all I care. I never want to see him again."

"You don't mean that."

"I do."

"I wanted to tell you something." Lily paused, chewing on the edge of a fingernail. "I've met— someone."

"What? And you didn't invite him to the wedding!"

"Flight 741 for Manila is now boarding at gate three," a disembodied voice droned over the loudspeaker.

"I gotta go." She gave her twin a huge hug. "When I get back I want to meet this special guy."

"Ah, it's kind of complicated."

"What are you talking about?"

"You know, I've always been a bit of an experimenter." Her twin chewed her bottom lip nervously. "Just forget about it, you'll miss your flight. I'll explain more when you get back."

"Sorry, I'm so rushed, but I look forward to a nice long chat when I get back." She hugged her sister again.

Lily broke the embrace first, leaning forward, touching her forehead against Lacey's. "I wish you weren't going—that I could go with you. But I understand. And I'll take care of JR for you, no problem. Just be careful is all I ask."

A deep pang of guilt cut through her. Her sister had finally agreed to the trip after an hour-long standoff, after she'd glibly explained that the path ahead didn't appear all that fraught with danger—at least to her. Nobody, and especially no man, was going to get in her way. Because she had the proof, it hadn't gone down the way they were all saying. And Athena was going to 'fess up if she had to throttle it out of her. Then, if that didn't work, she'd head to Vegas to confront the sister she was currently keeping on ice, the ashes safely tucked away as leverage.

Lacey swallowed hard, glancing back at her sister, who was watching her walk down the corridor to the boarding area, a nervous smile twitching on her face. Was she being too impulsive this time? Too curious? She straightened her shoulders. Of course not. It was how she'd always been. Plus, she had a job to do and a grieving friend waiting for answers. Repositioning her backpack, she turned and strode confidently onto the boarding bridge and into the airplane.

Without company, the trip lagged. She hated to admit it, but she missed Will. He was such fun, making everything go smoother. In self-defense, she read everything in sight, including the airline's instruction manual for what to do in an emergency. Scintillating reading. She checked her watch for the umpteenth time. The plane was scheduled to land at midnight local time. She envied the gentle snores around her. At least some people had found a diversion.

"Can I get you anything?" the cabin crew member asked again as he did each time he passed through on a check of the passengers under his care.

"No, I'm good. Is the plane on time?"

"Yes. We'll be landing soon. You headed to Manila on business? Got someone to show you the sights?" he asked.

"Yes, thank you." She didn't even feel like flirting with the handsome, attentive man who smiled so charmingly each time he stopped to speak with her. Perhaps her ego had taken too direct a hit? That sucked.

The lights of the city soon twinkled across the horizon out of the side portal, beckoning and yet elusive. *God, please give me the answers I need this time.* She braced for landing with all the other passengers at the captain's request, her stomach lurching at the overriding worry of how such a massive structure could stay in the air. The primitive part of her brain was convinced it just wasn't logical.

She bounced from her seat and into the aisle as soon as the massive engines slowed, unfortunately along with all the other passengers, struggling to move forward in the long, boring, far-too-hot line to debark. Will's private Learjet came to mind. She sighed. He had it so easy with all that family money, while she had to make do in seat twenty-six A, swallowed up by the maddening crowd.

The push to get a taxi went just as well, taking forfuckingever, and she made the hotel in a fabulous mood, wanting to strangle someone. Anyone.

"I'm sorry, miss, but your reservation was canceled. You didn't arrive before our deadline and our policy is to give away rooms that are unattended. Surely, this was all explained to you when you booked? You didn't pay for the night's stay ahead of time, which would have guaranteed your reservation."

"Because I was unaware. There must be a room available somewhere in this joint?" She was tired, sweaty and just generally pissed off. How to make the imbecile see reason? *Ah, pull a Will. Offer a bribe.*

She slid a few bills across the desk. "Perhaps this will help?" she asked all sweetness, flashing her teeth before gnashing them.

"Let me check once more." He palmed the pesos, slipping them into his pocket. "Someone might have checked out in the last few minutes." He got busy on the keyboard of the computer. "Ah, luck is with you, a room has opened up."

"Fantastic." She rolled her eyes.

"Do you want it?" he asked pointedly, obviously not impressed with her attitude, pinning her in place with a stern look.

"Yes, please." She squeezed out a pretend smile. "And I need it for a few days. Any problem with that?"

"No, but you may need to check back with me on that to make sure we can keep the reservation open each morning."

"Fine. Whatever."

"Here's your room key."

She took it, nearly yanking it from the clerk's outstretched fingers.

"Have a good stay, miss," he added, a smug grin accompanying his remarks.

She turned and stomped to the elevator. She ignored a guy watching her intently from across the foyer, who made her uneasy for some reason. The man, dressed in black pants and a white shirt, had looked up at the noise her boots made as she crossed the floor, giving her a quizzical stare. He just seemed a tad too interested. Maybe he didn't see too many redheads in Manila? She took note of his appearance, taking in his sharp features and thick mustache. It was standard in the private investigator game, keeping alert to who was around.

She stepped inside the elevator and stabbed the number for her floor. Will never seemed to mind bribing people, but she tended to get pissed off. Then a twinge of guilt hit. *That's because being what most people would call beautiful means blithely traveling Easy Street, Lacey, making you spoiled, feeling you always deserve the best.* The words of a former friend came back to haunt her. *Have I really gotten that entitled?* The thought pained her. *I earned my way, right? Worked damn hard to become a good PI?* She was just tired. A good night's sleep would clear her mind. What were a few pesos, after all? The guy probably only made peanuts at his job.

She hurried to unlock the door of her hotel room, then set her small suitcase holding her surveillance equipment down carefully on the desk and tossed her backpack on the bed. A shower, a sleep and she'd be ready to roll in the morning. She had made a sound plan on the plane and intended to stick to it. First up, the governor's son's residence. The connection between Danny and that dirtbag — it wasn't just coincidental and she was getting the intel to prove it.

She unpacked her few belongings, grabbed her toiletries and headed to the bathroom for a shower to wash off the day. Sliding between clean sheets twenty minutes later, she drifted off to sleep, only to be woken by the racy lyrics of someone singing drunkenly in the outer hallway. It was not amusing his partner either, who kept trying to shush him up, and that noise was even more annoying than the original singing. She rolled over in frustration, punching the pillow into a more comfortable position.

She was about to get up and check through the peephole when a slight rustling nearby caught her ear. She strained to listen. It was followed by another furtive sound. Her blood froze. Someone was in the hotel room. And here she lay unarmed, unable to bring a weapon on the commercial flight. No knife, no bear spray, no gun under her pillow. She blinked, focusing on a dark shape rummaging through the items on the desk. Nothing else for it then.

Starkers, she leapt from the bed, forcing her adrenaline-fueled limbs into a classic defensive mode, arms raised to chest height, feet well planted on the carpet, ready to do battle. Nothing like a fully naked, pissed-off, well-prepared person to scare away a would-be thief. At least she hoped so. Her heart was hammering so loudly she was certain people could hear it. But the furtive sounds only escalated when the invader turned at the noise of her getting into position, scrambling to face her, dropping something in the process that bounced toward her. She glanced down. Her kit bag of tricks. *Damn it, I hope nothing's broken.*

For good measure, she let out a banshee yell like a Scots battle cry, loud enough to wake the dead. If she was going down, she'd go down fighting.

* * * *

It took all night and well into the next day, but finally all the children were moved to a safer location. Exhausted, nerves jangling from hours spent at the controls of the huge bird, Will checked his watch, adjusting the time shift in his head. *Fuck.* His heart sank. The wedding was over and the happy couple were already blissfully enjoying their honeymoon. He needed to explain. He envisioned the scene in his head. Lacey at the altar alone, Lacey in the photos alone, Lacey in the reception line alone. No, she'd never forgive him. But damn it, he had to try. If he hurried, he'd be back in Winnipeg in a few hours and be begging at her door by noon. He set a course for home.

The trip seemed to take forever, but finally he landed the jet. Home. *Never felt better.* He raced to his vehicle parked by the hangar.

Thirty minutes later he was prepared and pulling up in front of Lacey's. He grabbed the bouquet of three dozen red roses from the front passenger seat of his Mercedes sports car, gathered all his courage, and took the front steps of the Cameron twins' condo two at a time. He rang the doorbell, hoping she'd let him in. Give him just one minute to explain. Hell, even thirty seconds would be enough. Why did Lacey, who he outweighed by a good eighty pounds and loomed at least eight inches over, scare the bejesus out of him? He shook his head. It had to be her wild Irish-warrior-goddess spunk. Something he admired on one hand and dreaded on the other. Made her unpredictable. Though, if he was a betting man, he'd lay odds that today she would throw the flowers back in his face with a generous amount of swearing. She could put a longshoreman to shame when she got wound up. And, of all the things that could wind her up, the one he'd just pulled probably topped her better-not-do-it-to-me list. Not now. Not ever. He prayed he could get ten seconds to explain. All he needed.

The door opened to reveal Lily. "Will, you're home!" she said, all smiles. "You had us worried."

He gave a rueful grin. "Yeah, couldn't be helped, I'm afraid. An emergency came up and I had no choice but to handle it right away." He quickly explained the rescue of the children, watching Lily's eyes grow rounder and larger as she took in the information.

"Wow, that's the best reason for missing the wedding I could've imagined. Come on in. I'll put those flowers in water for you."

"I was hoping to talk with Lacey. She here?"

"Oh — you don't know. No, Lacey's not here. She flew back to Manila last night."

"What? No, it can't be! It's far too dangerous for her to be there alone." The flowers dropped from his nerveless fingers onto the floor. Lily's expression turned to one of horror as his words sank in.

He turned and raced down the stairs, ignoring Lily's pleas, yanked the driver's door open and jumped in behind the steering wheel. Lily was hurrying down the front steps after him, her panic visible on her face. He buzzed down the side window and shouted at her, "I'll bring her home. You wait here," before starting the vehicle and slamming it into gear.

He stomped on the gas pedal and fishtailed down the street, fighting the wheel for control. He grabbed his phone—the way ahead was clear—and called the airport to have maintenance fuel and prep the jet. *Damn it, Lacey, why can't you try to act like a sane person and consider safety first? This time, when I get my hands on you, it will be far worse than a promised spanking that I didn't even carry out.* He'd obviously gone too lightly on her, and that was why she had him wanting to run off in ten directions all at once, just about driven out of his mind with worry.

Chapter Twelve

"It is easy to stand with the crowd. It takes courage to stand alone." — Mahatma Gandhi

Whew. Lacey slumped onto the bed, her legs gone shaky and useless from the receding adrenaline. The intruder she'd confronted had run out, slamming the door behind them in their haste to get away from the madwoman. *Thank God.* It could have gone another way entirely. This was one incident she was not sharing with the Ringers or anyone. What next? Right, report the event. She pulled on some clothes and called the front desk. Her mind was a bit wonkier than she'd care to admit if she couldn't remember first things first.

"I'd like to report an unknown person in my room." She took a deep breath to steady herself. "They were trying to rob me."

The night guy seemed rather unconcerned when she explained nothing appeared to be missing — perhaps such a thing was just more common here — which had

Lacey finally giving up the attempt and heading off to shower away the fear and sweat. At least she'd get a jump on the day. Next order of business, rent a car or preferably a small van. Easier to park on the street and watch a residence. Who knew how many days it would take to find definite proof of what she suspected to be the case? She hoped it wasn't just fanciful dreaming.

While she waited for the clerk to file the paperwork on the rental, she kept a careful watch on the comings and goings of others in the vicinity. Though she was fairly certain the robbery attempt had been unrelated to her reasons for being in Manila, she couldn't be one hundred percent certain. The clerk handed over the keys to the vehicle and she thanked him.

"You will need to bring it back full of petrol or the company will charge an administration fee to have it refueled," he warned her.

"Fine. No problem."

Her cell phone buzzed while she was busy loading her equipment into the back of the ancient miniscule van about the size of a smart car back home. She stopped to answer it, tucking it into her neck to keep her hands free. Time pressures were making her uneasy and this rust bucket looking near the end of its days didn't help.

"Lacey! Are you okay? Will was just here and he stormed out saying you're in danger! My God, Lacey, what's going on?"

She sighed. She didn't need this right now.

"I'm fine, Lily. Calm down. I'm on the case. No problems. Will's exaggerating. It went fine last time."

Ten minutes of soothing her sister before she could get back to business. But Will was on his way now and that fact alone sent a surge of a good feeling racing through her, remembering it wasn't her twin he wanted. And her twin certainly didn't want him. Of course, he was still a man. *And, don't forget, a good friend, Lacey.* Oh shit, what was he going to say about her once more going off half-cocked? And no way could he know about last night. The clerk, she'd better bribe the clerk.

She slammed the back door of the van shut—only way it would close anyway—ran back inside the hotel and reached the desk partially out of breath.

"Ah, the guy from last night, the clerk, could you get him for me? I need to speak with him."

"Sorry, miss, he's gone home. Perhaps I can help?"

She drummed her fingers on the desk, thinking. *A note.*

"I need to leave him a message."

"Certainly." The man waited expectantly, pen in hand.

"Ah, I would prefer to write it myself."

He handed pen and paper over and she scribbled a few lines.

"Do you have an envelope?"

The clerk handed her one, a little too interested in what she was doing. She turned away and added some bills, licking the shallow triangular side, making a face at the bitterness of the glue and sealing the contents inside.

"Please see he gets this," she said, handing over a few more pesos.

"Of course." All smiles, the clerk tucked the envelope away under the counter. Lacey prayed it got into the right hands and hurried back to the van.

Fifteen minutes later, she parked outside the residence she intended to target and turned off the motor. The van ticked a few seconds longer, the timing off, before the older-style engine finally relaxed and shut up.

She crawled into the cramped space behind the driver's seat. Time to go to work. The procedure was soothing, something she'd done more times than she could remember, laying out the usual equipment. Of course, hours from now, she'd become bored. But right now, on the hunt, she was invigorated, certain she'd get the answers she sought.

The morning passed with no movement detected inside the dwelling but plenty of sweat trickling down her own body. *Like a damn tin box, this van, no air.* In desperation, she turned on a small personal fan to throw a breeze her way. She continually scanned the area with her tiny but mighty digital camera, certain she'd see someone or discover something. She'd found a pretty good spot too. The upper-class part of town featured trees and bushes. Unless she was unlucky, no one should take note of the van parked between other service vehicles a hundred and fifty yards away.

She watched the driveway leading to the two-story mansion intently, expecting any action to most likely occur there. A cherry-red Maserati sat waiting near the garage, haphazardly discarded some time during the night. *Party house.* Exactly what she expected, having met its slimy occupant, Marcus Salang, at Club Ten.

She finally caught a glimpse of two people moving about in the conservatory. A good selling feature, it stood just to the side of the four-stall garage, the room being blessed with multiple windows. *Sweet.* She began a series of head shots, hoping they'd turn her way. One did, Marcus Salang revealing his mug. Who was the other person — a woman? *Come on, turn my way.* But whoever it was, they had an annoying ability to be uncooperative and avoid a good photo. *Fuck.*

Intent on capturing the second guy's elusive image by hitting the shutter button multiple times, Lacey didn't hear the sound of the van's side door being forced open until it was too late. Just as the second person revealed herself in the conservatory, a smelly rag was thrust in front of her face, held tightly over her nose and mouth. Her body instinctively jerked back from the offensive, cloying odor, but she was trapped by the steering wheel. Her head swam. Chloroform. She slumped forward onto the steering wheel, distantly hearing the van's horn blaring — that worked even though the door locks and AC did not — and fell into unconsciousness.

* * * *

Slowly, painfully, she came back to wakefulness and found herself lying prone on an uncomfortable cot. Alone. Something tied around her mouth. She tried to move, to sit up, but a massive headache exploded in her brain at the smallest movement, making her stomach roil violently. Queasiness and nausea collided, a hot mess in her stomach. *Unfuckingbelievable.* Trying not to throw up, she swallowed a few times, not chancing moving again. Using her eyes only — even her eyeballs ached — she sleuthed around the room to take her mind off her rolling belly. Small. Open storage shelves on one wall. Filled with tins and bags of food items, floor to ceiling. At least she wouldn't starve. That is, if they would untie her hands and hand her a freakin' can opener. *Be brave. The warrior may be shattered in mind, body and spirit, yet will not give up. The warrior knows that one's strength lies in many areas, spiritual as well as physical, and the melding of the two creates true power.* The words soothed her battered body.

But thirst grew by the second, her throat scorched by the chemical compound they'd forced on her. She licked her dry, cracked lips. Wished for water. First thing she'd ask for when they came to check on her. *Damn chloroform.* The seconds and minutes ticked past by, but no one appeared. Had she been forgotten? With no way to know the time, she found the dislocation of being adrift in an unknown situation and place the worst kind of punishment. But, and it was a big but, if they hadn't killed her straight away, they probably had other plans. Even that dismal concept chilled her to the bone. Though it took her mind off her extreme thirst and pulsating headache for minutes at a time while she postulated theories.

She was too physically uncomfortable to sleep, too worried anyway. She rolled onto her side on the cot, her hands losing feeling, tied too tightly. Who would find her? She hadn't left any word at the hotel about her location. *Fucking dumb, Lacey,* she chastised herself. Maybe Will was right? She did run off half-cocked at times. And look where it had led her this time. Right into a fucking trap.

Then she remembered who she had seen through the conservatory window. Her mind cleared as the clouds parted. *Holy fuck. What was Athena doing with Marcus?* They had appeared friendly, or at least the young woman had stepped closer to the man just before she — Lacey — had been rudely interrupted by the men barging into the van.

Her thirst grew stronger, making her confinement intolerable. Rolling this way and that, no position gave her any ease. Her bladder felt about to burst when footfalls sounded outside the door and it opened.

* * * *

Will scrambled from the taxi, slamming the door shut. He ran up the hotel steps two at a time and rushed through the foyer to the front desk. A clerk was busy with another couple who appeared to be making a reservation, but he had no time to wait.

He stormed up to the uniformed clerk, pushing past the pair, who stumbled out of his way.

"Excuse me. We were here first," the male of the couple said, voice raised in anger or surprise at being rudely interrupted.

He ignored him and looked right at the startled clerk, whose fingers froze on the computer's keyboard. "Lacey Cameron. Is she here? Have you seen her?"

"Ah, sir, these people were here before you," the clerk said.

"It's a matter of life and death," Will said grimly. He'd pull the clerk right across the desk by his skinny neck if he had to.

"Oh," the man said. He began keying something into the computer. "Yes, she booked in last night. Then rented a van early this morning." He looked at Will. "Will you be staying with us as well, sir?" He looked as if he hoped the reply would be in the negative.

"I have no idea, but that's unimportant right now. I'm looking for a friend who's gone off on her own and could very well be in real danger. I need to find her. To make sure she's okay."

"Of course, sir. Do you have a photo? I could show it around and see if anyone has seen her."

Will dug his cell phone from his pocket. His personal screen image was of Lacey at the Red River Ex, an event hosted by Winnipeg each June at the Exhibition Grounds near the racetrack on the west side of the city. She had sat beside him on the Ferris wheel, her favorite ride that she explained she had to do every year. Usually with Lily. But this time she'd asked him as her twin had a bellyache from too many Little Donuts, a fair favorite. Of course, Lacey had bossily insisted at their going up after dark to observe the city's lights.

He swallowed hard, staring at his favorite photo of her, her hair flying free in the breeze, a halo of fire, her face lit with the inner light of mischievousness that was all Lacey. He'd caught her at an open second, with no defensive barrier raised between her and the viewer. The perfect moment.

But, with the obvious being drilled into him at every twist and turn this trip, this wasn't the real Lacey, the one driven by demons to get herself into messes that he didn't want to see her involved in. At least not anymore. And now he had a churning gut from her latest escapade, certain something bad lurked in the dark underbelly of Manila. A mess he was about to be pulled headlong into. And after she'd promised no more of it.

He handed the phone to the clerk, his mind strengthening with a fresh resolve. *This is the last time, Lacey, I can't take this anymore. Not when you don't even try to change. To mature. How could our night together mean so little to you? It changed my world – why not yours?*

"Yes, I saw her this morning. Hard to miss." The clerk's expression shifted from concern to one of appreciation, staring at Lacey's image.

"And?"

"She was in a hurry, as I remember. She may have left something for the night clerk? An envelope I think?" The guy began rummaging round under the desk, looking like he had misplaced it.

Will pulled a few bills from his pocket and slid them across the counter under his palm to hide them from the couple still milling around behind him.

The clerk took them and hid them away then pulled a sealed hotel stationery envelope from under the counter.

"Ah, yes, here we are. But it's addressed to the night clerk, not to anyone else. Maybe I should hold on to it?"

Will grabbed it from the man's hand. "Sorry, mate, but I have no choice. Lacey might be in mortal danger and this might help."

The clerk pressed his lips together, choosing not to comment, but giving a slight acknowledgment with a small nod.

"Hey, now, we've been waiting forever," the man behind him complained.

"Yes, we need to get —"

The couple's annoying, whining voices vanished from Will's consciousness. He concentrated on striding across the foyer to the taxi stand, tearing open the note and reading it as he hustled along.

Please don't share the knowledge of my room being broken into with anyone. I'm working undercover and the information shared with the wrong person might cause problems. Lacey Cameron, room 517.

His fear was more than justified. His heart in his throat, he gestured for a taxi. Sitting in the back seat, he thought hard about his next step. Yes, Jomar might be able to help. Misgivings poured in — the policeman was worried about danger to his family. But what other choice was there? The man had connections.

He pulled out his cell phone. Meeting away from the police station might just work. He was checking through his contact list when his cell rang. Number unknown. Local. Who was it? No one in Manila had his private number.

"Hello."

"William Thornton?" The calmness of the man's voice filled Will's mind with apprehension. He listened for any nuance, any background sound. Because he already knew in his heart. *This* was the call.

"Listen carefully. You want to see your woman alive again, you will get ten million American dollars, smaller bills — nothing over a hundred. Do you understand?"

"That's a lot of money. I will need time to gather it. I will need to fly home to Canada." His mind raced. That was far more ready cash than he had available.

"You have forty-eight hours. I will be in contact."

"Wait!" The man ended the call. *Fuck.* He'd wanted to demand to talk to her. Make sure she was okay.

He tried calling back, but of course the number was blocked. The man had already dumped the burner phone.

"Where to, mister?" the driver asked, turning around and giving him a speculative look after being party to the call.

"I'll pay you double rate just to sit still until I'm certain."

The man shrugged. "Your pesos."

He called the police station. No help for it with recent developments. "Lieutenant Jomar Versoza. William Thornton here."

Jomar came on the line a few seconds later.

"Will, what's going on? I told you —"

"No choice. Lacey's been taken. I need to see you. Now, for the love of God, man."

A ragged sigh erupted on the other end of the line. "Twenty minutes, same as before."

"Thank you." Will hung up and gave the driver an address. His mind raced with things that he needed to accomplish. He sent a couple of texts, not wanting the driver to overhear anything else.

He paid the man and asked him to wait. Now that they had Lacey, he was pretty certain his own ass would be safe, at least until he had their money. Then all bets would be off.

He climbed out of the back of the cab, feeling years older. Straightening his shoulders, he strode down a couple of blocks before slipping into the café, alert for any suspicious activity. They might have someone watching him and he did not want to lead them directly to the lieutenant.

He ordered coffee that sat untouched while he waited, the seconds ticking away. *Where is he?* The twenty minutes stretched to forty. *Christ, is he okay?*

Just when the unknown became unbearable, the lieutenant slipped inside the door, headed his way. Stone-faced, Jomar sat down across from him.

"Coffee?" the waitress asked.

"Ah, sure," Jomar said, licking his lips. He nodded his thanks when she poured it. He leaned in, resting his elbows on the tabletop, clasping his fingers tightly together, head forward. "Tell me what happened."

"Lacey was taken. They just called for a ten-million-dollar ransom. I'm in the process of getting it together."

"They give you proof of life?"

Fear churned his stomach. He swallowed against the rising bile. "No. They hung up."

"How long do you have?"

"Forty-eight hours. Have you heard anything?"

Jomar hesitated. He knew something. Will pounced. "What? For fuck's sake tell me!"

"I can't. I told you to take her and leave. Why is she back here, for God's sake? Putting us all in danger?"

Will's patience snapped. "I don't know why she came back, except that she cares about her friends. Too much. She wanted to be sure about what happened to Daniel Wright. She was following a lead. Information that the body might not have been Danny's. Something about a tattoo."

"This is dangerous territory, as I told you before. My family has been threatened. I can't help you. I'm sorry."

"For God's sake, you have to. It's your sworn duty." Will pressed hard, racking his brain for a solution. The answer came in a flash of inspiration. "I can help you. I own a private jet. We can get your family out. Set you up in Canada. Whatever it takes. But please, for the brotherhood of our being soldiers together. Please. Help. Me."

Jomar looked undecided, torn up, his eyes dark and bleak. Will bit the inside of his cheek so hard the metallic taste of blood coated his mouth.

"Do you have a plan?" Jomar finally asked.

Will let out a deep breath. "No, but I will have. You have my word. What do you say? Will you help?"

"I can't promise you anything. But I will try to find out what I can. But first, you must make my family safe."

"I will—make your family safe, you have my word. Thank you, Jomar. You're a good man."

"Don't thank me just yet," he said, shakily. He gulped the coffee and stood up. "I gotta go. I'll call you. Don't call me at the station again. When can you fly my wife and children?"

"Can they be ready in a couple of hours? I need to fly to Canada for the ransom."

Jomar checked his watch. "Make it seven p.m. and I will see they're ready. That's three hours from now."

"Fine."

The man hurried away, vanishing into the crowded street.

Will let out a deep breath. There was a lot to plan now. People to pull onboard. And what would his own family think of all this? His father would be angry, that was a given. Probably no help there. Might be bad publicity, circumventing Canadian customs. But weren't a lot of people doing that right this moment? Flooding across Quebec's border? What was one more family to make safe in an unsafe world?

Will got up from the table, a plan of action in mind. But better to make his calls where there was no chance of anyone overhearing. He left a couple of bills on the tabletop, then headed out onto the street. Jumping into the taxi, he instructed the driver to return to the hotel. He needed to check out the contents of Lacey's computer.

A bribe at the desk got him handed her room key in short order. In her room, he found the abandoned computer on the bed. The room retained the subtle scent of Lacey's flowery perfume, giving him such a flood of emotions he held on to himself by the thinnest of margins. He swiped his hand over his dampened eyes, his body giving a shudder. He slumped down dizzily onto the bed, his hands shaking too much to work the keyboard.

"Damn it, Lacey, why the fuck did you have to put yourself in harm's way?" he said out loud, letting the anger out.

No answer.

There came a laugh in the hallway from a group passing by. He grabbed the computer and went to work on obtaining her password. He was well trained by the military in the art of hacking, had even had some useful pointers from Lacey, and within ten minutes had it unlocked, able to check her recent files on the case and related searches. Another twenty minutes and he had a clear picture of her recent activities. A Google street search showed the residence she had bookmarked for surveillance. *Fuck*. No wonder she had been targeted.

He set the computer aside. *Time to make the call.*

"Hello, son." His father's casual voice suffocated the line, using up all the oxygen. It denied who the man really was, his overbearing need to keep control of everything around him.

"I need your help."

"Really?" With the echo of that one word slicing into his heated brain, Will shut down his belief the man would ever consent to help him. But he had to try, for Lacey's sake.

"Yes, Lacey Cameron's been kidnapped. She's—we're in Manila working on a wrongful death of a friend. A ransom of ten million has been demanded for her safe return. And I was thinking—you know that old money from that deal gone bad you set aside in the safe—I think that would be the perfect choice—just flushed out with, say, a hundred grand from my bank account. And to get help with her case, I need to bring the policeman's family to Canada as there have been threats on their lives. Him too, after he helps me find Lacey."

"What the fuck's going on?" his father shouted so loudly Will winced at the pain that stabbed his eardrum.

"Will you help or not?" he demanded, pulling the phone away from his ear.

A moment of dead silence.

"Figures," he muttered. "No political mileage in this one, eh, Dad. Just the satisfaction of doing the right thing. If you won't help, I'll do it all myself."

"Of course I'll help you. You are my son even if you don't act like it. But I demand something in return. Are you prepared to come back and work for us?"

"Not if you expect me to work in the crafting of armaments for supplying a war that kills and maims people." *God, please don't ask this of me right now.* He was weakened, worried sick about Lacey.

"That's our most lucrative business. Besides, any war has to have its weapons. You know that. What, you wanted to throw rocks at the enemy? And right now, you're asking for ten million from that very business. What does that say about you?"

"Nothing good." He heard the defeat in his tone. His soul deadened with the idea of going back to help with the devil's work.

"Never mind. I won't hold you to it."

"What?" The fish hook was removed from his brain. "What do you mean?"

"I mean, I will not ask you to work on that business. I'm thinking of making changes anyway. Moving away from manufacturing into more high-tech companies. Something I hear you're good at with your hacking skills. But, I warn you, it will take time to avoid a financial hit. I can't shut down the business immediately."

Now he tells me. First make me sick, then pull the hook out. Resentment then relief flooded in. For his father, it was a hell of a concession. The biggest one he'd probably ever made in his long life of accumulating material wealth, his most obvious driver. More important than time with his family, proven over and over in the past. One of the reasons Will wanted to do it differently, if and when he was blessed with his own family.

"Yeah, I could help you with that. Future's information — driven by technology, at least until we run out of oil."

"Good." His father made a strange sound, clearing his throat. "What do you want me to do?" The gruffness of his father's tone was a further surprise.

He laid out the plan to his father, the first bridge built between them in years. Temporary or not, he'd take it.

228

Chapter Thirteen

"I have the strength to endure it all." — *An Israeli soldier*

Lacey struggled to sit up as the man advanced into the room. She managed to awkwardly position herself against the back wall of the storeroom. Her hands useless, she used her thigh muscles to keep herself upright, hampered by having her feet tied together as well. She'd managed to work the rag over her mouth down her chin, and it now hung around her neck, making it easier to breathe.

"Who are you?" she demanded, taking in the man's appearance. He wore jeans and a black T-shirt, nothing remarkable about him except the coldness in his dark eyes. He looked to be in his late thirties, average in every way except his work. *Who kidnaps people except real assholes?*

"None of your fucking business," he said.

"Could you untie my hands at least? I need to use the restroom. And I'm damned thirsty. Hungry too. Is this any way to treat another human being? I'm Lacey, by the way. I live in a small city in Canada. Perhaps you've heard of it? Winnipeg, Manitoba? Heart of the continent. I have family there." *Tactics 101.* Make him see her as a real person to gain sympathy.

"I know who you are," he grunted. "Hold out your hands."

She pushed herself away from the wall, leaning forward so he could reach her bindings. It was a horribly vulnerable position. She held her breath, waiting, felt him tug at her arms before they dropped free to her sides. Blood began flowing back into her hands, two heavy lumps dangling from her body. She winced at the sudden pain when feeling returned, rubbing at her chafed wrists, rolling her tight shoulders.

"Thanks."

"Sure. Leave your ankles tied if you know what's good for you," he warned, pointing at her feet. "Toilet's in the corner, water and food on the shelf. Can I get you anything else, princess?"

"No, you've done quite enough," she said, working very hard to keep the sarcasm at bay.

Still, he eyed her suspiciously. "Okay, keep quiet and we'll get along fine."

"How long do you intend to keep me here?"

"Not my department, princess. What, you got a ball to go to?" He grinned at his small joke.

"Yeah, maybe, if I can find my other glass shoe."

He snorted. "Sure."

Keep him talking.

"Where am I?"

"Like I'm going to tell you."

"Am I being ransomed?" *God, I hope so.* At least they'd keep her alive for a while. Proof of life. Not that anyone she knew could afford to pay a ransom. Except Will.

"No idea what they've got planned for you. My job is just to keep you here. Hopefully in one piece." The last was a definite threat.

"And keep me alive?"

He shrugged as if it didn't matter one way or the other to him what his instructions were—he'd carry them out. Her heart chilled at the knowledge.

"What's your name?"

His eyes narrowed. "Why do you need to know that, princess?"

"I can hardly call you Handsome Thug Number One." She gave him an innocent smile, all dimples and flirty eyelashes. *Yuck. What a girl won't do to stay alive.*

His eyes widened for a split second. "Call me Hector."

"Handsome Hector it is."

"What are you playing at?" he growled.

"Nothing, just being observant. You have a family?"

He shrugged again. "Sure, doesn't everyone?"

"Wife or kids? Do you live close by?"

"You ask a lot of questions. I gotta go."

She nodded. *Always be agreeable. Mimic their speech patterns.* "Sure, I gotta do some stuff too."

He gave a dry chuckle. "Yeah, eat, drink and be merry while you can."

He turned to go.

"Can I have something to read? Anything you can find, even a dictionary or a phone book is better than nothing. It's going to be a long day." *Please, dear God, just let it be one day.*

"No promises. I'll see what I can rummage up."

"Thanks, very nice of you, Handsome Hector." She added a sweet smile for good measure.

He grunted. "Anytime," he said, closing the door behind himself. The clicking sound of his locking it soon followed.

She scooted off the bed, intending to head over to the chemical toilet half-hidden behind the shelves. A wave of dizziness halted the attempt mid-hop. She sat back down abruptly to steady herself. Damn it, but she hated feeling weak. She took a deep breath. On the second try she managed to use the rudimentary restroom facilities, rinsing her hands in a basin of tepid water and drying them on her pants, then grabbing a bottle of water off a shelf and downing it in a few quick gulps. Wiping her mouth with the back of her hand, she surveyed the shelves. *A convenient weapon might be a bit too much to hope for?*

She inhaled a bag of potato chips while going through the dismal offerings. Other than taking a shelf apart and using a steel leg as a weapon, nothing else stood out at her. And no tools. She tried budging the shelves, testing their weight. Even putting all her weight behind them, she had no luck in moving them. Far too heavy, loaded down with bags of flour, sugar and rice.

She drank another bottle of water, thinking. She checked every square inch of the ten-by-eight room, finding nothing of value to aid in escape. No window either. *Good choice for keeping someone hostage.* She surveyed the shelves again. *Hmm. Maybe.*

Sounds erupted at the door again and she hopped the few feet to the bed and sat down.

"Found this," he said with a grunt, handing her a tattered magazine. She glanced at the cover. *Better Homes and Gardens.*

'Thanks." She took the offering.

"Got to tie your hands again."

"Could you do it in front so I can read?" she asked.

He scratched his head, eyeing her.

He pulled a length of thin rope from his back pocket and waited for her to hold out her hands. She obliged. "Not too tight, please. My hands still hurt."

He glanced at the angry red marks, shrugging, before looping the cord around both wrists in short order, tying the knots like a Boy Scout. "You should have stayed home, princess, if you wanted to stay perfect."

"Anyone else here with you?" She'd heard voices while scoping out the room, the conversation inaudible.

"You think I'm going to share that with you?" he said with a snort.

"Can't blame a gal for trying, eh, Handsome Hector."

"Stop calling me that. It's just Hector."

"Fine, I was just trying to be friendly." She played at pouting, pretending her feelings had been hurt by the exchange.

"You want to be friends, princess?" he asked, his voice changing. *Fuck.* She'd gone too far.

* * * *

Will drummed his fingers on the steering wheel of the nondescript van he'd rented. He'd gone out of his way to make sure he wasn't followed to the address Jomar had given him at the last possible moment, the concern over being the one to ensure the family's safety weighing heavy on him. His stomach in painful knots, he scanned the street for suspicious activity.

He had tried to leave nothing to chance, setting up a military-level plan of action that had a very good chance of success. But — and there was always a but — if things didn't go off without a hitch, the cost was not something he wanted to think about.

Fuck. Hurry up. He wanted to get moving. Action provided relief from worry with no time to ponder, or think about Lacey. His mind struggled to keep from heading in that direction. It would only bog him down and make it impossible to concentrate on what mattered at the moment — getting Jomar's family to safety so that he could focus on rescuing her.

There they are. Jomar exited the back door of his house, shepherding his small family in front of him. The young daughter he held in his arms, clinging to his neck, her face half hidden. A baby was bundled up in the arms of a young woman, her expression worried, her movements jerky. Will jumped out of the driver's seat, moved quickly around back and helped them into the vehicle.

"I'm going back for the luggage," Jomar said, scurrying away while Will settled the little girl, who looked to be about three years old, on a seat, buckling her in securely. He helped the woman next. She thanked him in a soft tone, seeming too shy or too scared to say much. Fear. It made a whole lot of sense in their precarious situation. Jomar was back in short order, carrying two huge leather suitcases and a stuffed canvas carryall bag. He piled them inside, then jumped in himself.

"Go!" he shouted at Will, his tone sharp.

Will hurried around the van and squeezed in behind the wheel of the small vehicle. The rudimentary seat didn't accommodate the large body of a former football player. And those few seconds it took him to move from A to B, vulnerable to a target leveled at his back, the focus of a sniper's crosshairs, chilled him to the bone. The sense was so real his neck and spine tingled and it was all he could do to keep from turning around and shooting randomly, the way he would in war to send a message or hold the enemy at bay.

Tense, his hands clenched tight on the wheel, he drove as fast as he dared toward the airport, getting to the fueled and ready-for-takeoff Learjet his main focus. Safety and freedom waited on Canadian soil. He kept his eyes constantly on the street ahead, scanning for unusual activity, alert for an ambush. Had someone been watching at Jomar's residence?

He prayed, something he didn't normally do. But right then, right here, it felt right. He swiped at the stinging sweat that dripped constantly in his eyes, the air conditioning in the van not up to the sweltering weather. Or a constant adrenaline feed from the occupants. Jomar had to be as edgy as him, maybe more so — this was his family they were dealing with. The traffic became denser, hemming the van in on all sides. Horns barked, drivers screaming, angry at other drivers and the life they endured. The dismal smells of the city grew sharper, the petrol stink annoying his nostrils. *What's the holdup?* His heartbeat picked up, thudding as if he was trying to outrace the devil.

The traffic inched along. Had there been an accident? He craned his neck, trying to see what the holdup could be. Or even if there was one. Manila traffic had more natural snarls than Winnipeg by a ratio of a thousand to one.

"What's taking so long?" Jomar barked from the back seat. Will took the chance and turned around, taking his eyes off the road for a split-second, wanting a quick assessment of how the man was faring. The lieutenant had braced himself on the carpeted floor on his knees, his arms around his family, his face white and desperate. Sweat ringed the underarms of his uniform shirt. His daughter sucked on her thumb, making Will's heart squeeze painfully. The innocent victims always did him in. He swallowed hard, glancing away.

"Darn traffic's backed up," he said, keeping his eyes forward. He patted his side, the firearm reassuring in the light of the delay. He was carrying illegally, but he had to defend this family. No matter what it took. No matter if he too landed in jail. *But please, God, don't let it come to that.* Who would help Lacey then? He couldn't see anyone else in his family taking the chance of coming to Manila to rescue her. He shook his head, his stomach roiling.

Traffic continued to inch along, drivers gesturing angrily, exhaust fumes building. Intolerable. They'd all be poisoned long before they got to the airport at this rate. He checked the GPS device. Five minutes out. *God give me the strength.* Rain began to fall, lightly at first, then in torrents in a matter of seconds. Monsoon season had arrived early. He switched on the wipers, the rhythmic swiping back and forth sluicing the flood water away, but only where they could reach. Visibility dimmed considerably beyond the arch, affecting the periphery. More sweat trickled down his body.

What the fuck else could happen? Maddened by the slow progress, the unending rain and the poor visibility, he tensed further, his body imitating a coiled spring, so tight his muscles ached from the strain.

The passenger door of the van flew open suddenly, a man jumping in the front seat beside Will.

"What the fuck!" he swore, reaching for his gun a second before recognizing his friend. Jack.

"Sorry, didn't mean to startle you, mate," Jack said, checking the back of the van where the family huddled together.

"What are you doing here? Fuck, I nearly shot you," Will asked. Not that any help would be turned down at this juncture.

"I was worried. You were taking so long I grabbed a taxi and spotted you in traffic." Jack wiped his wet face with his sleeve. His clothes were soaked. The torrent had not let up.

If Jack had, someone else could. Even in the downpour. "Traffic's a bitch," he said, agreeing with him. Then he remembered there was a child in the back seat and lowered his voice, correcting his swearing. "Glad to see you. I could use the help if this thing goes south."

Jack gave him a rueful grin, patting the gun under his flak jacket for emphasis. "What are friends for, eh?"

As though his friend had brought good karma on board along with his physical presence, the traffic gods suddenly took pity, and traffic began moving in the right direction. Forward.

When he swung the wheel, turning the van onto the road leading into the private section of the larger airport where the jet waited, Will let out a deep breath. *Just a few more minutes, that's all I ask.* He refused to think about the dangers of coming back here. Tomorrow could take care of itself. Jack looked just as relieved as he did, nodding once and staring out through the front windshield between the raindrops. "Just about there, buddy."

Quiet murmurings came from behind him. The family also recognized they were close. So close. He drove as quickly as he dared across the tarmac toward the plane. Restlessness filled him. An urgent call to arms. He didn't care how hard the rain gods taunted. Nothing would keep him from taking off, the family safely stowed inside.

Ten minutes later, Will was behind the controls, Jack in the co-pilot's spot. He spoke over his headphones to the tower, awaiting instructions. Taxiing onto the runway, busy with the multitude of details for takeoff, he had no time to worry. He soldiered through the next twenty minutes before they were finally in the air, headed west. If only Lacey were with him, he could breathe a real sigh of relief. But leaving her behind was the hardest thing he'd been asked to do. Even in war he pulled fallen comrades from the battlefield. But this was the right thing to do, no matter how much it hurt.

"Want anything, buddy?" Jack asked, rummaging in the cooler once they were safely airborne.

Extreme thirst registered. He'd been perspiring and was down a liter.

"Water, please. Then coffee."

Jack handed him a water bottle, unbuckling his seatbelt. "I'm going to check and see if the family needs anything."

Will nodded and drank the water in a few quick gulps. A slight vibration of the plane gave him immediate pause, his hand freezing in mid-air, all senses on high alert listening to the jet's ambience. The last thing he needed right now. Engine trouble.

* * * *

Hector leered at her. "You're damn lucky I was warned to keep my hands off the merchandise. Apparently, you got an admirer, princess. Doesn't like to be second in line."

Yuck. Admirer. Right, I bet he meant the governor's son. But why would he have her snatched? Take such a chance? Unless the connection to Danny made him even dirtier than she imagined? Danny had liked to gamble. Marcus Salang liked to gamble. They'd met at least once. Were they close friends? Ten to one this case was connected to the gambling, just not in the way someone had made it appear behind the Dollhouse. And Athena would throw her hated brother-in-law to the wolves just for the hell of it, likely spilling everything she knew to the guy. Making her an accomplice. If only she could get back on the case. Get out of here and dig for more information, because this case stank to high heaven. And she could not live with herself until she got to the bottom of it.

"You know, I have very rich friends. Willing to give a generous premium for my release."

"Phhtt. You have any idea how insane it would be for me to go against the ones behind this little scheme? My life wouldn't be worth one plugged centavo," he said, using the smallest peso coin available in the Philippines for reference. Heck, they didn't even have Canadian pennies in circulation anymore, she thought, remembering the giant cookie jar she'd filled with the bright copper coins over the years. How many pennies in the giant jar? Made a fun question at dinner parties for curious guests. No one had ever been close to guessing, except Will. *Darn it, can't get him out of my mind today.* And, oh boy, was he going to be furious about what she'd stepped into.

"Sure, sure. But I know my friend can pay far more than your friends can. Maybe even set you up somewhere real nice."

"Nice try, princess. But I do just fine. Besides, my family's here."

She shrugged with indifference. "If you change your mind—let me know. I would just need my phone back to make the call to arrange things."

"And using the tracker, in they come. Not going to happen. Besides, your phone is a jigsaw at the bottom of a garbage can."

"Waste of a good phone," she muttered as her jailer left her alone. Foreign country, kidnapped, stripped of her electronics—not her best day. Kind of up there with the time she'd fallen down that crater in the band of holes, Pisco Valley of Peru, famous for their Nazca Lines. Busy checking for mineral content and hoping for gold or silver, she'd ended up stranded for two days without water after tumbling in and twisting her ankle. Just her luck it had to be one of the deeper ones and the desert had non-existent cell phone reception.

By the end of the second day, with things about to take a nasty turn, she had carved into the hard-earthen sides of the embankment enough toeholds with her handy Leatherman to get purchase to boost herself up and over the top of the hole. Using the knife on the tool, she'd fashioned a suitable walking stick from a nearly fossilized tree limb and walked out of that damn desert. Didn't stop her from going back a year later with new intel. And that trip had paid off big time. Her nest egg was growing with each adventure.

She successfully untied herself—*lots of practice at how to deal with ropes, the trick being to get them to secure them in front of the body.* She picked up the magazine, anything to get her mind off her current reality, but kept returning to thoughts of Will. Why had the sex been so damn good? Just thinking of it sent her mind and body reeling off into another dimension. Maybe because they were friends first? Was that it? The way they had come together, like he knew exactly what to do and how to do it to cause her the most pleasure — it defied description. She swallowed hard, her body thrumming with instant lust. Maybe it was for the best she'd thrown herself at him when she'd had the opportunity. At least they'd always have Manila. The words spoken by Bogie in *Casablanca* made her smile. Now that was a city she hadn't visited yet. *Paris.* Next up on her bucket list.

Another thought struck. Just how angry was this little blunder going to make Will? She chewed on her bottom lip. Not her problem — she'd only done what she had to. She'd do it again in a heartbeat to help a friend, but plan for a different outcome, of course.

She let out a long breath. *I need to tell him I'm sorry, though, for placing him in danger.* What was he doing right this minute? No doubt doing whatever he could to get her home safely. A stab of conscience hit her hard, right between the eyes, making them sting with unshed tears. She felt suddenly undeserving of such loyalty, having placed her best friend in harm's way by her own actions. *Damn.* Such realizations sucked. She needed to get the hell out of there at the first opportunity. Keep him safe.

* * * *

Will swallowed hard over the lump lodged in his throat, worrying about Lacey. He knew she could handle herself, had proven it many times, but this was Manila. She could up and vanish and never be seen again, just like her friend Danny.

"How are we doing?" Jack asked, glancing over at him. Will had filled him in on the strange vibration.

Will grunted. "Still not sounding good. I think I'm going to join a monastery after this. Women, nothing but trouble." He had reduced their air speed, hoping to limp back to Winnipeg.

Jack snorted. "That's as bloody likely as a fish not needing water, bro."

Will shook his head. "I've been working on putting my playboy image to rest."

"Yeah? That's going to break a lot of hearts. What's brought this on?"

"Just want to move on with my life," he said, keeping one ear tuned to the engine.

"Good for you, buddy. Is it Lacey causing all this? That girl would break anyone's heart. Doesn't need anyone."

Will ground his teeth. "She's got a lot of good qualities, too. Always there for her friends." And the most exciting, most amazing woman he'd ever met. Even if he did spend a lot of his time chasing her, he wouldn't change a thing. Except for this time. This one was bad. "Tell Jomar to come up front. We gotta talk."

"Sure."

Jomar slid into the co-pilot's seat beside him. Will gave him a glance. *Looking better, his eyes clearer.*

"How's the family doing?"

"Fine, thanks. Going to be a hell of an adjustment, of course, but at least we'll all be together. You're a good man, Will."

"No different than any other. Just have the advantage of resources." He gave a rueful nod to the jet he was piloting. "Family money."

"You might have been born rich, but many rich men never help others. That's what makes you different. Don't lose sight of that."

"Tell me what you know about Daniel Wright's case. What's been going on?" If the plane went down over the Atlantic Ocean, God forbid, he'd have the information relayed to Lily and the Canadian government. It was the best he could do.

* * * *

The minutes dragged, each second a damned eternity. The lack of a clock wasn't helping. What was going on? Where was Will? She'd thrown down the magazine in disgust hours ago. She'd read everything she'd ever need to know about home decorating, including the ads. And she had no interest in it, had always left most of that kind of decision to Lily, who had a flair for it.

A sharp click of the lock disengaging in the door. *Finally.* Her legs ached from standing at the ready. She bent down and picked up the ten-pound bag, waited.

Hector came in, holding a plate in his hands that gave off the sharp bite of garlic. "My missus—"

She dumped the partially opened bag of flour down on his head, the white dust particles flying everywhere, the room vanishing instantly within the swirling cloud. The plate of food splattered its contents all over her before crashing to the floor. Hector, struck first by the weight of the bag before it exploded, lurched about, his hands over his eyes, trying to rub the flour obscuring his vision away. Coughing erupted when the powder hit his lungs. Her lower face covered by a rag, Lacey raced through the doorway and right smack into a man pointing a gun at her chest.

She grabbed for the weapon and tried to wrestle it away, forcing the barrel toward the man and away from her body. He was strong, but desperation made her stronger. A gunshot rang out. The recoil of the gun, the barrel instantly hot from the explosion, burned her fingers. She stumbled and went down on her knees, then, scrambling to her feet, raced for an open doorway. A hand reached out and clutched at her T-shirt, stretching it out and dragging her back. She kicked out at the obstruction, trying to get away, her feet slamming into body parts with piston accuracy.

A whoosh of involuntary sound. The man let go. *Must have connected with a sensitive area.* She lurched to her feet, her legs filled with determination, adrenaline pushing her onward. Daylight. She ran for it. Shouts behind her. On the other side of the door was an alleyway. She barreled down it. Legs pumping. Straining for distance. Strange cooking smells permeated the air she breathed, essential oxygen she sucked into gasping lungs, uncomfortable with humidity and extreme heat.

At the end of the narrow street, she paused, debating. Which way to go? She had no idea where she was. Nothing was familiar. A back alley with decrepit buildings surrounded her on both sides. Hemmed in. Sounds of commotion behind her. A loud shout followed.

"Stop!"

She couldn't help herself — she turned to look back like a foolish heroine in a horror movie. Hector was gaining on her, still covered in flour, righteous anger contorting his expression. A second man followed him, bending over in discomfort. *Must have connected with his nuts.* Relief filled her. No one had been shot. She fled, her legs pumping hard, feet slapping the rough ground, no time to worry about a strain or Charlie horse in her calf. She had no idea where she was headed. Didn't matter. Getting away and back to Will and Lily and the Ringers was all she cared about.

She ran for blocks and blocks, ducking and knocking into people who gawked back, her wild state not reassuring to her fellow humans. At least some of the flour blew off her clothes and hair, along with other chunks of more disgusting debris. She ran full out until she heard no further pursuit, then ran some more. Exhausted after what had to be hours of running, she bent over at the knees to steady her breath on the hot sidewalk, lungs aching from the strain. She patted herself on the back for staying in shape, running five days a week, plus the occasional marathon.

She straightened up. Good. No sign of Hector or his henchman. *I need a phone.* She rubbed her eyes in disbelief. Was it a mirage? Across the street sat the Dollhouse.

She looped across the street, working her way between the honking traffic and outraged pedestrians. A nice normal day in Manila. At the entrance she stopped, considered her options. The *mamasan* would turn her in, no doubt. Best to hang around and wait for Nina or Layla. She moved to the sheltered side of the building and stood in the shadows. Thirsty beyond belief, but with no money to pay for anything, she had no choice but to cool her heels and keep an eye out for Hector.

She stood still for a few minutes, but no one came by. Too early in the day or was this the one day they were closed? Wait a darn minute. *Yes. Isn't the Dollhouse close to Athena's?* That would be better, getting two birds off with one stone. Checking the street, eased by the short rest, she hurried off. Confronting Athena. The very idea gave her strength and determination. A few minutes later, she turned onto the right street, jogging at an easier pace.

The house appeared deserted. She slipped around to the back of the small home, pretending to be cutting through the yard, stopping and peering into a couple of windows. *Hmm. No discernible activity.* She tried the back door. No luck. Locked. She looked around the yard, searching for the right tool, spotted a fair-sized rock and a garden hose. *Perfect.*

Chapter Fourteen

"Money is only a tool. It will take you wherever you wish, but it will not replace you as the driver." — Ayn Rand

Will and Jack stuffed the American greenbacks into large black duffel bags. Ten million cash took up a lot of space. The jet had been serviced and the mechanics had pronounced it sound. And if it wasn't up to the task, he'd beg, borrow or steal another. Less than ten hours left. At least the family was safe, his father was still onboard and he was mentally prepared. *Get Lacey home.* That was now his only focus.

"Where's Jomar?" Jack asked, snapping the buckles of his co-pilot harness into place.

"Told him to stay with his family. Besides, I know what I need to know," Will said bluntly, checking the aircraft's gauges. He'd sent an operative to Las Vegas and the wife had confirmed it. He shook his head. The shady tale was hard to believe. And the last thing he wanted to do was to put Jomar, a family man, at risk.

Bad enough Jack had insisted on coming along. The second team required for the job he'd already sent to Manila, awaiting his signal. He prayed it would do.

Jack pursed his lips, declining further comment. He didn't need to point out that they could have used the policeman's help.

Will taxied the aircraft onto the runway in preparation for flying east toward the Philippines. Holding his breath, he lined her up, gave her full rein and thrust when their turn came to lift off. The jet behaved, quick to respond to his every touch. He adjusted the controls, the skyline of Winnipeg vanishing from the horizon when the aircraft rose above the clouds. This was the part of the journey he liked best.

* * * *

The lights of Manila twinkled around him as Will taxied into the private hangar reserved for his arrival. He'd been on edge for the entire flight, not as confident about the jet as he would have liked to be. He prayed it would get them back home, safely. Jack had sat quietly beside him the entire trip, no doubt preoccupied with events ahead.

His and Jack's part of the plan was simple. Meet the kidnappers' demands and get the hell out of Manila. He hoped never to see the place again. Only one memory remained, the best night of his life. Maybe all they would ever have. One perfect moment. That was if everyone even survived the coming battle.

"Sorry to be putting you in danger once again, buddy," he said to Jack, bringing the jet to a complete stop.

Jack shrugged. "So, you owe me another one. One of these days I'll come knocking on your door for a favor."

"Whatever you need, you know that."

"I know, bro."

They disembarked, piling the duffel bags into a nondescript van Will had bought, sight unseen. The oppressive heat caused the pair to sweat profusely during the task, and Will climbed into the van first, switching on the air conditioning to full blast. His skin prickled, and not just from the heat. Someone was watching their every movement, a given under the circumstances. By now they'd know that Jomar and his family were long gone, taking away the element of surprise. All Will and Jack had were the money and the resolve to end this thing.

They drove straight to the hotel. Now it would be a waiting game until the kidnappers contacted them again. They didn't try to hide their movements — they wanted the criminals to know they were back in town, ready to do business.

"I'll guard the money," Jack said casually. Will had parked in the hotel lot in a bit of shade. He turned off the motor. Rolled down the window partway.

"No, we'll both wait here. They know we've arrived. They'll call soon. Our team's in position to act as soon as they call." No way was he placing his good friend in more danger than necessary.

"Suit yourself."

Eighteen excruciating minutes later Will's cell phone rang. His stomach roiled at the sound. This was it.

"You got the money," the disembodied voice said. It wasn't a question. Eyes at the airport all right. And at the hotel.

"I need proof of life before I hand it over."

"You're in no position to make demands."

"Seems only fair when I'm paying ten million dollars. Or don't you watch the movies — know the accepted way this thing usually goes?" Will kept it light, praying he'd hit the right tone.

A short silence.

"Okay. But it will take time."

"We got time."

"Not as much as you think, padre. I'll be in touch." The line went dead.

The van's temperature rose higher from the heat and two adult male bodies. Will turned the motor back on, blasting in cold air. That was the one thing he'd insisted on from the company he'd bought it from.

Five minutes later his phoned dinged with the incoming message. Will closed his eyes after checking out the image attached. *Thank you, God.*

"Okay, she's alive," he said to Jack. Or at least she had been a few hours ago when the photo was taken. She had to be. He couldn't believe otherwise.

"What now?"

"We wait to find out the drop-off point. Exchange the money for our girl."

Jack grunted.

Will sat, his body vibrating, waiting to be called into action. His hand grew sweaty from holding his phone so tightly.

His cell rang. "Drop off the merchandise at the warehouse one block from the police station you visited earlier this week. You got that? You have thirty minutes."

"On my way. You'll have my woman there?"

"Of course not. You'll be given instructions for her whereabouts."

"Not good enough. I want her there. I need to see her before I'll turn over this amount of money."

A moment of hesitation. Will could almost hear the wheels turning. How experienced was this kidnapper? He sounded younger and more privileged with each call, as though he thought himself a very cool hipster.

"Okay, we exchange at the warehouse. You got no backup anyway on our turf. But don't bring in any weapons. Leave those behind — in the van."

Right, figured. They had someone following their every movement. Course, that kind of money bought a lot of cooperation in Manila.

He sent the text to the other team and turned to Jack. "Let's roll."

Pulling up at the warehouse, it appeared deserted until a man-door opened next to a loading dock. They jumped out of the vehicle, Will in the lead. Jack had his back.

At the open doorway, Will hesitated for a moment. He had no idea how this was going to play out. He sent up a silent prayer, then stepped through the opening. A handful of men in full-face, blank-white masks stood about. The cool, dimly lit warehouse contained shelving filled with cardboard boxes, some of the contents strewn about, mostly cheap-looking knockoffs of clothes and other consumer goods. A large table stood near the group of men, surrounded by a pile of cheap white plastic chairs.

The one in charge gestured impatiently at the waiting men. "Bring the cash inside." It was the guy who'd made the phone calls, from the sound of his voice.

"Where's Lacey Cameron?" he demanded.

"All in good time. First, we check the money. Then you get the girl."

"Is she here?" he asked.

"Do you think I'm that stupid?" the man said with a harsh laugh.

The seconds ticked by as the men dragged the heavy bags of money into the building and hefted them onto the long banquet table. Will held his breath, praying as they made a production of counting it and finally pronounced it exact.

"Okay, you got the money, where's Lacey?" Righteous anger fueled him. *What the fuck is taking so long with the other crew? Is the job done?*

"Hmm, that might be rather more complicated." The guy's cell phone rang and he held up an imperious finger to quiet everyone before condescending to answer it. *Finally.* Will watched the man's body language. He stiffened considerably, like a cock on the walk.

"Fuck! When did this happen? Okay, okay I hear you."

The man slammed his phone down on the table, his face white with strain. He marched right up to Will, pointing his finger at his chest. It was all Will could do not to grab it and break the digit off right there and then. "You did this, you double-crossing scumbag."

"Insurance. I couldn't be sure that you would hold up your end of the bargain." Will forced himself to remain calm. Now all the cards were on the table.

"Do you know what you've done? Who you kidnapped? The entire police force will be coming for your severed heads. Your life isn't worth jack-shit now, asshole."

"I'll take my chances. Soon as we leave the country safe and sound, he'll be released. He's not kidnapped, just restrained for the moment. Big difference. Besides, you get paid either way. Right? What's it to you?"

The guy didn't answer. Thinking it through, obviously. He paced up and down, his crew wisely remaining quiet.

"I gotta make a call." He stomped some distance away.

It sounded like he said, "You got to be kidding me," the mask muffling his words.

"Sit down, you're making me nervous," he ordered his crew. They sat.

"We got a big problem. Turns out she's escaped," he said, shaking his head in disgust.

Time hung suspended. Both sides stared the other down, the stunning, unexpected twist throwing everyone and everything off-kilter. Will tried to think. To focus. He had had the upper hand, holding Marcus Salang as the price of admission. But it was only meant to keep things running smoothly, not change the deal. Paying the money would guarantee cooperation at the most basic level, predictable human greed. Taking it off them now would set the hell hounds loose, a situation he'd pay big bucks to avoid. And the timing had been so delicate. His team couldn't have grabbed the governor's son until the meet had been set up. And now it looked all for naught. *Where are you, Lacey?*

* * * *

Lacey wrapped her T-shirt around the rock she'd picked up from Athena's back garden, turned her face away to avoid flying glass and broke the window. She knocked the last deadly shards out of the frame. With the sun slipping below the tree line and shadows dappling the lush green grass of the postage-stamp-sized yard, she climbed inside the quiet house with the coiled-up garden hose clutched under her arm. Shaking the bits and pieces of glass from the fabric, she pulled the shirt back over her head. She wrinkled her nose at the sharp odor. Between her sweat rings and the house smelling stuffy from being closed all day, she was hardly going to be a treat for Athena. *Good.*

She had to get word to Will, try to prevent his trying to rescue her. If her actions got him hurt, she'd never be able to live with herself. In a desperate race against the clock ticking ominously in her head, she searched for a phone, but it was in vain. No phone, just a docking station for charging one. *Why did landlines have to go out of fashion?* The sounds of a car, then a door opening and closing alerted Lacey to company. She pressed herself against the back wall of the house by the door, peering out of the side window.

Athena came into sight, walking past the side of the house, loaded down with packages. A key scraping in the lock sounded. Thank goodness she hadn't noticed the broken window yet. Lacey picked up the hose she'd connected to the kitchen tap and held it behind her back. The door was pushed open and she tensed, waiting. Athena spotted Lacey and stopped in her tracks. "What the hell are you doing here?"

"I've come for some answers. And I need to use your phone."

"I don't have to do anything you say. In fact, I want you to leave right now before I call the cops." Her eyes widened, taking in Lacey's bedraggled appearance. She set the parcels down on the kitchen table and pulled out her cell phone, looking pretty damn sure of herself.

Lacey let her have it, the hose turned on full blast, making her foe stumble back in surprise. She rushed the woman, tackling her to the kitchen floor. She tied the hose around the woman's shoulders, effectively pinning her arms to her sides, and knocking her phone out of her hand in the process. Her elbow pressed to Athena's windpipe, she straddled the woman, who gave up the struggle fairly quickly. *Smart woman.* She reached for the abandoned phone and punched in Will's cell number. *Please pick up.*

"Will, it's Lacey. I'm at Athena's. Please hurry." She rushed out her entire message in case they were interrupted.

"Lacey—thank God. Are you all right? I'll be there right away. We're ten minutes out barring bad traffic," Will barked into the phone. *Best sound in all the world.*

"Thanks, I'll be waiting." *You came through for me. Again.* She swallowed hard, blinking back tears. She had a sudden wish to shower off the crap still clinging to her hair and clothing. *Not going to be a pretty picture today.* Not that he'd care about that. He wasn't at all about appearances. One more thing to remind her how foolish she'd been.

She began trembling uncontrollably, holding on to the soaking wet Athena for dear life. She had come so close. Too close. She was going to change her ways. She grabbed hold of her emotions with difficulty. She straightened up, not wanting the woman to see her weakness. Life could take away a lot of things while the clock relentlessly ticked forward, but it couldn't take away her essence. Who she was. A woman who needed to straighten out her life. *Not every day one is given a second chance.* If no one got hurt today in these final few moments, she was going to change. Give back to society. She didn't know how yet, but it was going to be a lot more than just showing up once in a while to help serve at the homeless shelter.

"You smell bad. Could you let me up?" Athena whined, wrinkling her nose in disgust.

"First you're going to answer some questions."

"Fine, but I could answer them standing up just as well."

"Not feeling you're the most trustworthy person right now. I saw you at Marcus Salang's."

The woman's eyes grew wider. "You know about that?"

"I know all about it. You might as well confess and save me the trouble of throttling it out of you."

Athena crumbled like a deck of stacked cards blown over by the wind. "I didn't want to do it, but Danny—he said he'd hurt my sister and nephew if I didn't help on this end. I'm sorry, I shouldn't have done it. But I did it to protect them. You can see that, right? I only spent time with Marcus to make sure we keep a lid on this thing. It's insane what they cooked up. I keep expecting the roof to fall in, even if Marcus has the connections."

"Danny would never do that. Hurt a child."

"He swore he would. He was a different man after those men started coming after him for money. If you don't believe me, I have proof on my phone. Look at it—I saved all his text messages and a video."

Lacey gave her an impatient glance, but did as she asked when the woman didn't appear to be lying. Her heart sank at what she found. *Damn it.* Danny had done what she said. She shook her head, not wanting to believe it of a man she'd cared about. The one video

Athena had taped was the most damaging, proving her assertions.

"He was in debt from gambling. And he was into drugs. Wanted the insurance money to pay off the goons after him. Have a nice nest egg to set up here — get his own place. Him and Marcus are good friends. Love to gamble—and do other stuff together." She blushed when she said those words before pressing on. "He promised to share the money with Marcus, too. Angel had to go along with it. Please, you need to help her. Let the authorities know. She needs to stay out of prison. Her son needs her." The words poured out in an avalanche of emotion. Athena really believed she was sharing the truth.

"I don't know." Lacey shook her head. There was too much to take in right now to be making promises she might not be able to keep.

"Please, she's innocent." Athena began to cry, tears rolling down her pretty features. Lacey took pity on her then. Sincerity shone through in the young girl's face. No matter what else, she cared about her sister just like Lacey did about hers.

"Okay, I'll see what I can do." She swallowed hard, finding it unbelievably difficult to imagine that he'd changed so much, had become someone she didn't recognize at all. *But then, people change all the time, right? It's up to them to decide whether it's for the better or for the worse.* Strangely, the thought made her feel more in charge of her destiny. Even on the heels of such a devastating blow, she had a frisson of hope. "Where's Danny now?"

"Hiding out at Marcus'. He knows he's safe there, at least as long as he hands a share of the money over to him when it comes through."

"Protected by the governor's son. No wonder we've been blocked at every turn." The whole sorry mess fell into alignment for her. *Faking his own death – didn't see that one coming.* And the thing that most upset her was that bringing the pair to justice wasn't bloody likely. Well, at least she could keep them from financial reward by whistleblowing on them to the insurance companies involved. The date stamp on one of the photos would be proof enough.

Loud car sounds changed her focus. Was this it? Her heart began beating rapidly.

More agonizing seconds passed by.

Then Will was striding in through the open door. He looked so good, confident and in control. Bigger than life. She sighed at the surreal vision, her heart expanding three sizes in her chest and tears prickling behind her eyelids. He was followed by Jack. Seeing them set her free. She got up, releasing the half-drowned Athena.

"Hey, beautiful," he said, grabbing her into a bear hug, making her stumble full force into his arms. She held on to him for dear life, tears welling up.

Jack grabbed Athena to keep her from interfering.

"Oh, Will, you're okay! Thank God!" She buried her face into his broad chest, breathing in the intoxicating essence that was all Will. The best fragrance in the entire universe. His warmth flooded through her, giving her strength. She didn't want to let go.

"Are you hurt?" he asked, tugging her away from his body to stare into her eyes.

"No, I'm okay. Just need a shower." She gazed up into his warm brown eyes, sensing herself falling into their velvety depths. Falling into him.

"You look different somehow. Everything okay?" He'd just rescued her, but she felt a slight reserve in him, a certain tenseness around his eyes and in his stiff body. The past two days had been a terrible strain, no doubt. She wanted so much for things to be perfect between them, a hell of a lot to ask considering what she had just put him through, but she would make it all up to him. No matter what it took. A definite promise. She had crossed her own personal Rubicon today and there was no going back, not that she wanted to.

"I don't think this is the place to hang around talking. We need to get out of here right now," he said, not answering her query.

"What about Athena?"

"I'll be fine. I won't call anyone either. You just help Angel, okay? That's all I ask."

Lacey nodded. "You have my word. You can let her go, Jack. I believe she means it."

"If you're sure? I can tie her up if you want," he said, before moving forward and hugging her. "So glad you're okay," he murmured into her hair before letting her go.

Will led her by the hand to the waiting van, assisting her into the front seat, then getting into the back right behind her. Jack got in the driver's side. Not being able to see Will bothered her. She wished they were seated side by side. She just wanted him to hold her, tell her they were going to be okay. A huge lump obscured her throat, making it hard to breathe.

"Let's go, Jack," he said.

"You really okay, Lacey?" Jack asked, giving her a quick perusal before placing his attention back on cranking the steering wheel of the van to the right to merge with traffic. Lacey watched the police station fly by the window a few seconds later. *Pure craziness.*

"Yeah, sure, I'm okay." She gave him a bright smile. No, she was not okay, but she'd never, ever admit that. *A warrior sucks it up. Okay, just making that up, but if the code were being written today, they'd use it.*

Will remained quiet. She needed to get him talking. "What happened today? Did the kidnappers ask for anything?"

He grunted. "You don't want to know, Lacey, trust me."

"I do want to know. I'll pay you back if it cost you anything, I promise."

"You got ten million in your back pocket?" Jack said, earning a sharp hiss of breath from Will.

"What! Really, they asked for that much? And you just paid it?" Scandalized, she spoke without thinking. "We gotta go back, get the money!"

"What did you want me to do? Leave you here? Not an option, beautiful. And it's too late to go back. Too dangerous." He shrugged. "Just paper anyway. It's you I can't replace."

"I'll make this up to you." She frowned, rubbing her tender shoulder, thinking his attitude a bit cavalier about that kind of cash. *Must have hurt the socket when I fell onto Athena. Nothing broken, thank goodness.* "That's a lot of money to come up with in short order. How did you manage it?"

"Compliments of the family business."

"Really." *Oh boy.* Didn't Will want to be less indebted to the company? Wasn't that what he'd been saying for some time now? And she'd just single-handedly landed him right smack-dab in the middle of it. She swallowed hard, a flush that defied the air conditioning breaking out on her body. This time it truly was all her fault. *But I had to know what happened to Danny, right?* The thought did not ease her immediate pain. And now, she did have the information that Megan needed. She shook her head slowly. Megan wasn't going to like what she had to tell her. She'd have to fudge it somehow, save her friend any pain she could. And yet, her brother was alive. A reason to celebrate. Normally.

"I don't want to talk about it anymore. What's done is done, Lacey," Will said in a neutral tone, then took a cell phone call, effectively ending the conversation. That he didn't blame her somehow made it far worse. Adrift and cut off, she sat flummoxed, uncertain of her next move. Not a situation she was equipped to handle.

"Yes, it's done. Meet you there."

He made another call, his tone terse. This was not the warm Will. This one was all alpha male. She'd never seen him on the battlefield, so maybe this was how a soldier acted? But she sensed this went deeper. A terrible worry crept in. *Just how badly have I messed things up?*

"We need to take a short side trip to Pakistan. You okay to go? Do you need to see a doctor first?"

"No, I'll be fine. Yes, please, do whatever it is you need to do. I won't stand in your way." She had already caused more than enough trouble for her best friend.

"Charlie will be there, so if you need anything, he has a medical background and can help."

"Charlie's in Pakistan?" Good Lord, what had she been missing out on? She felt like an ostrich pulling its head out of the sand.

"You'll see him soon. He's working on something for me."

She was about to ask what when she looked out of the window to see they'd arrived at the airport. Thank God. *Now, just let us get away okay and I won't ask for anything else in my lifetime.* A part of her knew she couldn't keep that promise. It would never be in her nature to sit on the sidelines and be safe.

They boarded and Will took the captain's spot while Jack sat in the co-pilot's, leaving Lacey to sit behind them. She envied Jack but didn't make a fuss, buckling herself in.

"What are we waiting for?" she asked as the minutes ticked away, the two men at the helm.

"The other team detained Marcus Salang at his house to make sure the men did the right thing."

"You kept the governor's son hostage?" she asked, her voice rising in disbelief.

"You think they'd let you go otherwise?" Jack asked, turning around and giving her a steady look.

"No, I guess not." No wonder Will was on edge. Another vehicle came barreling into view on the tarmac, its tires screaming as the driver slammed the brakes on, parking it nearby. Two men disembarked and ran for the jet, climbing up the short flight of stairs two at a time and jumping into seats near her. They both appraised her and nodded greetings. Big men, they looked like they could handle themselves. They were packing heat under their black jackets.

"Everything okay?" Will asked them.

"A-okay, boss," the older of the two replied, running his hand over his bristly, graying brush cut. The second man remained silent and only gave a brief nod of agreement.

"Good. We're heading to Pakistan first." Will turned around without waiting for a response and got down to the business of getting the Learjet off the ground.

"I need to let Megan know what's happened," Lacey said once they were on their way. That was going to be a difficult conversation, one she dreaded with all her heart, but it had to be done. "They took my phone." She shook her head slowly. "I still can't believe that Danny's alive. He had me so fooled."

"Sorry about your friend's betrayal. Soon as we land, you can borrow my cell." Jack added a reassuring smile.

"Damn, and my computer's in Manila." No electronics, no clothes and needing a shower in the worst way. *What else can go wrong?*

"No, I have it," Will said. "I picked it up from the hotel along with your other things."

"Thanks." Of course, that was how he knew about Marcus' involvement. He'd hacked into it. She could hardly complain about that, though it rubbed her the wrong way.

"I brought some of your clothes. They're in the back in your carryall. Go ahead and freshen up—lots of hot water. And the weather promises good flying today," Will said.

At least something was going in her favor, and the jet had a nice bathroom. She unbuckled and hurried to retrieve her bag. She glimpsed her reflection in the bathroom mirror and froze. White powder dulled her hair, food chunks stuck to strands of it and there were trails of black mascara under her eyes. *I look like a freakin' zombie!*

In a whirlwind of activity, she got down to work, ignoring her bruised shoulder. No wonder Will had kept his distance with her looking like this. Lacey ignored the small voice that reminded her that Will had never cared about appearances.

Thirty minutes later and it was a new woman who stepped from the bathroom. Dressed in a white sundress that made her feel girly with its full skirt, she oozed confidence walking back down the aisle to take her seat. The men noticed, all except the one she wanted to, Will appearing too busy in the cockpit to spare a look her way.

Lacey's special scent drifted into his personal space, making his head swim with suppressed longing. He'd been overcome when she'd slipped so freely into his arms, had held himself together by only the slenderest of margins, wanting nothing more than to crush her tight to him and never let go. To see her in such a state, to think of her treatment at the hands of those ruffians, made him physically sick. He'd pay all the money he had or would ever have to keep her safe.

But it was his heart he had to protect now. He couldn't afford to be taken in again. She would just abuse the privilege and run amok in his life, breaking his heart over and over. Because that was who she was and she refused to change. He loved her spunk, her adventurous spirit, but it was going to be the death of her and he didn't want to be around to watch. Couldn't be around to watch. *Then why do I feel so bad for making what should be a wise decision? And why does it feel like my heart is breaking? But what other choice is there? If there's a God in heaven, please keep Lacey safe*, he prayed like he'd never prayed before.

He shook his head, swallowing his grief, and focused on getting the jet to Pakistan safely. *A warrior keeps his*

own counsel, even when the world's imploding around him.
A sudden thought came to mind, pushing aside his sorrow.

"Jack, could you give Lacey the report on Daniel Wright? It's in my briefcase."

Jack leaned down and opened the slim Samsonite case, extracting a flat manila folder. "This one?"

"Yeah, thanks."

Jack turned around and handed the folder to the man behind him, who handed it over to Lacey.

"What's this?" she asked, taking it from Jack's hand.

"Some recent intel on your friend Daniel Wright," Will said.

"Okay. But I think I pretty much got the picture from Athena."

"He planned this whole thing with Marcus Salang."

"Yeah, that's what Athena said. He was blackmailing her and his wife, threatening her son." Lacey visibly shuddered, obviously finding the words hard to comprehend even saying them out loud.

"I'm sorry, Lacey, that your friend turned out to be this way," Will said. "It sucks to know our trust is misplaced."

"Yeah, kind of does. And I'm sorry too, Will, you must feel I betrayed your trust. Can you forgive me?" She swallowed hard. Saying such a thing out loud, with others listening, went against all her natural instincts to shut herself off from taking responsibility for her actions she deemed necessary. But something in her gut said time was running out.

Silence followed her confession, the men around her averting their eyes, making her feel an even bigger fool for speaking up.

"We'll talk about this later. But thanks, I appreciate the apology," Will responded in a neutral tone, keeping his cards close to his vest.

Lacey drummed her fingernails on the arm of her seat. So much needed finalizing and here she sat cooling her heels. Sitting still always made her jumpy. Too much time to think.

The sound of the engine whine changing to a lower pitch alerted her. *Finally. Time to land.* She sat up eagerly, managing a smile for the other men involved in her rescue. She was reminded that the operation had cost a small fortune. *How on earth am I going to make a cool ten million plus to pay Will back?* A sudden tightness in her stomach made her press her lips together. She'd need to become a fortune hunter extraordinaire to make that happen. *At least I have a lifetime to manage it. Heck, I might even need to consider robbing banks.* The insane idea made her giggle nervously, catching the disapproving eye of the man with the salt-and-pepper hair.

She looked away and waited her turn to disembark. Stepping off the plane, she hurried down the few steps. Benazir Bhutto International Airport. The small group, led by Will, made their way through customs and into waiting cars.

Seated in the front passenger seat of the SUV next to Will, who was driving, she had to ask, "Where are we headed?" After Manila's experiences, Islamabad, Pakistan had to be better, right? Will cranked up the air conditioning, giving her a quick glance.

"Charlie's with the children about an hour out. Are you hungry? We can stop to eat first, though there's food there as well."

"No, I can wait," she said, ignoring her stomach that indicated by its constant squeezing into a rather painful ball she was hungry. She desperately wished they were alone, and not with prying ears in the back seat where the others were.

"There are children with Charlie?" she asked belatedly as what he said registered. She reached out and placed her hand on his forearm, needing to touch him. The electrifying warmth flowed from his flesh and pooled in her belly, her body instantly remembering that amazing night in Manila. She wanted another night like that—many, many nights like that. He casually moved her hand away to fiddle with the radio, searching for a working station. *He's slipping away from me.*

"Yes, Charlie's working on helping the children who were victims of the Afghanistan war. He's hooked up with MIT in the US and working on providing an inexpensive, more natural movement prosthetic created on a 3D printer that can be made right where the children are. He's a genius at it too, using a 3D laser scanner to model the limb perfectly. I'm grateful he's agreed to help. It's going to revolutionize the industry and help millions of people around the world."

Lacey swallowed hard, tears threatening. She felt about as low as a human being could. *How much material and supplies would that ten million have bought?* She shook her head, trying to keep from crying.

"I'm so sorry about the money, Will. I mean it. Somehow I will manage to pay you back."

"Forget about it. What's done is done, beautiful." He gave her a reassuring smile that broke her heart.

Tears spilled over. *Damn it.* This was not like her. She looked out of the window, her fist pressed to her mouth to keep the sobs inside. To keep the others from hearing. The knot in her throat filled it, aching in sympathy for her crime. Maybe not criminal, but an ethical crime at the very least. *How am I going to look those children in the eye knowing how much money's been wasted on one human life? My life.* She had to change. Her life was not working anymore. And here she sat with a good man who knew what he wanted. A true Canadian hero, and about to visit with another, Charlie, the most unassuming man on the planet.

At the compound, Will clicked the transmission of the older model SUV into Park, Jack jumping out to open the gate wide enough for the vehicle to enter. Lacey took in the low-lying structures surrounding three sides of the courtyard that made a U-shape around them. Nothing remarkable about any of them, built of bricks and mortar, common to the region.

Seconds later Charlie's beaming, welcoming face appeared in the doorway of the largest building in the middle of the U. *Same old Charlie.* She swallowed hard. *Time to put on a brave face.* It was the least she could do.

She hurried across the dry-packed earth and right into Charlie's warm hug. She held on tight to the lifeline.

When they pulled apart, he gave her a look of assessment. "How you doing, kiddo?"

"Oh, you know, same old, same old. Getting my ass into trouble," she said, not happy about her shaky-sounding tone. *Try harder.*

"I heard. You sure you're okay? They didn't hurt you?" His expression of concern made her take a deep breath.

"No." She shook her head. "I jumped on someone and wrenched my shoulder a bit, nothing serious. Nothing like that time in Northern California on that gold-finding expedition." She absently rubbed the scar on her forearm from the surgery to reset the broken bones, then hugged her arms across the front of her body.

"That was a bad break. That arm giving you any trouble?"

"No. I'm fine."

Will joined them. The men shook hands, Will giving Charlie a clap on the back. "How's it going?" he asked.

"Fine. We're pretty much all settled in. You want to meet some of the children, Lacey? Oh, Will, I nearly forgot to tell you, a reporter, name of Porsha Evans, called and said she's doing a feature on you? I didn't share anything, told her you weren't here."

"Good. Thanks, Charlie."

"I'd love to see the children," Lacey said. She ignored the name of the interfering female and the roiling in her stomach. These were the children she'd stolen from. How could she ever make it up to them?

Charlie took the lead, ushering them into a long dormitory-type room. Children were sprawled or sitting everywhere, a couple of white-coated attendants hovering nearby. Some of the children were playing simple board games like snakes and ladders or checkers, others lying quietly on their small cots. But they all had one thing in common. Missing limbs.

"Looks like you've got everything under control," Will said, surveying the scene. "Had a chance to set up and try the 3D printer and scanner yet?"

"Printing one as we speak. It's going to be going day and night until everyone's taken care of." Charlie's face split into a happy grin.

Some of the children looked up at their arrival, surveying the visitors with big, dark eyes. One small child covered his head with a blanket, peering out from inside the cocoon.

"I've brought some good friends to visit with you," Charlie said, keeping his tone reassuring and low.

"Is it okay if I say stop by and say hello?" Lacey asked, wanting nothing more than to give each child a hug. She held herself back with great difficulty, digging up a bit of rare control. This was not all about her — these children had been through too much.

"Come, it'll be fine." Charlie took her arm. "I'll introduce you around."

"Thanks, Charlie."

Will strode over to a cot, sitting down beside two of the children, asking to join in their game. Lacey hugged each child in turn, taking the time to find out something about them, hearing stories that tugged at her heart, all the while keeping Will in the perimeter of her vision. He was totally at home with the visit, getting the children to open up. Soon small giggles began to fill the space, the high-pitched sounds of young voices a tonic.

"Perhaps you'd like a break? Some food or drink? You must be tired after your ordeal," Charlie asked after an undeterminable amount of time had passed.

"I hadn't noticed till now," she answered truthfully. Exhausted about summed it up.

"Come, I've got dinner planned."

"That would be nice. Do you have much help here?" she asked. She looked around for Will, but he was nowhere to be seen. Somehow in the past few minutes he'd left and she'd missed it. She wanted to get him alone so badly she could taste it. She had to make this right. A glimmer of hope for them was the only thing keeping her going in her extreme tiredness.

"Enough. Security is tight. We've got a good cook as well. That helps a lot. Some of these children are in sad shape and they need a lot of proper nourishment to heal."

"I can only imagine," she murmured, ashamed of her own attitude. She'd never appreciated all that she had, her birthright, born into the great, generous country of Canada. Something niggled at her, something she was supposed to take care of. She slammed her forehead. "Good grief, I can't believe I forgot to call my sister! Lily must be frantic. Can I use your phone?"

"Sure," he said. He reached into his pocket and handed his over as they walked down the narrow hallway to the kitchen. "If you want privacy, I'll give you a few minutes. Join me when you're ready."

"Thanks, Charlie." Her fingers flew over the keyboard, entering Lily's number.

"Hello, Cameron Agency." The sweet voice of her twin sounding like she was in the room right there with her brought another prickling of tears. She took a deep breath.

"Hey, Lily, it's me." She closed her eyes, turning her back to the corridor, drinking in the moment, prepared to concentrate on only speaking with her sister. Her precious sister she hadn't been certain she'd see again.

"Lacey! How are you? Are you okay? My god, I was so worried. When Will went flying off after you, I just about had a heart attack. You didn't say it was that dangerous. What were you thinking?"

"I'm sorry about that. I wasn't thinking, I guess. Please, forgive me, sis. I'm going to change. Hell, I need to change. I've been just running roughshod over everything and everyone for so long and it stops now. I promise, I'm reforming."

Dead silence.

"Where have you put the real Lacey? You mean it? You're going to be more careful?" Lily's tone held hesitation. Like she couldn't believe what she was hearing. She couldn't blame her. She had been a force to be reckoned with for too long, a one-person tornado.

"I do. I still intend to do what we do in the business, of course, just be more circumspect. Think of others first on occasion. I should have listened to you all along."

"Wow. That's great, Lacey." Her twin's voice changed, all notes of concern vanishing and her tone filling with enthusiasm.

"And talking about change, I need to make some things right ASAP. My ransom was paid by Will and his father's company. I'll be paying them back if it takes my whole lifetime. So, I want you to check with the doctor downtown for me, you know the one I mean, right?" She didn't want to say his name over the phone as a matter of course. *Never know who's listening in.* "All my jewelry, including the jeweled cross I found in Florida, will have to go on the block. Even Mom's pearls." She said the last part with a huge lump in her throat. That would be the hardest, letting go of the last remaining item of her mother's.

"No way, I'll buy them from you. Fair market value. How much was the ransom?"

"An even ten million. It sickens me when I think of how many families, children, could have been helped by such a substantial amount. And Will paid it to save my stupid ass. He's so much more than I deserve. And after I had escaped too. It just sucks big-time."

"That is a lot of money, but that's a rare cross. It should cover a part of it. And you also got some other nice gems to sell in your collection. Too bad. You've been collecting those treasures for years now."

"Yeah, well, it can't be helped. They're just material things, after all." She hesitated for a second. "I'm afraid I've got distressing news about Danny." She went on to explain the harsh facts to her stunned audience. She sighed when she finished. "I'll tell Megan. I gotta go, Charlie's waiting."

"Give him and Will my love."

"Of course." She ended the call and took another deep breath. What was done was done. She was about to call Megan, then stopped. Telling her over the phone didn't seem right. As soon as she arrived home, she'd visit her in person. Megan deserved that much. She turned to walk down the hallway and bumped right into Will's broad chest, the man in question standing suspiciously close by.

"Oops, sorry," she said. He had a strange look in his eyes, seeming almost embarrassed by something.

"Did you mean what you said to your sister?" he asked as if he couldn't help himself.

"You were eavesdropping!" she said, accusing him, more than a little perturbed.

"Sorry, I was just coming to get you. I figured you must be hungry." He stopped talking for a moment and ran a hand over his hair that looked suspiciously wet. The fragrance of clean soap and a light musk that was all Will filled her nostrils, making her senses leap, confirming a recent shower.

"I'm starved, all right," she admitted, giving him a look. If he had heard what she said to Lily, then he must have questions. Her heart began to beat quicker. Was this the moment? Could she finally tell him what she felt for him? What she had discovered these past few difficult days?

"Lacey —" His eyes held an emotion that worried her. Suddenly, instead of wanting to spill everything, she was afraid. Afraid she'd messed everything up.

"Let's talk after dinner, okay? I have a lot to tell you and I want to be able to concentrate when I do. Things I should have told you a long time ago."

"Okay. But tell me one thing now."

She nodded. "Sure."

"Did you really mean it when you told Lily that you were going to change? Not take such big risks like you did in Manila? And so many other places?"

"I —"

"Will!" a feminine voice called out, interrupting, making both their heads spin around. Porsha Evans.

He went still by her side. Porsha advanced down the hallway, looking far too pleased with herself. She'd tracked down her prey.

"Porsha, what on earth on you doing here?" he asked.

"You are a hard man to get a hold of, William Thornton, but I was in the area and needed a bit more info for my article, so I thought — what the heck, I'll just come by in the hopes you could spare a few minutes. I hope that's okay? That I didn't interrupt?"

"You just happened to be in Pakistan?" Lacey asked, bristling with instant devil-red anger. She could've sworn the woman had grown horns since they'd last met, popping through that shiny black hair.

"Yes, on another story. Sorry, can't share what it is. All hush-hush. But when I learned you were close by, Will, it seemed the perfect opportunity. And your father did say unlimited access, right?" Her tone was all honey and brightness. Totally fake.

But Lacey barely heard her through the surge of intense heat clamoring through her bloodstream. *Bitch. Knew exactly how to play it.*

"Right," Will said, rubbing the back of his neck in that telltale way he had. *Hmm, so Will is not pleased about the reporter's unexpected visit. Good.* She choked down her agitation at the woman's uncanny appearance. Compared to the last two days, Porsha was small potatoes. *Right? Then why am I ready to claw her bald? Guess you can only fix one human foible at a time.*

"Will and I were just about to have dinner," she said with a warning look. "Your timing is not the best. Perhaps you should consider making an appointment?"

"Fine, but I'm here now." She gave Lacey a nod, dismissing her, taking Will's arm. "This is amazing, what you are doing here. I just finished talking with Charlie and he's filled me in on all the good work you're doing together. Is this what you've been hiding from the world? That's crazy. They should know about this. You're a true Canadian hero, Will."

"I needed more time. I didn't want to alert the wrong people until everything was in place. As it was, we had to bring the children from their home country to the relative safety of Pakistan."

Lacey clenched her fists at her sides, itching for an excuse, any excuse. *Fuck this.* If Will couldn't handle one snoopy far-too-sexy reporter... Another part of her quietly added, *he's just being polite, Lacey.* The two sides of herself arguing, she hurried away in the direction of the kitchen. Let the pair of them work it out. She was beyond famished, and angrier than she cared to admit. Change was hard-earned for this Cameron.

"Charlie, that smells wonderful." She moved to the stove, breathing in the delectable odor of spicy food cooking, giving him a smile.

"Yeah, well, I hope you like it. It's a new recipe I've been working on. And it's our cook's day off, so the timing was right." Charlie's fair skin lit up with a goodness that was all Charlie. She gave him a sideways hug while he fussed.

"You're the best, Charlie. A tonic for my soul."

"That reporter staying for dinner as well?" he asked, his freckled, open face questioning, his brows knitted together.

"She's certainly pushy enough to invite herself," she retorted, grabbing a teaspoon from the table to nab a bite of the food right out of the large soup pot.

He chuckled. "Yeah, I gathered that. But, in Will's eyes, no one holds a candle to you. Surely you know that, kiddo?"

"Maybe," she said, giving him a smile. "I'm going to change, Charlie. I need to think of others first, like you do. You have a heart of gold, while I go running off with no thought to others."

"We all have our strengths, Lacey. You're generous to a fault. I've seen it get you in trouble in the past — give things away that would have guaranteed your safety. And you're running pretty hard most of the time. Ever stop to wonder who or what you're running from?"

She stood dead still, teaspoon hovering over the simmering pot of stew.

She cleared her throat. "You're good. You should be a shrink."

"Charlie's the wisest man I know," Will said nonchalantly, filling the doorway with his huge frame, all sexy enticement, wearing his pants low on his hips with one hand tucked in a pocket, surveying them standing at the stove.

"Where's your girlfriend?" she asked, giving him the stink-eye.

He shrugged. "Had to move on to another story. And Porsha Evans is definitely not my girlfriend. I happen to like spunky redheads that are always getting themselves in trouble."

"Oh, yeah?"

"Oh, yeah."

"So, where do we go from here?" she had to ask. The very air felt electrified.

"I'm thinking to the table for food, then back to my room for a long, long talk."

"Works for me," she said with a grin. Never in her life had the air needed clearing more. But was she going to be able to explain it all? To tell Will why she was the way she was? Or did she even really understand it all herself? All she could do was state the facts in the end and hope he could make sense of them.

"Grab a plate — chow's on," Charlie announced. "I'll go get the others." He left the room, limping slightly.

Silence descended. Lacey chewed on her bottom lip, standing over the gigantic pot of food. A colorful mixture of rice and vegetables, the fragrance of saffron wafting up from it making her salivate.

"Fill your plate, Lacey, before they join us. Jack has a legendary appetite and the others will be starved as well. It's been a long day," Will warned, grabbing his own plate off the pile on the counter near the stove.

She scooped a large ladleful onto her plate, then swung a leg up and over the bench seat of the long picnic-style table, getting down to the wonderful business of filling her stomach. The table also featured fresh, hot biscuits and a couple of pies, one apple and one blueberry. *Manna from heaven.*

"Hmm, this is damn good," she said between forkfuls of tasty rice and bites of biscuit slathered in butter.

Will dug in, finishing his food before the other men even made it back to the room.

"Hope you left something for us," Jack joked, lining up with the others in front of the stove. Charlie stayed back, watching the men take their fill, looking happy providing for his guests.

"Are you done, Lacey?" Will asked.

She glanced over at the dessert choices. "What kind of pie do you want? Apple, blueberry, humble..." she asked innocently, widening her eyes at him.

"Humble has a nice ring to it, beautiful. Though I can't imagine it tasting better than the honey I was blown away by just recently."

She nodded and got up, hiding a grin at the lust instantly sizzling between them, remembering Manila. "Thanks, Charlie. Catch y'all later."

Chapter Fifteen

"There are only two ways to live your life. One is as though nothing is a miracle. The other is as though everything is a miracle." — Albert Einstein

"Where's Charlie got us sleeping?" Lacey asked, following Will down the hallway, dragging her feet, suddenly nervous as hell.

"It's not grand, but he's managed a couple of private rooms. The others are in the dormitory. Space is tight, as you can imagine."

"I can sleep in the dormitory if it helps," she offered. "I've slept on the cold desert floor before. No problem."

"Don't worry. You're not taking anyone's spot. Charlie's got his own private quarters."

They were being too formal. Lacey's heart dropped. She wished she was on the other side of this talk. Or better yet, not talking, just connecting like they had in Manila. She sighed. Loudly.

Will stopped in his tracks and took her by the shoulders. "You sound like you're being led to your execution. What's the matter? I just want to talk with you. Figure some stuff out."

"I know, I know, but I don't understand it all myself. I run off willy-nilly and shit happens. I want to do the right thing, I do, I swear it, Will." She looked him right in the face, trying to get him to see.

"Slow down, beautiful. I think you've been running all your life. But from what?"

Tears threatened. Why was it so damn hard to open up? She took a deep breath, needing to steady herself. Even with her best friend in all the world giving her all the support she could have hoped for, family shit still hurt to the core, and caused the most damage. "My dad"—she paused, swallowing hard before continuing—"was harsh with my mom, really harsh. And I couldn't do anything to stop it. I couldn't wait to get away. To have my own life."

"When you say 'harsh', do you mean abusive?"

The tears spilled over. "Yeah, I had to punch a shark to figure that one out," she admitted.

"You punched a shark?" Will's eyes darkened with horror. She could see him even through her bleary vision.

"Not one of my smartest moves, I'll admit, and I will never do it again," she promised, crossing her fingers over her heart in a shaky gesture.

"Did you mean what you said to Lily? About wanting to change? Stop being so impetuous and running towards danger?"

She swallowed hard, feeling the old anger rising, trying to see a better way. "I had an epiphany while in Manila that I need to tell you about."

One of the security guards began to make his way down the hallway, his boots ringing on the stone floor. He nodded in their direction. The man looked to be on patrol.

"Let's go inside and talk in private."

She followed him through a doorway into a small bedroom. Will shut the door, effectively closing off the rest of the world. He stood there, looking so real and concerned, and yet unapproachable in some ineffable way, a mysteriousness that was all Will. The part that worried her about men and made her hesitate. Always. Perhaps she was too damaged by all she had witnessed? But at least she could try to explain. He deserved that much after what she had put him through.

She sat down on the edge of the bed and rubbed her shoulder with the Ringers tattoo for courage. She'd need all the luck she could muster. She'd rather face a shark attack than be vulnerable, and look where that had gotten her.

Will crossed his arms over his chest, remained standing. So, it was all up to her. She cleared her throat.

"Being a prisoner, it changes you. And made me think back to all the times you've been there for me. I began to see I should be running toward you, not away from you." The raw words hung between them.

He cleared his throat this time. "I don't want you selling your mother's pearls. I won't allow it."

Don't tell me what to do. She stifled the anger, standing too near the cliff, every subtle nuance mattering. "Lily's going to buy them. They won't leave the family that way. But everything goes to auction to pay you back. No ifs or buts on that one."

"Fine, but you don't have to do that. I'm far richer than you realize. And there's something I need to tell you about the cash used — "

She interrupted him, sick of talking about money. "I don't love you because you're rich, I love you for you."

"Lacey." His voice sounded strangled, hoarse and real from her confession. She hadn't known she was going to say it, but there it was.

"You don't have to answer me right away, I know I've caused you so much grief, but I do intend to mend my ways. Turn over a fresh page and write a better story."

"Do you really mean that?" His tone hoarsened further, but his eyes gave the gift of hope.

"I do. And I'm talking about a forever kind of love story. One I know that's never going away," she said, then cleared her throat to go deeper, to bare her soul. Will was more than worth it. "You know, when you went away to war, every night was an agony for me. Something I've never shared with you or anyone before. But I knew you had to do that. That it was a patriotic duty you had undertaken. I understood, made myself deal with it. I know I go running off half-cocked sometimes, but I feel that duty as well. Like the obligation I undertook for Megan Wright. Sure, I could have gone about it better, waited for you and that's what I guess I want you to understand. I can't not be who I am, but what I can do is try to stop and think first, consult with you, and choose the best course of action, with your help. Would that work for you?"

"Yes. A thousand yeses on that one. That's all I ask. I love you too." He moved to the bed and took her into his big, warm, loving arms. "I've loved you since I first met you and you got all hissy when I stepped on your mermaid tail." He smiled a little at the memory. "But you've been scaring me for years. Your impetuous ways. And this last time— If I lost you— I don't know what I would have done. I couldn't go through that again." A tear traced down the curve of his cheek and shame filled her that she had made this warrior bend so low, had caused him such pain and torment.

"Oh, Will, I'm so very, very sorry."

They fell into each other's arms.

"My beautiful Lacey, I can't believe you love me too." He hugged her so tightly she could scarcely breathe, crushing her to his broad chest. "I'm not going back to war. If you can make a concession, I can as well. Fair's fair, my beauty."

She raised a hand up to trace his handsome profile, the stubble rough and masculine. He stole her breath away and the flutters gathering in her stomach pushed her forward, toward a better future. "Thank you. I love you in so many ways, William James Thornton III. Friend…confidant…lover. And it's a very precious thing. To find it all in one special, incredible person."

He kissed her then, his lips capturing hers in the most wonderful way imaginable. Sliding across the sensitive flesh and waking all the tiny nerve ending. The heat pooling deep in her belly made her moan softly.

"Careful, my beautiful Lacey, you'll make my ego too large for this body. To think I almost lost you," he murmured against her mouth, his voice catching. Raw and real with emotion.

"With the size of your body, not going to happen. You're stuck with me now," she joked back, a sudden lump in her throat. It had been a close thing, too close. His seeming to be slipping away from her during the past few hours had been a torture she never wanted to endure again.

She trembled, a rush of emotion swirling in her brain. He used his strong hands to slide down the curves of her body, lighting the flames. She let herself be caught up in that burst of lightness and pleasure, let herself really be all she was for the first time in her life, holding nothing back. Finding a new level of being, a new footing to move forward with, she laid her hands on him, running them over his broad, muscular chest.

"Oh, Will, you feel so fine," she said, softening against his hardness. He groaned, moving one of his hands to her breast, his fingers grasping a nipple. It pebbled tightly in response, making her center grow hotter and wetter with each intimate caress.

"I need you too," he said without preamble, letting her go long enough to tear off his clothing. She let him help remove hers and the last barrier standing between them dropped away.

Her body tingled with lust, her soul rising. The want was much more than merely physical, but a burgeoning spiritual need necessary to reconnect them. To prove their intentions. It grew white-hot inside her, pressed her into action.

"I want you—now," she said, her breath ragged with desire, her cheek pressed to his chest, breathing in his delicious scent that made her heart sing with joy.

"Oh, my beauty," he murmured, picking her up and depositing her on the small cot. It barely held them, but it didn't matter. He hovered above her, keeping his heavy body from crushing hers until she grabbed his shoulders and tugged him down onto her, proving she was more than ready for him. He entered her without preamble, the heat and force of their joining making her cry aloud.

"Did I hurt you?" he asked, stopping.

"No, far from it. I need this. I need you." She encouraged him with her heels pressing into his sides until their bodies blurred with movement, driving them toward ecstasy.

Each thrust cemented their intentions, sent their souls entwining, their flesh enabling the intense connection to be the one. At the pinnacle, she let out the excess of emotions, tears running down her face to soak into the pillow under her head. He collapsed onto her, cradling her, his essence filling her.

"I love you, Lacey, more than I can say. More than the moon and the stars and the earth beneath our feet. More than all the words written, that is how much I love you." A tear escaped, falling to join with hers, and she tenderly wiped it away. Her eyes locked with his where the truth lay deep and real between them. A deep well of fresh truth, a fresh chance, overflowing and swirling around them, made her more than she was alone. Made her the best she could be.

"I had no idea you were a warrior-poet, Will." She pressed a shaking hand to her chest, seeking to explain, too. "I feel you here, in my heart, where everything is possible. And I will love you always. And in all ways," she said. "You have my solemn promise."

Chapter Sixteen

"Time is too slow for those who wait,
too swift for those who fear,
too long for those who grieve,
too short for those who rejoice,
but for those who love,
time is eternity." — *Henry van Dyke*

"Ah, beautiful, I have something I meant to tell you sooner, but we got a tad busy last night and it completely escaped my mind. Promise you won't be mad," Will said, grimacing and running a hand through his hair. After a night spent in each other's arms, Lacey could not imagine anything he could say or do that could possibly upset her.

"What's the deal?" she asked, pausing in pulling on some fresh undies after a quick shower. She thrilled at his reaction, his eyes raking over her like a man possessed.

"Maybe you'd better finish dressing first. Otherwise, I might forget again and I need to come clean."

"Maybe I want you to forget," she teased, knowing she was grinning like a fool in love. Love. Not nearly a big enough word for what she felt for this man. "And maybe seven times isn't enough. I think you may have just turned me into a nympho, handsome."

He sat down on the side of the cot, averting his eyes, patting the spot beside him. "Come, sit down."

"Sounds serious." She finished dressing and sat. The cot squeaked under her, and she suddenly wondered who else had been party to their spectacular reunion.

He took her by the shoulders and stared deep into her eyes. "Promise me no running away."

"Christ, now you're scaring me, Will. Spill it."

"The money, the ten million."

"Yeah, what about it?"

"Promise me you won't be mad."

"Okay, I promise not to run off half-cocked. And why does this feel like a test?"

"Maybe it is. But the ten million wasn't exactly real."

"Not real? They didn't ask for ten million?" She was confused now.

"Yes, that was the sum specified, but years ago, one of the shadowy arms contracts my father set up—which will *never* happen again—paid with counterfeit bills. Really good and expertly crafted, and would pass most tests, but not real. Most of the money left in Manila was totally fake. All except for a hundred grand."

"Shit, you're kidding me, right? And after all the flak I took for it. Damn it!" She got to her feet, literally seeing hell-red explode like fireworks over her vision.

"You said you'd be okay—that we could work anything out, right?"

"This was a little more than I expected. Give me a second to process."

She moved a few paces away, thinking, considering, then crooked a finger at him. "Oh, come here, lover boy," she cooed.

"Now, Lacey—" Will got to his feet and ventured closer, watching her every movement as if she was a cobra about to strike. "It just slipped my mind is all."

She squinted her eyes at him, waiting. When he reached for her, she was prepared.

"Hiii yeeee!" she exclaimed, springing into proper karate defense mode, using his momentum and unpreparedness against him. Her right foot moved like lightning to take out his moving leg. She crouched down, and he was over her shoulder and hitting the floor in one smooth operation. *Sweeeeet.*

A satisfying whooshing sound from her victim indicated the air being driven from his lungs.

She quickly straddled him, giving him no opportunity to get to his feet.

"Remind me not to hide anything from you." His voice was a bit wheezy, but she knew she'd gone easy on him. Relatively.

"You'd best remember not to be messing with me," she warned. She shook her head, imaging the scenario in Manila when the gangsters discovered the truth, then began to laugh out loud. "Can you just imagine when they find out that the money's fake. Ha! I'd love to be the proverbial fly on the wall."

She punched him in the biceps, none too lightly.

"Ouch! What's that for?"

"For not telling me sooner. Making me suffer."

"A warrior poet helps his fellow man — or woman, in this case — gain further knowledge and understanding of themselves."

"Bull!" she snorted. "You're making stuff up now. I say you wanted to drive the lesson home."

"Maybe," he teased, reaching up and slipping a hand behind her head to pull her down for a kiss.

"No time for round eight. We got that thing to do. Remember? Something about not wanting me to get away and calling in the bet you won in Manila? And, judging by this performance, you'd better strike while the iron is hot or miss your chance, my handsome lover boy."

Will slipped his hands up her back, caressing her skin as he went, his lips descending and sliding down her neck, kissing that spot under her ear that drove her crazy with lust.

"Hmm, maybe just one hour won't change anything," she murmured, forgetting entirely what they had spent the night planning. What little time they had between lovemaking, that was.

Epilogue

One week later in Paris, the City of Lights

"Dearly beloved, we are gathered here today in the sight of God to join this man and this woman in holy matrimony. Not to be entered into lightly, holy matrimony should be entered into solemnly and with reverence and honor. Into this holy agreement these two persons come together to be joined. If any person here can show cause why these two people should not be joined in holy matrimony, speak now or forever hold your peace."

The minster paused in his recital, making Lacey tremble. Thinking of something and doing that something were two very different things. She glanced up at Will, knowing what getting them to this place in one week must have cost him. How he had managed to cut through all the official red tape, like probably bribing everyone in sight for permits and licenses, was beyond her. But his standing like a beacon at her side right now, dressed in his black tux and snowy white shirt, his boutonniere blaze-red like the matron of honor her sister Lily's dress, whatever it cost, it was more than worth it.

Everyone else wore what they could find on such short notice. Will had insisted on this quickie wedding, saying he would not let her get away a second time, and he'd caught her at the right moment, when she needed most to prove her decision to change, to embrace their lives together. She felt her heart fill with a swoop of intense emotion, remembering the moment when he'd said they'd been engaged too long as it was, and she bit her lip, hardly able to contain it. She turned her mind back to the ceremony, not wanting to miss anything on this one and only day she was ever getting married.

"Marriage is a sacred union between husband and wife and shall remain unbroken. It is the basis of a stable and loving relationship and is a joining of two hearts, bodies and souls. The husband and wife are there to support one another and provide love and care in times of joy and times of adversity."

Will gave her fingers a light squeeze and a loving look that melted all her reservations away.

"Who gives this woman in holy matrimony to this man?" the minister asked.

"We do!" the Brass Ring Sorority sisters sang out as one, making Lacey smile broadly. Even Casey and Truman had made it, part of their European honeymoon. And guess who won the Disneyland trip from the stag and shower? None other than Rebecca, winning it by default when the first couple had to beg off. They'd fallen through the ice of Lake Manitoba getting their fishing shack off before spring breakup. They were going to be fine, but it couldn't be more perfect, because Rebecca needed it to gain the opportunity to kiss her duke. And the sooner, the better. Lacey sighed with the romance of it all, remembering her pole dance for Will and what that had started. She pinched herself, just to make sure it wasn't all a fabulous dream, all these happy threads of her life.

They exchanged rings, and when Will slid hers on, he leaned down and kissed her finger over the ring as if to seal the deal, the gesture so romantic tears prickled the backs of her eyes.

Lily leaned over and hiss-whispered in her ear, "Don't you dare cry. You'll ruin all my hard work."

She sucked it up, and when it was time for their first kiss, when he leaned down to capture her lips with his own, she let herself feel the moment. The glorious now. The moment she never expected to have in her lifetime. Her life was taking an incredible turn, opening up to embrace a husband and home, and hopefully children, all adding to the fullness of traveling the globe together. No matter the common wisdom — she, Lacey Anne Cameron, was going to have it all — go for the gold. Will pressed his lips for long, incredible moments over hers, centering her, making her want that golden life all the more.

Being best friends first had worked for them. She knew him inside and out, and her life was in good hands, the hands of a man who cared about her to the bone. A man who'd insisted on giving the sword to the Manitoba Museum of Art ASAP and with her approval. Who was going to be featured in Maclean's magazine next week as a national war hero, which was why they'd stay in Paris until the fervor died down. Even insisting that Porsha Evans had helped them in getting to where they were — on top of the world. Maybe. She'd never say it, but if the woman had taught her one thing, it was how much she was going to make sure no other woman ever got her hooks into her man.

"I ask you now to make your vows, one to the other. Lacey?"

She looked into Will's eyes, licked her lips and watched as he tracked the action.

"I, Lacey Anne Cameron, promise to entwine my life with yours, to laugh with you, to love with you, to be true to you, and to share all our days together. To be there for you come what may."

"And I, William James Thornton III, promise you all of the above." He paused for a smile, continuing, "Furthermore, I promise to keep you safe, to protect you, to harbor you from the storm, and when you need space to be the warrior I know you to be, to not interfere, but to stay by your side and assist you all that I can and with all that I have. That I do solemnly swear. Today, and all the days I may live."

Will's well-thought-out words spoken with such true conviction brought comfort, but, most of all, freedom. Freedom to be who she was, to live her life to the max, and to do it right. What else could a warrior ask for?

Want to see more from this author? Here's a taster for you to enjoy!

The TETRAD Group

Racing the Tide

January Bain

Excerpt

Day One: 5:13 a.m.

The bed trembled, its legs jerking and thudding about in a kind of macabre dance. Cole woke instantly. *Is this the big one?* The king-size bed shimmied and rattled a few more times, then settled back down, coming to rest slightly askew on the hardwood floor of his bedroom, the earth having released its rage. *Another fucking tremor.* He ran his hands through his sweat-damp hair, glancing over at the bedside table.

Five-fourteen a.m. He slid his gaze from the clock to the picture, as he did every morning, ready to administer his daily punishment. During the long night of sleeping intermittently, he had made up his mind, but now, looking at her face, he couldn't do it. He couldn't dishonor her memory in that way. *Especially not in that way. The coward's way.*

His mind zeroed in on the single event defining his life, the day haunting him every second the clock ticked. The day almost a year ago when he'd pulled into his driveway after a voice message he could make no sense of. Finding the front door ajar. Walking down a hallway so silent he could hear the pounding in his skull echoing his slamming pulse. Finding the bathroom door shut against him. One more obstacle. Turning the handle as slow as a swimmer in deep water, finding it unlocked, his throat tight and aching. The creak of the hinges. The door swung open. His vision darkening around the edges as he took in the horror of the scene. The heaviness in his chest that made him sink to the floor, gathering her into his arms. *No. Oh, God no. Not like this.*

His cell phone rang in the dead stillness of a house that had once been a home, jerking him back into the present. Swallowing hard, he picked up the phone from the table, turning his back on the photo of his wife and himself mugging for the camera in happier times. The words of his father haunted him. *'A real man never cries, son, no matter what'.* Did he mean even if the worst thing that could happen, happened?

"Yeah." He managed one sharp word.

"Hey, Cole, it's Jake. How's it going?"

Hearing his friend's voice ratcheted down his anxiety, put the cap back on his demons. Had it been only nine months ago that they had put Kastrati and his son away for crimes against humanity? The one bright spot in the past year had been the whirlwind operation involving Jake and his new wife, Silk. Teaming up, they had been successful in putting the Kastrati crew, a cartel that had been on his radar for some time, behind bars for trafficking in women and drugs.

Silk had borne the worst of it, when the son's senseless drunk-driving had left her sister and her sister's unborn child dead on the streets of LA. She'd even gone after the man herself when he'd been released on a technicality with the help of high-priced lawyers—she'd been waiting with a high-powered rifle across from the courthouse to take him down. And that was how she and Jake had met. Better than a dating agency, Cole supposed. A more awesome and skilled pair of operatives he could not hope to meet. Jake with his brilliant and fine-tuned military skills and Silk with her PI's investigative knowledge and dedication. She was almost as obsessive as he was about taking out the bad guys.

When he didn't answer right away, Jake asked with a hint of concern in his voice, "Did I wake you?"

"No. A fucking tremor managed to do that this morning. Seems the San Andreas fault is unhappy these days. Playing with us mortals and reminding everyone who's the boss. Other than that—I'm fine. How's the new family?"

He cleared his throat and focused on the present. He got up and padded into the living room to open the drapes, staring out at a world that appeared normal, on the surface, anyway. He knew better. A dark abyss lurked underneath, just waiting to swallow a person whole. *Not going to happen. Life is precious, even when crawling through hell.* Staying there kept Mathew's memory intact and he'd not give that up for anything. Someone had to remember his little boy. *Keep him alive.* And someone had to try to save others. Do what they could. *Choose me.*

"Great. Glad you're okay. We were wondering if you've got the time to come our way for a visit?"

"Sure, what's up?" He recognized Silk's excited voice in the background as she insisted, "Just ask him already!"

Now, it was Jake's turn to clear his throat. What was making his friend who had undergone the horrors of war nervous? "I had intended to wait until you got here, but you know our Silky. Well, here it goes. So, we're in the process of starting up our own company — The TETRAD Group. I think it could be right up your alley, Cole, with your need to rush in and rescue others, not to mention that your skills and abilities complement Silk's and mine perfectly. You know we shone as a team when we worked together to take down the Kastrati crew a few months back. Silk and I still talk about it all the time, thinking — hell yeah, we can do more. All of us, together, taking on cases for people who have nowhere else to turn. We can go and do things even law enforcement can't and yet have their support and insight because Quinn Malone's already on board with his far-reaching connections. I know you've worked with him lots in the past. He can bring a slew of abilities to the group, what with his undercover operative skills from working as a FBI agent and his former career as a lawyer. He knows the law inside and out, just like you do. Isn't that where you met? At law school?"

"Yeah, Quinn and I competed for top honors in our graduating class." *A long time ago and in a land far away.*

"What do you say, buddy, want to come to Vancouver and discuss it? Become one of the four founding members? Our aim is to help people who have trouble going to the local authorities — you know — do whatever it takes to make a difference and protect the innocent. Like you've been doing already. But with your tech savvy, hacking skills, undercover experience and understanding of the human mind, we would be unstoppable. Strength in numbers with a diverse range of overlapping skills brought into the mix from all of us. We'll stand together, strong and proud. Make a difference in this world that's desperate for more heroes."

Do I? Maybe this is what I need. A complete change. And working together on cases meant so much more could be done. He had an admiration for the like-minded, married pair of Jake and Silk. And he'd worked off and on with Quinn over the past few years, his contact with the former FBI agent proving invaluable to his own personal crusades when he'd used up every bit of knowledge he could throw at criminals allowed by law, and then some.

The guy was the best. Knew how to play the dual role of human being and undercover agent and not mix up the two. He always got which side of the law he was on. Cole understood first-hand how hard that could be, acting at being one of them without becoming one of them. Learning to live with duality. It was hard enough infiltrating a motorcycle club or a drug cartel, but when he'd taken it to a far more disgusting level to get close to the nefarious perverts of NAMBLA, the North American Man-Boy Love Association, and had to listen to their sickening conversations and self-justifications, well, that took it to a level Cole found he was unable to deal with, though Quinn had gone on a righteous crusade and brought the fuckers down. Even having to talk Cole off a ledge when he'd threatened to blow up the convention center where the group was holding one of its secret annual meetings. Cole had to admire not only his dedication, but his loyalty to the cause and to friends.

Hell, Quinn even had a sense of humor about his undercover work, sending one criminal to jail when he was posing as a drug dealer and having the asshole call him from there to ask him to "raise bail". He'd done that all right. Raised it to a million with the help of inside officials—not quite what the creep had meant. Though the time when Cole had posed as a hitman-for-hire in an online sting to take down a dirty lawyer looking for a revenge killing on a business partner and his innocent wife—that time had cemented the loyalty of their friendship when Quinn had smoothed things over with law enforcement. Things have a way of going awry when Cole worked a case driven by emotion, lack of sleep and an intense drive for justice. No apologies. *It's who I am.*

People said they looked alike, but Cole could never see it, at least not anymore since he'd lost so much weight and Quinn now outweighed him by a good twenty pounds. Sure, they both had dark, military-short hair and brown eyes, but that was where the similarity ended. Besides, his nose had been broken playing basketball—being so big and tall had made Cole a favorite on his college team. *God, those were simpler days.*

In a blink of an eye, the series of cases they'd been involved in flashed through his mind, pushing him to a quick decision.

"Sure. What the hell. I'll come up, see how things work out on a trial basis. Not much going on right now, anyway. Kind of between things. I can close up shop for a few days and not a soul would know I'm gone." He shrugged, staring out of his front window at a neighbor now watering his lawn. "I'll catch a plane tomorrow and text you the time."

"Great! That's great." The palpable relief in his friend's voice was nice to hear. Made him feel needed, something he'd not experienced for a long while. He ended the call and strode into his office, where he booted up his laptop to check out airline reservations. He found a flight with a layover in Denver and booked it. *God, I need coffee.*

His phone rang again. *So much for coffee.*

"Cole," Jon said before he could even say hello, the hard edge to his friend's tone unusual. *Hmm. What now?*

"Hey, Jon, I was just thinking about you. Great minds think alike. Just planning on calling you about dropping by and visiting tomorrow. I have a layover in Denver planned." Jon lived in Denver, had for the past fifteen years, since his daughter Sara's birth, his and Rose's only child. "How you doing?"

"Been better, but it'll be good to see you. How about you? How you holding up?"

"I'm okay. What's up with you?" A tightening of his stomach muscles made Cole straighten in his chair, all senses alert. He shut his laptop lid and homed in on the voice coming over the phone, paying careful attention to each nuance. In the psychology courses he'd taken, he'd discovered the subtle clues for what a human being wanted to share or tell a listener were there, not hidden at all.

"Sorry, it's just business. So much going on right now. Crazy busy — you know how it is. But you're going to be here soon, so we can talk then."

It was damn well more than just business. But it was also obvious Jon would never say whatever was troubling him over the phone. Cole would get to the bottom of it tomorrow, that was for damn sure.

"I'm okay. Got an interesting job offer I'll tell you about also, if you're sure you have the time?"

"Sure, we'd love to see you. You know how Rose dotes on you." Jon's voice softened, sounding more himself, when he spoke of his wife. A good woman, Rose. Cole swallowed hard, regret riding him hard.

"Okay, tomorrow it is."

Cole hung up the phone, his nerves on edge. He went into the galley kitchen, filling a cup with instant coffee and adding hot water from the special machine that kept water hot or cold all the time. He drank it standing over the kitchen sink, surveying his neglected backyard that had used to be his pride and joy. The bright red swing set he'd sweated over a few years ago needed a coat of paint, its rusty surface beginning to lean. *Yes. Past time to move on and do more.*

About the Author

January Bain has wished on every falling star, every blown-out birthday candle and every coin thrown in a fountain to be a storyteller. To share the tales of high adventure, mysteries, and full-blown thrillers she has dreamed of all her life. The story you now have in your hands is the compilation of a lot of things manifesting itself for this special series. Hundreds of hours spent researching the unusual and the mundane have come together to create a series that features strong women who don't take life too seriously, wild adventures full of twists and unforeseen turns, and hot complicated men who aren't afraid to take risks. She can only hope the stories of her beloved Brass Ringers will capture your imagination as much as they did hers when she wrote them.

If you are looking for January Bain, you can find her hard at work every morning without fail in her office with two furry babies trying to prove who does a better job of guarding the doorway. And, of course, she's married to the most romantic man! Who once famously replied to her inquiry about buying fresh flowers for their home every week, "Give me one good reason why not?" Leaving her speechless and knocking her head against the proverbial wall for being so darn foolish. She loves flowers.

January loves to hear from readers. You can find her contact information, website details and author profile page at http://www.totallybound.com.